PRAISE FOR *A LILY IN THE LIGHT*

"Anyone who loves a study of human behavior under catastrophic circumstances will be swept away by Fields's dynamic prose and intense psychological suspense."

—New York Journal of Books

"What makes this debut novel so engrossing is that it focuses on those left behind to deal with the trauma of such a tragedy."

—*Red Hook Star-Revue*

"*A Lily in the Light* draws you in immediately . . . the storytelling is sharp."

—MarieClaire.com

"A deftly scripted and reader-engaging story told with a distinctive narrative style, *A Lily in the Light*, by Kristin Fields, is a compelling and entertaining read from beginning to end. An impressively crafted psychological suspense novel by a master of the genre."

—Midwest Book Review

"Fields brings new light and language to the relentlessly terrifying and ever-present subject of lost children and the horrifying fallout that, here, grips the reader from start to finish."

—Martha McPhee, author of *Bright Angel Time* and *Dear Money*

"Heartbreaking and compelling, *A Lily in the Light* is a revelation of what it is to lose yourself and come home again."

—Kimberly Brock, award-winning author of *The River Witch*

"Honest, heartfelt, and at times wrenching, Fields's novel exposes every heartache and raw nerve of her compellingly flawed characters, touching on the many ways we punish ourselves and those we love when life leaves us feeling powerless—and how we must ultimately learn to forgive."

—Barbara Davis, bestselling author of *When Never Comes*

"*A Lily in the Light* captures family in the throes of chaos. A journey through guilt and suffering and the world of ballet, culminating in the miracles achieved through both. Fields is an emerging literary talent, and her debut, deftly written, uncovers the heart of family and forgiveness."

—Rochelle B. Weinstein, *USA Today* bestselling author

"Poignant and gripping, Fields's writing will break your heart and put it back together again."

—Kaela Coble, author of *Friends and Other Liars*

"A haunting and beautifully rendered tale of survival and the careful tending to a wild and desperately needed hope. Highly recommended."

—Therese Walsh, critically acclaimed author of *The Moon Sisters*

"Magical and gritty by turns, Esme's story—of family and the search for self—is as radiant as it is unforgettable."

—Sophie McManus, critically acclaimed author of *The Unfortunates*

A FRENZY OF SPARKS

ALSO BY KRISTIN FIELDS

A Lily in the Light

SASKATOON PUBLIC LIBRARY
36001405133154
A frenzy of sparks : a novel

A FRENZY OF SPARKS

A NOVEL

KRISTIN FIELDS

LAKE UNION
PUBLISHING

This is a work of fiction. Names, characters, organizations, places, events, and incidents are either products of the author's imagination or are used fictitiously. Any resemblance to actual persons, living or dead, or actual events is purely coincidental.

Text copyright © 2020 by Kristin Fields
All rights reserved.

No part of this book may be reproduced, or stored in a retrieval system, or transmitted in any form or by any means, electronic, mechanical, photocopying, recording, or otherwise, without express written permission of the publisher.

Published by Lake Union Publishing, Seattle

www.apub.com

Amazon, the Amazon logo, and Lake Union Publishing are trademarks of Amazon.com, Inc., or its affiliates.

ISBN-13: 9781542022446
ISBN-10: 1542022444

Cover design by Philip Pascuzzo

Printed in the United States of America

Dad, this one's for you.

Chapter One

The bolt slid back from the latch easily, but the doors were rusted shut. Oxidation from water on metal. The canal flooded when the moon was full and the tide was high or when rain came on suddenly enough to flip leaves to their underbellies; that was when the water lapped over bulkheads and rolled up the street, gobbling concrete and lawns, sometimes getting as high as the front porch, where the bunny hutch sat next to her mother's tomato plants.

Today the sun was a hazy ball in the sky. There weren't any airplanes. The tarps on the new houses across the swimming canal flapped in the breeze. There were only a few minutes until her mother would ask for help before everyone came over for coffee and cake after church, as they did every Sunday. The metal door was hot beneath her foot as she tugged at the other until it sprang open, jarring her shoulder, stale musk rising as strong as when she lifted a lid off a saucepot on the stove. Gia flicked on her flashlight and took the first few steps into the cool basement air, where she'd certainly find chemicals.

The basement dripped. Weathered posts cut into the earth every few feet to hold the house up. The flashlight made a fuzzy circle on the ground, on the old kitchen cabinets where her father stored junk tools, empty paint cans, wood varnish, sprays with faded labels. Holding her breath, she flipped a can; a skull and crossbones warned against touching, the ingredients unpronounceable, even for Gia. She was thirteen, the best reader in her class, but couldn't be bothered with Nancy Drew or *Tiger Beat*, not when *Silent Spring* claimed people were poisoning the world. Even the author had died of cancer, which proved chemicals built up in living things until they killed them.

It was happening here, right at Mr. Angliotti's house. His wife had died a few years ago, and his three grown kids lived on Long Island. Mass was said for his wife at Our Lady of Grace every month, and he always sat in the first pew when her name was read. He watered her rosebushes and had planted a fig tree, which didn't fruit because it was too sad. Gia couldn't remember what his wife had looked like, only that she'd thrown steaming buckets of pasta water into the garden instead of down the drain. Gia's family wasn't related to the Angliottis, but they had lived on the same block for so long they might as well be.

Last week, when Mr. Angliotti had been reading his newspaper on the stoop, Gia had ridden by on her bike, streamers flapping lazily in the heat, when the birds had suddenly gone quiet, and then they'd spiraled onto the lawn. Birds didn't fall. It was wrong and had stuck to Gia's bones, so she'd dusted off the book Sister Gregory had given her before summer vacation, rereading the parts about orange groves where people fell down dead or bees making poisonous honey, the places in the book no longer far away and fairy-tale-like but right here.

They'd put the dead sparrows in a garbage bag, and three days later, men in white suits had taken the tree down with a chain saw, carting away branches, leaves, and trunk until all that was left was a stump.

They were probably Soviets testing a new radioactive signal or something, a Cold War weapon, dissecting those birds in an underground bunker. Her brother, Leo, said it was a stupid idea. Her cousin Ray said sparrowcide was a thing, and yes, he'd heard of it, and the cats were next—but Ray was usually full of it.

The scariest thing Gia could imagine was sucking in poison all day. It was everywhere: in the hose bulbs that watered lawns; in the wax on supermarket fruit; soaked into thin berry skin; in the trails planes left behind when they took off over her house from John F. Kennedy, so close kids playing in the street jumped for the underbellies of the metal birds, hoping to touch them if they timed it right; or in the oily rainbow slicks in the canal. She'd found these in one week. Chemicals were everywhere.

"Gia!" Her mother's voice was muffled from above. Plates clattered. The lawn mower revved outside; a shadow passed in the square of light through the basement door. It was time. These buttoned-up chemicals couldn't have killed the sparrows. She should have known there wouldn't be anything important down here, not where the floodwater could get it. She did a quick search for fish bones, but only pebbles crunched under her Keds. That was another thing her mother wouldn't be happy about, dirtying her Keds.

The lawn mower passed again, closer. Gia shut the cabinets as the lawn mower stopped, spinning a blade over the same patch of grass, opening up its insides. How did grass bounce back week after week? Like hair or fingernails.

The basement door slammed shut. The bolt latched. Gia had to blink back the darkness, even with her flashlight. Trapped, she found the things in the cabinets scarier now, leaking stuff that would soak into Gia's spongy lungs until she suffocated.

"Shit." Gia pulled her T-shirt over her mouth, banged on the door with the butt of the flashlight, rattling the battery until the light sputtered out. Not even a line of light came through the basement doors. The mower was on the other side of the lawn now, near the garage. If it was her father, he wouldn't hear her. If it was her brother, he'd probably done it on purpose.

She sat on the dark steps, damp seeping into her shorts. At least she'd changed out of her church clothes. Her mother couldn't be mad about that too.

She closed her eyes, waiting for the mower to cut out so someone would hear her. If it didn't, she'd dig a tunnel. Solving problems without adults was good practice for taking the boat out alone. She imagined the bay now, saltwater air filling her nose, waves lapping over the sides of the boat. There were probably a thousand centipedes down here. And spiders. They could see her in the dark, but she could not see them. Her breath left a hot, wet spot on her shirt. Just a few more minutes. She was bigger than everything down here, top dog in the basement animal kingdom.

The lawn mower stopped. *Please,* Gia prayed, *let it be Dad.* She banged on the door until her fist buzzed. Yelling meant breathing the air down here. No. The soft thud the sparrows had made when they'd hit the grass was enough to keep her hand over her mouth. She banged harder.

The door sprang open, the sudden sun blinding.

"What'd you expect from playing in the basement?" Her father, Eddie, smirked, rubbing his hand through his hair, spiky with sweat. "Playing" was for kids in miniature plastic houses with food that snapped together. Gia was not "playing."

"Promise me you were not looking for chemicals."

The blue ink anchor on her father's arm came into focus, done on a navy cruiser. He always knew. It was the most annoying thing about having a cop for a father. Even off duty, he still angled to the side, never baring his full chest, one hand ready where his holster would be, and he listened to what people weren't saying instead of the words coming out of their mouths. She couldn't lie, so she said nothing.

"Your mother's looking for you."

"Did she actually leave the kitchen?" The words shot out. Too far. Gia braced. She wasn't too old to get smacked.

He held up one warning finger. Thankfully, it was the first one today.

"Your rabbits are back." Her father threw the oily lawn-mowing towel over his shoulder. "Whoever took 'em didn't want any part of the babies."

Gia darted off, the flashlight swinging against her thigh. A cardboard box had her stolen black rabbit and red-eyed white one, plus five pinkish babies, too small to open their eyes yet. They'd been gone one morning, the latch swinging, maybe a joke, but now she picked them up, nestling them in her hands. All five fit together as snug as a single breathing thing. She'd never seen anything so small except mice or fiddler crabs, but this was different. Their backs were warm under her fingertips, new hearts beating inside paper-thin skin.

"Don't get too attached," her mother, Agnes, said from the doorway. "They won't all make it."

And some would be dinner one day.

Gia nodded. She understood; you cleared your plate even if it turned your stomach, but she could feed them lettuce or strawberries sometimes, let them hop on the grass, keep them safe from chemicals. Animals with eyes on the sides of their heads were designed to detect danger instead of pursuing it. That was where Gia could help them. They were otherwise helpless in their box.

"Put more straw for the babies; then I need you inside."

Her father set up folding tables next to Nonna's old statue of the Virgin Mother and the peony bushes she'd planted when Gia had been born. The green parakeets on the phone wire hopscotched over each other, someone's pets set free. Her brother was riding a bike in the street in lazy circles, one of the castoffs Uncle Frank had brought home from the dump, with her cousin Tommy on the back. At fifteen, Leo was already too tall for it. His knees stuck out like open car doors on either side. He slowed down long enough for Tommy to kick over an empty garbage can.

A window popped open across the street as Leo circled back toward the house, and Joseph Salerno's mother stuck her head out, still in rollers at noon.

5

"Leo!" she called. "Hey, Leo!"

Leo slowed to a stop. Her father rested the folding table against his leg and turned to watch.

"Next time you fight my son, don't hit him in the face. He couldn't see right for a week."

Leo smiled and waved. The window slammed shut. He was the best fighter in the neighborhood. Everyone wanted to fight him in the lot behind the rectory, even scrawny Joseph Salerno. Instead of worry lines creasing her mother's forehead, she was smiling, shaking her head. Even her father smirked as Leo threw the bike down on the lawn. He earned straight Cs to Gia's As and broke more things than he fixed, but their parents called him old stock, a leftover of their life on the Lower East Side, where men did pull-ups off fire escapes and got into scraps over crooked looks. Leo had been born with it even though he'd never lived there, even though they'd moved here to get away from all that. It made for good war heroes, cops, firemen, people who could stomach danger.

"How come he never has to help? He didn't even go to church." Neither did her father, not even on Christmas or Easter, because he'd heard too many unanswered prayers in the South Pacific. He studied instead, his GED books spread around him on the kitchen table.

"Women pray." Her mother stepped aside in the doorway, handing Gia a peach apron. "Men move heavy things. Now come on."

Her mother could type eighty words per minute and moved like a typewriter ribbon, light on her feet, mousy curls springing around her head. She scheduled jurors for court in Queens, but on weekends, she was always barefoot, carried cigarettes in her apron pocket, stripped the beds on Sunday morning before church and hung them to dry on the line afterward, thumbing through *Reader's Digest* with a glass of milk and a cigarette for recipes she would never make. She had the same wiry build as Leo, the same blue eyes and slightly disheveled look, as if the wind had blown them around for a few minutes and suddenly stopped.

That was probably why she favored Leo more and her father favored Gia. They were mirrors of each other.

Gia tucked the last rabbit into the hutch. It wavered on its gummy legs, sniffing her fingers, eyes dark under the pink lids. Gia moved him closer to his mother, nestling him in beside the others. Food rabbits shouldn't have names, but this one was Buster.

Inside, Gia didn't complain about pouring milk from the big container to a small one or putting sugar cubes in a bowl with a tiny spoon, even though it was ridiculous, just like ironing shirts or polishing spoons or wiping down the kitchen wallpaper after cooking fish. Women's work stank. Polished silver wasn't necessary for survival, not like fishing or chopping wood. But at thirteen, it was expected of her. She hated it.

"When you're done, change into one of Lorraine's old dresses and brush your hair. A nice dress, please. No more shorts for today."

Gia groaned, wishing she could sit on the dock with her feet in the water and watch leaves float until she forgot about chemicals and becoming a young lady, but said nothing. One warning was enough, and she wanted to ask her father, again, if she could take the boat out by herself, so she wore the apron, poured milk, transferred sugar, and swept the kitchen without being asked before Aunt Ida and Uncle Frank pulled up in their convertible, top down, Aunt Ida's hair tied in a yellow scarf even though they lived only two blocks away.

When it was time to change, Gia dabbed her mother's day cream on until she looked like a wet shell, brushed her hair, bobby pinned the wisps behind each ear. Lorraine's old seafoam frock with the white collar was tolerable even though it came down past her knees and the seam itched, but it had pockets in front. When no one was looking, she'd carry Buster around like a baby kangaroo.

Outside, Uncle Frank was going on about the new houses across the canal having Westinghouse air conditioners, washer/dryer units, and dishwashing machines so the ladies could kick their heels up all day. In the kitchen, Agnes and Aunt Ida were talking about fertilizer for African violets, clanging plates. Her father lit the barbecue, making everything smell like charcoal and lighter fluid.

It was painfully boring. Uncle Frank and Aunt Ida stirred up a kind of disgust in Gia with the way they watched everything and stored it up to gossip about later. *Did you notice how the paint chips off the shutters? Or the grease on the stove? Where's their pride?* It made Gia miss the uncles she'd never met, her father's three brothers lost at war, who used to sit on the stoop in the Lower East Side and knew everyone in the neighborhood, playing cards with real bets, letting the kids see their hands. Getting stuck with Uncle Frank and Aunt Ida instead wasn't fair.

Gia lingered. Window light turned dust suspended in the air to gold, making Gia almost pretty in the mirror, not movie-star pretty, but more like a mer-creature who'd surfaced to see what land was all about. She hadn't quite grown into her nose or gotten past her fear of tweezers to fix her eyebrows, but her features were sharp and symmetrical. Hazel eyes and brown hair were a good combination, according to her cousin Lorraine.

There were footsteps on the stairs, and Lorraine smiled in her honeycomb dress and white headband like a magazine model on the hood of some fancy car, staring at the stars. Any pretty Gia felt evaporated. Plus she smelled like powdered sugar and warm butter from the bakery, a hint of anise from the amaretto cookies, almond paste. At seventeen, Lorraine took nursing classes and knew how to tap bubbles from an IV drip, pushed a cart of snacks and games around in the cardiac wing while the doctors joked about how she'd do the old men in just by smiling. Lorraine was perfect, but instead of being jealous, Gia adored her.

"Hey, you." She held up a little bag. "Makeup time."

Gia sighed as Lorraine set up shiny tubes on the desk. This was probably Agnes's idea now that Gia was starting eighth grade, but the extra attention from Lorraine was nice. Gia sat up straight, closed her eyes for the tickle of brushes and powders over thin skin, delicate bones.

A girl was a terrible thing to be most days, but Lorraine made it seem easy, even for Gia.

"Not a lot," Gia mumbled.

"It'll come off when we swim."

Gia smiled. After the boat, swimming was Gia's favorite. "But what about your mom?" Last time, crazy Aunt Diane had left her TV chair to wallop Lorraine because wearing bathing suits in front of boys was trampy. It had been disturbing, Aunt Diane wading into the canal in her housedress, the web of blue veins around her ankles amplified under the water, furious at something ridiculous.

The brush stiffened ever so slightly before moving again. "I don't think she knows what's what today."

There were always bottles wedged in Aunt Diane's armchair while Lorraine heated TV dinners. Sometimes, Aunt Diane talked to Uncle Lou's folded flag on the mantel. She'd been pretty before Uncle Lou had shipped off to become a pilot, skimming close to the ground to drop ammo before being shot down over Korea. The night he'd died, Aunt Diane had dreamed of his plane falling from the sky to the ocean, the moon on the water, gauges failing as the plane filled with smoke. She'd woken up screaming and scared Lorraine so bad she'd crossed the street in her nightgown for Agnes. But even Agnes couldn't calm Diane down. Two weeks later when uniforms had rung the bell, everybody had known why. Everyone said the real Diane had died with Lou.

"Open." Lorraine snapped a cap into place, held up a mirror. It was Gia, only with lashes and bigger eyes, sharper cheekbones. She wished she could try this on alone for a little while, break in this new Gia until it felt right, but the makeup was back in the zippered bag. It was time to go downstairs.

"C'mon." Lorraine held the door. "You look pretty."

Gia hid behind Lorraine. In the kitchen, Aunt Ida sprinkled paprika on deviled eggs as her mother cleaned a bucket of clams in the sink, sand dotting the counter. So much for just coffee and cake.

From behind, Agnes and Ida were definitely sisters: they had matching heights, the same A-line skirts, hair shades of the same mouse brown. It was hard to match these women and Aunt Diane to their stories about sleeping on the roof under a tent of drying sheets on hot nights, sharing clothes from the same dresser.

"The color came through fabulously after one . . ." Aunt Ida, who usually looked at Gia like mouse droppings in the dish rack, stopped midsentence, forgetting about her African violets and the lipstick-stained cigarette in the corner of her mouth. "Well, look at you!"

Gia reddened. With the blush, she must look like Raggedy Ann. Her mother turned from the sink, her face lighting up, genuinely pleased. There was no trace of the usual disappointment. A tiny soap bubble caught in her mother's short curls, but she didn't brush it away. She pulled off her rubber gloves and came closer, turning Gia's face left and right, nodding at Lorraine.

"You look like a doll," she said. "A perfect doll. Lorraine, whatever you used, we'll pick some up next week. Beautiful . . ."

Gia didn't have the heart to protest. No one quite knew what to do with the girl who hunted chemicals and preferred boats to boys. Even Aunt Ida looked impressed.

"Come!" Agnes clapped and handed Gia the tray of deviled eggs to take outside, proving Gia could be ladylike after all.

Gia prayed Agnes wouldn't make a fuss in front of the men: her brother; her cousins, Ray and Tommy; her father; and Uncle Frank. It was bad enough with Aunt Ida.

"The thing about shucking clams," Ray was saying, "is breaking the muscle. The fresher it is, the more it fights you, so you slit the muscle that's holding both halves together like this, twist off the top, then shove the knife under the body to loosen it."

Clam juice splattered his shirt. Gia stopped cold at the top of the steps. He was ripping a clam from its home. The table was piled with them.

"Wait," she said. "They're still alive?"

"Of course it's alive. You can't eat the dead ones." Ray pushed hair back from his face and slurped from the shell, wiping his chin, chewing on something that couldn't scream.

"Don't be a sissy, Gia." Leo fumbled with the shucking knife. Uncle Frank reached for another, drizzled hot sauce and lemon juice, his own shirt dotted with clam juice. Gia's eyes watered. It would burn that clam like hell. Leo's knife skipped, and a red line welled up on his hand. He put it to his mouth and held it there.

"Go on," Agnes urged, her hand on Gia's back encouraging her forward. The rabbits squirmed in their cage, shaking straw through the chicken wire, but that pile of shells, knives moving in half circles, shells tearing apart, piling on the table like the sparrows had under the tree. She missed the step, fumbling over her feet. The eggs splattered onto the fresh-cut grass. Her dress caught the drainpipe, leaving a gash where the pocket had been.

"You'll have to excuse her," Agnes explained as the boys hooted and Lorraine rushed forward. "She read some book, and now it's chemicals, chemicals, chemicals and what they do to animals . . ."

"What a sin." Aunt Ida fingered the torn pocket until Gia pulled away. Gia felt like she'd been splashed with lemon juice, her eyes watering as her mother's disappointment pulsed behind her, and Aunt Ida made eyes at fat Uncle Frank. At least Buster hadn't been in her pocket. She cut toward the canal, where the water would scrub her clean until she was just Gia again.

Chapter Two

The water was cold around her ankles, warming as it remembered her. The houses on the other side of the canal were empty, cutouts in plywood for windows and doors, crabgrass where newspapers would drop on weekday mornings before the sun came up. The new houses towered over the squatty bungalows, taller than the floodwater to protect the nice things inside. On Gia's side, there were salt-weathered bungalows with missing shingles, plywood was nailed to a window a street ball had gone through weeks ago, and crazy gray-haired Louann sprinkled cat food from her bicycle basket every evening for strays. The old side.

Gia inched deeper into the water, wondering why she couldn't be the right version of herself with her family, why everything she felt on the inside didn't match the things she did on the outside with them. All she'd had to do was put the tray of deviled eggs on the table, and she'd botched it. The torn dress turned a darker shade of seafoam. Getting past her belly was the hardest part, so Gia dunked, washing water over her head, melting away the makeup, hair streaming, dress floating. Under the water, she was nameless. Nothing was afraid of her, nor she of it. If she walked lightly enough, like a daddy longlegs, hermit crabs with fuzzy shells would brush past her ankles, accepting her as she was.

Gia opened her imaginary gills for air, adjusting her dress as she drifted. Being alone was a relief. She shouldn't feel that way about family but couldn't help it.

Gravel crunched. Gia pressed her eyes shut. She didn't want to talk. That pile of clams was too upsetting, especially since she'd swum for sandbars and filled buckets with them, clams spitting from their burrows to keep her away, but they'd been like rocks. Now she knew better. There were a lot of things she was starting to know better about lately, even more than her parents, who'd only done eight years of school.

"You missed it." Lorraine's voice was muffled in Gia's underwater ears as Gia resurfaced.

The sun turned Gia's eyelids orange, then black, like monarch wings. Poor Lorraine, always looking after broken things. The water rippled as Lorraine floated in, drifted past.

"Leo was showing off his motorcycle, and the brakes stuck. He took down the Salernos' fence. The whole thing. He flipped over the top, but he's fine."

Her brother was indestructible, so unlike the sensitive thing she'd become.

"It's safe to come back. No one's thinking about you anymore. And your rabbits are probably hungry."

Gia's stomach tightened. She hadn't thought to feed them. Of course they were hungry.

"Was the bike OK?" Leo had been gathering parts for weeks, working under a tarp bungeed to two trees in lieu of a garage. He'd promised her a ride when it was done, all the way to Rockaway.

"Eh. He was taking it apart when I left."

Gia cringed at all that careful work, the only kind her brother had patience for.

The sun had reached its highest point hours ago and was arcing back to the water. She didn't want to go back, not even to see the fence. Right here was perfect. The breeze shifted, setting off a chain of ripples. The air was charged like after a thunderstorm, when the swollen canal was off limits. She suddenly felt exposed belly up, the most vulnerable position for an animal. A car door slammed, and Gia righted herself and balanced on her toes, holding the dress to her sides. Lorraine did the same, lowering to hide the bare skin rising above her bathing suit.

"Afternoon, ladies." He was on the new side of the canal, parked on the crabgrass lot that would be a lawn one day, scattered with lumber and pipes. Leaning against a new brown car, so shiny his reflection was hinted at in the door. The engine was running, exhaust disappearing into the air. He was wearing a white dress shirt with rolled-up sleeves, the first two buttons undone. Her father said not to talk to people like him, no matter what, because nothing was free.

Lorraine gave a small smile. Gia did, too, just to be polite, but not too friendly.

"Nice day for a swim." He shook a cigarette loose from the pack. "Sure is hot enough. Might as well enjoy it before it's filled in."

He gestured toward the stretch of the swimming canal that led to the bay. "Too many mosquitoes. Nobody wants a BBQ with suckers floating around, am I right?"

He lit the cigarette and brought it to his mouth, which was full of yellow teeth, even though he was probably just a little older than Ray. He exhaled another plume of smoke.

"But bats eat mosquitoes," Gia said. Everybody knew that. If they filled the canal, it would break the cycle. Lorraine's hand drifted to Gia's elbow under the water.

"Bats eat mosquitoes," he echoed, picking on something stupid Gia hadn't said. The shallow water was suddenly more transparent in the sun, revealing too much of her dress above the water. She tugged harder to cover the parts different from his.

"My cousin likes nature," Lorraine said. "Don't mind her."

"But where will we swim?" Gia pressed on. How could they take away the pebble beach? Lorraine squeezed harder.

"In beautiful aboveground pools, my dear, with crystal-clear water just like the Florida Gulf."

Maybe on his side.

"And you"—he fixed on Lorraine—"are invited anytime."

Gia bristled. He wasted half a cigarette, grinding it in the dirt under his heel.

"What's your name, sweetheart?"

Gia dug her feet into pebbles and broken shells, wishing they could swim away. There was no point in not answering. He could find out easily. Lorraine brushed wet hair from her forehead and stared back at him, holding her ground on the underwater pebbles.

"Lorraine."

"Lovely to meet you, Lorraine. I'll see you around."

He gave one last look at the unfinished house and slid into his car, then glanced back through the side-view mirror before the car disappeared onto the street.

Lorraine waded toward the shore, where she rubbed a towel furiously over her arms and legs, her mouth set in a thin line. Water ran down Gia's legs. Pebbles cut into the bottoms of her feet. The dress suctioned to her, and she wished she had a towel to hide in, too, thankful they hadn't had to get out of the water with him watching.

"Look at me," Lorraine said finally, shoes in hand. "Do not ever—ever—talk back to people like him. Do you understand?"

Gia nodded, eyes stinging, wishing she'd kept her mouth shut, but it was too late now. Everyone knew to stay away from the fancy suits and cars and not to take favors, knew about the businesses that had burned down on Cross Bay and the people who had gone missing. Why had she forgotten when it mattered?

"Do not talk to them *at all* if you can help it."

But the new houses watched them through empty windows and doors. In a few months, they'd have sliding doors and kids on bikes spilling down driveways into the same streets as Gia's side. Even the canal would go away, blurring the line between them. The sun burned a little brighter in the sky, warming Gia's already hot face. He'd never even told them his name.

The walk home was silent. Water dripped from their bodies to the concrete, leaving a trail that would evaporate before sunset. Lorraine split off at her house, the TV flickering through the window as always. Gia crept through her back door just as the boys were drifting away in their usual huddle to smoke by the dock or waste time in Ray's basement. Inside, the women washed dishes while the tables and chairs were put away. The Salernos' chain-link fence was rolled up into a neat bundle and tied with rope, and there was one long tire mark in the soft earth.

Gia left the dress on her floor in a soggy heap, shakier now that she was home. What had she started? Maybe nothing. Maybe he'd seen her as a little girl and let it go, but the way he'd looked at Lorraine was upsetting, like something mean scraping the bottom of a boat. Her neighborhood was changing. Her body was changing, too, making her less invisible.

But filling in the canal was unnatural. Her family had been here forever, and mosquitoes hadn't carried them away. Storms hadn't washed them out. The water was a part of them.

She would apologize to Lorraine and promise to keep her mouth shut. She would tell her father about the man. There was nothing her father couldn't fix with his gun and shield, his star-pointed hat. People respected him.

Gia changed into the shorts her mother hadn't approved of and left as quietly as she could, stuffing lettuce leaves between the chicken wire for the rabbits before crossing the street to Aunt Diane's, where Lorraine sat on the stoop, tapping ashes from a cigarette, brushing them away with her toe. Everything seemed less easy for Lorraine right now than it had before.

"I was thinking." Gia sat beside her cousin. "We could tell my dad."

"No." Lorraine lifted the cigarette to her mouth.

Gia's father closed the garage door, smothered the barbecue coals. Lorraine didn't have a dad, so she didn't know when one could help.

"Yeah, but," Gia started, but Lorraine cut her off.

"Drop it." She ground out the rest of the cigarette. Gia reddened. "Let's go to Ray's. I can't just sit here."

Ray's house was three doors over with perfect white shingles and blue shutters. Marigolds and petunias lined the walkway in ceramic pots, twelve inches apart from each other. They left their shoes by the front door, tiptoed down the plastic rug protector, past marble heads on pedestals and sickening blue paisley wallpaper, without touching anything. Smudging the fridge had sent Aunt Ida to bed with two aspirin and an ice pack once after a polishing frenzy and a long rant about respecting her home. Gia kept her hands in her pockets now, which was fine because everything stank of bleach and potpourri.

The basement, though, was full of empty tanks where the turtles, a corn snake, and two baby alligators from Florida had lived until one had snapped at Aunt Ida. The pets had gone away after that, and Aunt Ida had stopped coming down here when the boys had put up pinups. They put out cigarettes in the cast-off furniture Uncle Frank found on his sanitation route and had bought a stereo loud enough to shake the paneling, cutting through the stench of sweat and boredom.

"Yeah, but we're losing," Ray's voice boomed. "Why else would they send more men?"

Gia held the banister, creeped out by the see-through steps.

"No, man, it's over. They're throwing more power to finish it," Leo shouted back, pausing from rolling a joint, the table littered with tiny twigs. "The US doesn't lose wars, man. It doesn't happen."

"Everyone can lose, man," Ray shot back. "Everyone."

"Shave my head—I'll go right now." Leo pointed at the **READY FOR ACTION** poster over the couch, stolen from the post office bulletin board.

Gia settled beside Tommy, whose hands were folded neatly in his lap, his hair combed to one side from church. He, like Uncle Frank, would find a way out of being drafted because where Leo and Ray were wiry and almost old enough, Tommy was younger and looked like the Gerber Baby. Aunt Ida still cut his meat and made his bed in the morning; he was too innocent to be anywhere near a gun, let alone fire one.

"What do you want to run around the jungle for?" It came out snippy, but she was curious. There were interesting things to explore in the jungle.

"C'mon, Gia." Leo mimed shooting a machine gun. "Village raids. Bombs. Sweating on a boat. Free cigarettes. Canned meat. Cruising alligator rivers and rice paddies. And . . . you know." Whatever he meant was lost on Gia, but Ray smirked and Tommy shifted. She should've known better than to expect an intelligent answer. He wouldn't care about anything that lived in rice paddies. At least no one was teasing her about the clams.

"Crocodiles," she said. "It'd probably be crocodiles because it's hot there."

"Same thing." Leo popped a cap off a beer bottle with his back teeth, and Lorraine winced. Metal on teeth was worse than dentist cotton. "Point is, either one can snap you in half."

"They're almost dinosaurs," Gia said. "Remember when Dad held you over the alligator tank in Florida? Why'd he do that?"

"Because I asked him." Leo took a sip, smirking, and gathered the twigs into a neat pile. "I heard they jump. I wish we still had the other ones." He pointed to the empty tanks. "We could've trained them to swim behind the boat and snap at morons we don't like."

He held up his hands and snapped at the air. Gia's patience for the basement was running out.

"But you want to really know why? Because how else can I be a Hells Angel? You think they'd want some kid from suburbia? No one here would take a bullet for anyone else, not if dinner was done or *Sullivan* was on. No way. It does not happen here."

Gia rolled her eyes. Who actually believed a Hells Angel was a good goal?

"What does your dad think about you being a Hells Angel?" Lorraine smirked. They all knew what the answer was. Leo took a long drag off the bottle and slammed it down.

"Same as he thinks about anything that isn't food on the table."

Leo looked at Gia, waiting for her to nod along and chime in, but she couldn't because it wasn't right, not when her father was doing the right thing. Annoyance flickered on Leo's face, and then he licked the joint shut, closing Gia out with it.

"Lorraine, you are sunshine down here," Ray said. She was perched on the couch arm, taller than the rest of them, her hair still damp from the canal. "Like the grand marshal of San Gennaro, ready for a parade car." Ray waved to an imaginary crowd.

Lorraine rolled her eyes, tossed a pillow at him, scattering the twigs on the table. Tommy dropped the stray twigs into a candle burning on the shelf. Green bits sank into melting wax. Tommy liked everything neat.

"My friend's been asking about you."

"Not interested," Lorraine shot back, hardening into a glimmer of the person she'd been by the canal before. "Tell him I don't go out with trash."

"You don't even know who it is."

"Doesn't matter."

The boys smirked. Gia smoothed her shorts, wishing they'd change the subject. Dating made her feel less like a real girl, at least here. It was different in Lorraine's room with magazines spread over the comforter as she tried on the clothes Lorraine picked out for her. There, she was less of a wild-haired troll doll.

"You're not seeing anyone, from what I understand," Ray said slowly.

"What's it to you?" Lorraine crossed her arms.

"Just curious."

"When's the last time you were 'just curious,' Ray?" But Ray only shrugged, eyeing Lorraine the way Gia's father looked at wood before cutting. Measure twice; cut once.

"I'm gonna make it with Flora this year," Leo said, lighting the joint he'd just finished rolling.

"That's disgusting," Gia spit. "Don't say that out loud."

"You know what's worse?" Leo pushed on. "The way dumb Joseph looks at you. You see him? Staring over the fence?"

"Shut up, Leo." Gia's heart pounded. Why did he have to embarrass her like this when it wasn't even true? She swatted at Leo, but it only amused him, so Gia hit harder until Ray cleared his throat.

"Well . . ." Ray took a small white rock out of his shirt pocket and put it on the table, grinning. It looked like something swept out from under the couch.

Leo turned it over in his hands, sniffed it. It was the size of his fingernail. "Where'd you get it?"

"I'm starting a little business," Ray said.

"Ray." There was a warning in Lorraine's voice. "What kind of business?"

Ray ignored her.

Gia glanced at Tommy, because they were a year apart and he was usually as dumb as she was with these things, but Tommy was expressionless. If they waited long enough, they wouldn't have to ask. Tommy sat back. The rock could've been a quarter or a deck of cards, only it'd be swept away if any parents came down for a can of tomatoes or something. That much she knew.

"I thought we'd give it a try on this lovely evening."

"Well, have fun with that." Lorraine stood. "I've got to feed my mother."

Gia followed because she'd already let Lorraine down once today, but what was it?

"Just wait," Ray protested. He had the look he got when he was dealing cards, doling them out in a circle as everyone scooped and flipped, knowing he'd somehow cut the deck in his favor.

"She's not gonna feed herself." Lorraine was already at the steps, her hand on the banister. Something had spooked her.

"It might help her too," Ray mumbled, and Lorraine glared. "I'm serious. Timothy Leary says LSD opens up people's minds. You're gonna argue with a Harvard professor? Just watch for a second. Gia, just wait."

Ray rarely addressed her directly. A record ended, and the basement buzzed with silence.

"What does it do?" Gia asked. Ray's eyebrow rose.

"Eu-phor-ia." Leo exhaled a cloud of smoke, stretching the word into an exotic place with leis of tropical flowers around your neck at the airport. "And more energy than a million cups of coffee."

He couldn't even sit long enough as it was. The scrapes and bruises forming on his arms and hands were proof. She wanted to make a snide comment about the fence but couldn't think of one fast enough.

"I'll show you," Ray teased, "so you'll know when you're at a party."

The only parties Gia knew had streamers and stick ponies, not the parentless kind with pillows, black light bulbs that made clothes glow, spinning bottles, and holding hands like Lorraine told her about. She inched closer, because she would be in eighth grade soon. Things were changing. Lorraine paused on the steps, staring toward the upstairs door.

Ray crushed the rock with the bottom of a beer bottle into powder, like in the fingerprint kits her father used to bring home from the station. He'd let her dust everything until oily prints appeared like magic on doorknobs, handles, forgotten glasses of water.

"The good stuff comes like this. Powder is junk."

Tommy and Leo leaned their elbows against their thighs. Was it working already, drawing everyone closer, or was it like the powders in her book that coated budding orange blossoms on trees or lay sprinkled in sidewalk cracks to stop weeds, only to cause sparrows to fall from trees? Or worse, like the invisible chemicals that got dogs or babies sick after they played on the floor or with their toys? But she wasn't scared. She was curious. This was more interesting than watching her parents thumb through the *TV Guide*, arguing over what to watch while a bowl of popcorn steamed between them.

"Then you taste it." Ray dipped his pinkie and rubbed it over his gums. "That's good. My gums are numb. The numb-er the better," he fake slurred, more animated now. He'd been waiting all day for this, and his excitement was contagious.

Leo reached forward, but Ray stopped him.

"Ladies first," Ray said to Gia. "Just a taste."

Gia let go of the banister, drifting toward Ray like a jellyfish in a current, avoiding Lorraine's eye. Just a taste. Leo raised one surprised eyebrow. Doing something before Leo made her bolder. She dipped her pinkie, the powder illuminating a maze of lines, as her head did circles around itself: oranges growing slowly in a grove, sprinkled with snow in Florida, so far from here. It was not the same thing.

Ray mimed a little circle. Gia imitated him. A bitter taste spread through her mouth, worse than grapefruit, then went cold.

Her face puckered. The spell was broken. There was nowhere to spit, so she swigged from the beer bottle on the table, too disgusted to care that Ray's girl-kissing lips had been on this bottle, but the taste lingered. She felt tricked, worse than the time they'd told her pickle juice was soda and wouldn't let her have any because she wasn't five yet, but she'd begged and they'd let her, then laughed into each other like hyenas. Why did she bother coming here? She stomped to the steps.

"Hey, hey, hey. Wait. I know. It's gross. You're right. Just let me show you the next part so you'll know." Ray tore off a chunk of a magazine cover and scooped the powder into a line on his fist, then sucked it up his nose until it was gone, flashing his hand at the end like a magician. Why would anyone do that after what she'd just tasted? But Leo's fist was out, which wasn't surprising, considering he was stupid enough to think Vietnam and Hells Angels were good ideas. Ray smiled at her. She'd passed some kind of test. *OK,* she imagined him saying. *You can join the over-ten club now.* Part of her still wanted to be let in.

Ray had wanted to be a doctor once. He'd cut an old white T-shirt in half, wear it over his clothes, listen to their heartbeats with two cups on a string, the echo of a beat traveling from cup to cup. "What seems to be the problem here?" he'd ask while their feet dangled from the makeshift exam table on the counter, covered in newspaper so it crinkled like the real kind, prescribing M&M'S in Dixie Cups or candy cigarettes to calm their nerves while Nurse Lorraine took notes on a legal pad. Leo's illnesses were always the best—tucking the lower half of his arm into his shirt so only his elbow popped out. "It was here this morning."

Uncle Frank had come home one night to this scene in the kitchen, stinking of stale beer. "Like any of you got the brains to be doctors," he'd laughed. "You'll be lucky selling encyclopedias." They'd stopped playing doctor after that. Ray never talked about what he wanted to be now. Maybe it was this.

"Hey," Ray called after them. "I'll pick you up later. We'll go for a ride."

A ride meant cruising Cross Bay, windows down, hollering at people they knew. She'd much rather be in the boat, dropping the outboard into the water with a splash, gliding feather smooth on black water until the bay opened up, gray and choppy, salt on her lips. Disappearing into the marsh to watch planes take off, looking for mussels, wind tangling her hair. President Kennedy had promised a man on the moon before the end of the decade, and Gia hoped her parents would let her take the boat out alone before then. That would be better than any walk on the moon. That would be eu-phor-ia.

"Shouldn't we leave room for *real* girls?" Tommy pleaded.

"What would they want with you?" Ray shot back.

Gia slammed the basement door. A Florida magnet fell off the refrigerator, broke in two neat pieces.

"Shit." Gia stuffed them into her pocket to glue and put back later, but Aunt Ida was already in the doorway, ghost white in her floral housedress and cold cream, ice clinking in her gimlet. She'd hated Gia since the time Gia had plucked all the translucent seedpods off her money tree and skipped around in a flannel nightgown, handing out "money" to every open hand, while Aunt Ida had made a big show of stuffing the stark branches into the trash and hauling it out to the curb. Her mother would hear about this for sure.

"Wind took it." Lorraine shrugged. Aunt Ida nodded even though the windows were closed, the whole house buttoned to shut out dirt, bugs, and problems that couldn't be scrubbed with bleach.

In the living room, Uncle Frank yelled out for another beer. As Aunt Ida shuffled to the fridge, wrapping a towel around her hand to open the door without a smudge, Gia wondered why anyone would ever want to grow up and be a woman.

Chapter Three

A flea bit a dog and died from its blood; insects died from vapors off poisoned plants. Bees carried contaminated nectar to a hive and turned it into poisonous honey: spreading, spreading, spreading. The book didn't always say where these things happened, but it was here. Gia was sure of it—in her sparrows and stray cats and the rabbit hutch or the canals that led to the bay and beyond to the ocean.

Outside of Ray's basement, the white rock felt connected to these things too. The day the sparrows had fallen, other birds had cut across the sky, gripped tree branches with tiny claws, oblivious to the ones on the ground, and for a moment, Gia had felt as if she were on the ground with her arms tossed out to either side, her hair in the grass, blank eyes staring at a regular blue sky. Something was happening to her while the other birds tugged worms from the earth. It was so upsetting she'd grabbed at herself to make sure she was whole before riding away on her bike, but the feeling persisted.

A horn honked outside. Ray. She wanted to get to the bottom of it. It was more important than riding around on Cross Bay, but that was hard to explain. The faded macramé owl on her wall gave her a silent hoot. Fine. She pulled on her shoes and swiped sticky lip gloss over her lips. More chemicals.

The stairs creaked under her weight, heavy with humidity.

"Where are you going?" her mother asked from the couch as a laugh track erupted on *Ed Sullivan*.

"Out."

"Where's out?" The volume lowered. This would not be easy.

"I don't know. Just a ride." The horn honked again. She almost hoped they'd leave her behind. The TV clicked off.

"I'll walk you out." Her father met her in the hallway. Gia wiped the lip shine off. Wearing it in front of him was embarrassing.

"Why don't you just tie a bib around my neck and stick a Binky in my mouth?"

Her father searched her face. Gia glared back. Leo never got walked out. This was worse than him dropping her at school in the patrol car, whooping the siren to see which circles of kids scattered. *None of them better be your friends.* How was she supposed to grow up like this?

"You're my daughter," he said. "Shouldn't I know where you go?"

"But Lorraine is going too."

"Even more of a reason."

The man at the canal flashed back into her mind. The wet dress was still in a heap upstairs. She wouldn't have minded her father's arm around her shoulder then, but now it was heavy, labored her walking, and felt more like ownership than protection.

The radio shook the car, scattering the parakeets. Lorraine's front door opened. She was still in her honeycomb dress, glowing on the dark porch like a firefly. Ray lowered the music, one arm dangling from the window. There was no shuffling, no quick hiding. Ray had anticipated this, which made Gia feel less grounded, like riding a bike on ice.

"Hello again." Ray smiled. His sleeves were rolled up, showing mismatched skin tones. Whatever that rock had done was hiding.

"Evening," her father said. Why did Ray always get such gentlemanly respect even though he was a kid too?

"What's the plan for this evening?" It sounded friendly, but something floated underneath. Her father leaned into the window like at a traffic stop for a "broken taillight." Gia inched away now that his arm wasn't around her. Lorraine picked her way over the uneven stones dotting her walkway, one arm holding her elbow, turning back to look at her house, chin quivering.

"Dad?" Gia whispered. He didn't look up.

"Just a ride, Uncle Eddie. Maybe grab a burger, a milkshake." He stretched the last word into two, snapping on the *k* like a broken rubber band. Leo and Tommy stifled giggles, but her father wasn't laughing. They wiped their faces clean and shut up real quick.

"We got plenty of food inside, you know." His eyes met Leo's. "Your mother saved you a plate."

Leo stared into his lap, his thumbs running circles over each other.

"That's real nice," Leo mumbled. Tommy's shoulders shook from the effort not to laugh.

"Well, you know, that's my point." The trap snapped closed. "It's not funny. In fact, it's disrespectful. You're punished for the fence but think you can ride around all night?"

The parakeets flapped wildly, neon green in the streetlight, bouncing the wire. So much for caring where his daughter was going.

"So I says to myself, *What could be so important for him to forget?*" He threw up his hands, mock considering. *Said,* Gia silently corrected, embarrassed. They'd been over this. Present tense. Past tense. Future tense. Grammar. He hadn't just stepped off the boat. No need to sound like it.

A silent tear rolled down Lorraine's cheek, catching the streetlight. She brushed it away. Everything was wrong tonight.

"And I couldn't think of one good reason, so let's go. Out of the car. Night's over."

"We didn't mean any disrespect." Ray held up his empty hands, trying to catch whatever was left of the night, but her father was angry-calm. It was over.

"My son should know better. It's disappointing."

Leo slid over Tommy, trying harder than usual not to fidget, but his face twitched. He rounded the car, the headlights washing him into a blur.

"Get inside." Eddie pushed Leo toward the walkway, but Leo was only wearing one shoe. "And what is this?" Eddie threw up his hands.

Agnes was in the doorway, a silhouette of a bathrobe. The rabbits stirred in their cage. Straw fell through the chicken wire as Ray coasted to the stop sign, but Lorraine was still standing in the street, holding her elbow.

"Show's over," her father said, softening when he saw Lorraine. Where was that same nice for Gia? "What'd she do?" he asked Lorraine, noticing her tears.

The house was dark minus the flickering TV in the window. Lorraine's chin quivered harder. It was puffy and red. Lorraine licked the tears away, holding her elbow tighter.

"Stay here," Eddie whispered, and he headed into her house. Gia stood beside Lorraine, sorry she'd lingered in Ray's basement now. It had probably upset Aunt Diane. Or the canal had. The TV snapped off. Something thumped. Eddie hauled a black trash bag to the curb. Glass broke. Diane screamed inside, but it didn't sound like words. Lorraine stiffened. Agnes put her arm around her even though they were almost the same size.

"Sleep over tonight," she said softly. Lorraine nodded. Eddie wiped his hands on his pajama pants.

"I'll walk you back in the morning when she's not a lunatic," Eddie said.

"Or less of," Lorraine mumbled.

Gia trailed behind as her parents walked on either side of Lorraine, who looked more like their daughter than Gia felt. Her father had cast her out like raw meat on a hook, just to get Leo. Now everyone would think she'd snitched. It wasn't right.

Gia sat next to the rabbit hutch. The big ones took turns drinking from the waterspout. The babies nestled in a ball. Even the rabbits ignored her.

Leo clinked a Slinky at the kitchen table. It fell, bounced on the linoleum.

A chair slid out from the table.

"What's going on with you?" her father said. Silence.

"You take down a fence, forget you're punished. You haven't mowed the lawn in two weeks and come home like this."

Leo mumbled something.

"The rain has nothing to do with it—don't give me that. Your mother tells me you took five dollars from the grocery jar and came home with nothing from the store. Something's not adding up."

"It's summer, Dad. I don't know. I put it back."

"Not according to your mother. Why would she lie?"

The Slinky started, then stopped abruptly.

"It's time you got a job."

Agnes made a little sound.

"Well, he's not studying," Eddie said. "So he should pitch in."

"School starts in a week. He'll have more to do then. They'll be busy again."

"It's not enough, Agnes, clearly. He rolls around in the dirt fighting every kid in the neighborhood. He's not studying then either."

There was a pause, then her father's voice, low. Gia strained to hear over the rabbits rustling. She stuck her finger through the wire to calm them.

"A man provides for his family and is good to his word. You have to clean this up, Leo, because I see how your face is moving right now, and I don't like it."

"He's nervous, Eddie," Agnes said. "You're upsetting him."

"Starting tomorrow," he pushed on, "you're getting a job. I don't care what it is. Bag groceries. Fix bikes. You'll pay for the fence first. After, you'll keep half; the rest helps your family."

He knocked at the table with his knuckles. "You didn't use your time well, so now it doesn't belong to you."

Leo knew better than to talk back. Sometimes Gia couldn't imagine her father at war, but other times, like now, she could picture him locking a torpedo into place, shooting without hesitation, without mistakes.

"Tomorrow, I want a full report on who you spoke to. Understand?"

Leo mumbled. A shadow shifted on the porch as Leo climbed the stairs to his room and slammed the door so hard the rabbits stopped drinking.

Why shouldn't he work? She helped her mother. The sting of being used eased with the new fairness, not that Leo would actually listen.

If Leo got a job at the supermarket, Gia would go just to see him in that stupid uniform. Or as a movie usher, tapping people on shoulders with a flashlight to stop them from necking like perverts. But her brother wasn't so bad. When Joseph Salerno had lifted Gia's skirt in front of his friends as a joke, Leo had rolled up his sleeves in the lot behind the rectory, wiggled his jaw, and knocked Joseph Salerno on his ass. Joseph's friends had carried him home on one side of the street as Gia and Leo had shared an ice cream cone on the other, Leo smelling like dust, Gia dizzy with the fact that no one would bother her again.

"You see that?" Her father's voice startled her. The moon above the canal was a perfect circle. "It explains everything. Always does."

The moon and sports were the only things her father was superstitious about, but the storm in Gia's rib cage couldn't be explained by the moon.

"You used me," she said, wishing for the calm of the boat, though the water terrified her at night, even with a full moon.

"When I was a kid, your grandfather made me pick coal from the street to heat the house."

"I heard that story already. And how you got an orange for Christmas. Or a baseball. Or how the milk bottle had the same crack every week. You told me a million times."

"And sometimes he told me to pick pockets to feed the family. If I got caught, I'd go to jail, and no one would bail me out. How's that for fair?"

That part of the story was new. Gia hugged her knees to her chest. Who would send their own kid to jail?

It was quiet between them. Tree bugs hummed. Heat lightning lit the clouds over the water. A car peeled off in the distance, maybe Ray's if they hadn't given up and gone home.

"You gonna stay with the rabbits all night?" He held the screen door for her, though it would've stayed open on its own.

"Going to." She sighed, thinking of his GED books. Kids weren't supposed to help parents with their homework. "You don't know how lucky you are," he always said. "All you have to do is go to school." She went on, "*Gonna's* not a real word."

"All right. Are you *going to* stay out here all night?"

The storm in her chest quieted. She followed her father inside, retracing her steps to the bathroom, and started the shower. Steam coated everything in a light dew as she stepped inside, ignoring the pink plastic razor her mother had left for her. If it didn't matter what Leo did, shouldn't it be the same for her? She could take care of her family, be good to her word, if it meant she could be anything.

Her father banged on the door. "Water's not free."

If it was true about streams and rivers and water running back to the same place, it must be true for water pipes and showers and the things Gia washed away. She shut off the tap. No need to burden fish with everything Gia couldn't be.

~

Gia woke to voices in the hallway. Her room was stifling hot. Hair stuck to her forehead, her nightgown to her back, the air thick. Dawn was breaking in the distance, a line of orange and blue hinting in the sky. Gia had a hard time sleeping, one of the few things she had in common with her brother. She tiptoed to the door. Even the floor was warm.

"And what do we do about this?" her father whispered.

"Maybe he got an early start. You gave him a lot to think about," her mother hissed back.

"If you really think—"

Gia opened the door, squinting at the light. Her parents were in their pajamas, damp with sweat, startled as if she'd crawled out of the linen closet instead of her own bedroom. Gia pushed away the annoyance that they'd forgotten about her again.

"Morning, Gia." Her father changed course as abruptly as a new weather front pushing the old away. "I'm taking the boat out if you *want to* come."

Heck yes. She scurried off to change, the mood shifting again in the hallway, sliding under her door, raising the hair on her arms. She should've listened longer before startling them quiet. Stupid. She brushed her hair and teeth, changed, put a few cookies into her pocket for breakfast, and waited for her father on the porch all before the light drifted up any farther on the horizon. It was still a wavering orange line. She wanted to see the sun come up on the water, turning the waves colors, but her father finished a cigarette in the kitchen, then stopped to pull up the crab traps at the dock, all three, before dropping them back in the water.

Gia untied cleat hitches, coiling rope on the dock.

"Can I do it?" she asked as they motored through the canal, the bay smooth ahead, no whitecaps, just shimmering sun.

"Sure." He slid aside as Gia climbed over the middle. The motor hummed in her hand. She couldn't see very well over her father's shoulders, his blue tattoo especially bright in the sun, but she knew the canal well enough to stay centered and prayed no floating sticks or branches or fishing line would tangle them up, proving she wasn't ready to go out alone.

"Which way?" The bay opened up ahead. She kicked the motor up to handle the current.

"Left." Toward the airport, a short trip, but at least there was one at all. The sun was already hot on her shoulders, the breeze finicky, keeping sailboats moored in the bay.

"Kill the engine," her father said when there was enough room to drift, threading fishing line through a hook. Gia's stomach rumbled, but she couldn't eat when the boat was drifting. She needed to be alert. The boat warmed in the sun, heating the soles of her shoes, as an airplane drove lazily on the ground, positioning for takeoff. He was using rubber bait, which meant he didn't care if they caught anything. She never felt bad for fish dumb enough to fall for rubber bait; they didn't belong in the gene pool.

They weren't far from the marshy shore. The bay was only a few feet deep, too shallow for whales or sunken ships, a disappointing fact that made the whole bay seem like a lie at first, but she'd gotten over it. He cast off. The hook splashed in the distance, reeled in, the rubber fish catching bits of marsh grass. Gia bit off a chunk of cookie, scattering crumbs in the wind for gulls, wishing she'd brought her binoculars. There were osprey nests around here. The babies had hatched a few months ago and would be leaving the nest soon, following the males and begging for food before hunting on their own.

"All right," he said after a while. "How do you know if the anchor's holding?"

Gia perked up. If she knew, he might let her out alone. It was a good sign. At least he was considering at all.

"Easy. By noting your position on land. If the boat moves in a circle, that's OK, but if the position to the thing on land changes, it's dragging."

"What do you do if the outboard gets tangled?" Her father cast off again.

"Cut the engine. Lift it up and cut it free. Also, watch for stuff before it gets tangled."

"What if you're drifting in a bad spot?"

Why would anyone do that? She searched his face for a clue, but he was staring forward, reeling the line back, cutting an invisible line through the water, the rubber fish trailing underneath. Maybe he wasn't talking about the boat anymore.

"What do you mean?"

"Everything's fine till you realize it needed more direction, but by then it's out of hand."

Gia was confused. "Maybe, maybe row if you can't motor and get to a better spot."

Her father nodded, but it didn't seem like he'd heard her at all.

"You know, start over. Try things a different way," Gia pushed on. A gull circled overhead, but the cookies were gone. There was nothing but crumbs in her pocket. The sun burned into her face, making her see spots. If he wasn't talking about the boat, then what was he worrying over?

"What if you're taking on water?" The line was back at the boat now, but he didn't pull it in, just let it dangle.

"Bail. Get to land," Gia said.

"What do you do if it's the middle of the night, middle of the ocean, and a torpedo's heading right for your boat?"

The marsh grass bent as a breeze raced toward them, changing the shadow on the water until Gia felt it on her face, whispering the answer in her ear.

"Pray," she said quietly.

"Never let praying be your only option," he said softly.

"Dad." Gia worked up the nerve. "When do you think I'll be ready to come out here on my own? I'm only two years younger than Leo, and he's allowed."

A plane raced down the runway before its front wheels lifted and the plane tilted toward the sky, aiming for the shadow of the moon. Gia's heartbeat picked up with it.

"Leo . . ." Her father sighed, choosing the right words.

"Is indestructible," Gia finished.

"No." He whirled in the boat. "Nobody's indestructible. Not anyone. Never make that mistake."

Gia stiffened, suddenly uneasy as she thought of that rock in Ray's basement, of the man near the swimming canal, of no one ever believing a dangerous thing was dangerous until it was too late.

Her father steadied himself, holding the seat ahead of him with two fingers.

"Fearless. Your brother is fearless. You are careful, considerate."

"And a girl," Gia finished, which was the only real reason Leo was better suited than she was. Her father reeled in the line one last time before setting the rod aside.

"For fun, why don't you row us back? Prove you could do it if the motor cut out."

Gia stared at the oars. This was her chance, only she'd never used them, never needed to. Her father smirked. He didn't think she could do it. Gia picked the oars up, thinking of the old cops pulling pranks on the rookies, how they respected the ones who bucked up.

The sun beat at her back. The oars were heavy, splintered from years of salt spray. Her first few tries didn't catch or caught on one side but not the other, spinning the boat instead of propelling it.

"All right, there you go. Flatten it out so it cuts like a butter knife; then flip before dropping them again."

The splintered wood spun against the soft part of her hands. Gia huffed, arms screaming, but kept quiet. Blisters pulsed beneath her skin. She pushed into the seat ahead of her, crunching her stomach, leaning as far forward as she could to stretch the oars farther, dropped them in, pulled back, pulling the muscles in her back and shoulders, down her spine, and under her arms so intensely she could feel the web of muscle and sinew that held her together pulling apart like the skin off a rabbit.

"Lean back when you pull. Push off the seat ahead for power."

Sweat burned her eyes, plastered hair to her forehead. *Reach, pull, repeat. Reach, pull, repeat.* Was it working? Her mouth was dust dry, the cookies sour on her tongue. She pressed her eyes shut, sweat welling on the lids. Her face would explode, like a potato in tinfoil for too long, but this was her chance. Her one chance. She couldn't blow it, not when he was trying to prove she'd fail. It would be easier without *him* in the boat, or if she were Leo. They both knew it. His feet were up on the seat ahead, calling instructions over his shoulder like he was helping, but really to make his point. She pulled harder. The marsh grass was moving. The boat was inching away from the airport. Or she hoped it was. She spit an acid taste into the water.

"OK, that's enough. Motor us in."

No. She pulled again. This time, a splinter ripped a blister. Juice ran free, making it harder to grip. The oar slipped. The boat turned. Gia bit her bottom lip, pressed her eyes shut again, blocking the sun overhead, the back of her father's calm head. She imagined the marsh grass sparkling in the breeze, catching this way and that, rooted into the water below, her herons and osprey and seagulls and currents, because she felt most alive here, most Gia. The blood in her veins running like a tide back to sea, pulling with the moon instead of her mother's wishes or her father's, causing this pulled-apart feeling, throat burning, acid swelling. She could not grow up and get married like Aunt Ida, pressing blouses and skirts to sit under fluorescent lights all day in low-heeled pumps, worrying over runs in nylon stockings or how many words she could type per minute or fretting over what to wear to a Tupperware party. She'd rather die.

"Gia, that's enough."

She kicked back again. The boat lurched with the effort. It was moving. Only her stomach was moving too. Bakery sprinkles and butter cookies rising in her throat. She forced it down until she couldn't and vomited into the water, poisoning her fish. She'd failed. Couldn't do it after all. Her father was right. He balled the back of her shirt in his hand to keep her righted, but Gia swatted it away. He held tight. She *would* take this boat out alone—with or without permission. Gia's stomach emptied, heat burning under her skin. She picked up an oar again, but her father yanked it free and tucked it under the seats.

"Motor us in."

The last of her fight was gone. Gia struggled, jelly limbed, to lower the outboard without bouncing it, then to pull the cord hard enough to catch. She got it on the third try, fumes filling her nose, making her queasy again. Water lapped up, splashing her face, offering a cool spot on her hot cheek, promising that the water, at least, knew how much she was struggling, offering just a little comfort.

Her father sat ahead, legs up on the front seat, head back on the middle, the oars and fishing rod tucked into a pile beside him while blisters welled on Gia's hands. She thought of that rock and all the energy it could give her: a million cups of coffee. She needed that now.

"Next time," he said lazily, eyes closed, the sun on his face, "we'll practice getting the outboard untangled."

Leo hadn't done any of this, nor had he asked permission. The trees along the canal were dotted with the first yellow leaves. There wouldn't even be much time left with the boat before fall. Gia dragged a hand through the water, cooling her blisters. She'd tried to do things the right way, but her father didn't leave her much choice. Gia hardened around the idea like mud on bones, cementing it into place. She would just take the boat.

A bigger boat passed by ahead, white and yacht-like with a fancy sun shield and captains' seats. A dock flipped down in the back with a swimming ladder, full of men in bathing suits and slicked-back hair. One sat at the back, leg dangling under the lifeline, his toe lost in the split of the water parting for the boat. He raised a hand to his forehead in a mock salute. Gia ducked slightly behind her father. It was the same man from the canal. She was sure of it. Even the bay was changing. She wouldn't let him stop her from coming out here alone either.

"You know," her father said after the marsh grass ended, "I don't like the way your brother looked last night. You know anything I don't? Like what he's doing over there with Ray and Tommy?"

The houses rose around them on either side of the canal, Howard Beach on one, Hamilton Beach on the other. Boats rocked against weathered docks, tethered on Monday while everyone worked. A feather floated past, gray white like the rock, but the canal was still, quiet, listening. Her voice would carry. The rowing still burned. Why should she make this easier for her father, the investigator, especially when he was using her like bait again? She focused on the dock ahead, thankful when he didn't turn around.

"No." Gia cut the motor and drifted slowly into place. Her blisters stung as she tied off the boat at the bow and stern.

"Nothing you've seen him take or do that seemed different?"

Gia thought of the powder again but shook her head, maybe too quickly, focusing on the knots. Her father nodded. Gia was playing dead, but he'd circle back later like an eagle or a hawk, because little animals scurrying in the undergrowth were hard to catch on the first pass as the world rushed past.

Another plane lifted into the sky. Gia imagined an anonymous someone watching from a tiny window as they covered the boat with a tarp and made their way back to the weathered white-shingled house in silence.

Chapter Four

As soon as the screen door slammed, Gia kicked the ground until her shoe turned green and her toe throbbed beneath the nail, wishing she, like Lorraine, had no father to teach her lessons only he thought were important. She hated him for it. He wasn't even actually stopping her from taking the boat. The key still hung by the door with the others. But he split Gia's thoughts, making her doubt herself. His voice always won, in *her* head. The pain in her toe dulled the ache of rowing and the blisters and the confidence she'd lost this morning.

Across the canal, workers in sweat-stained T-shirts swarmed the hollow houses. Tools pounded on beams, reminding her of microorganisms in the grass, thousands, stamped dead in her fit. And she didn't hate her father. Her eyes welled with angry, tired tears. She just didn't want to be weak. Her own body had proved him right.

The parakeets bounced on the telephone wire. *Get up,* they said. *There's a whole day of summer.* Cicadas revved their hummers. The heat was heavy. They were right. It was too early to be tired and sad. The rabbits stirred behind her. They were hungry.

Gia forced herself inside, tore lettuce leaves from the fridge, and took a box of Life cereal for herself, ignoring the measuring cups Agnes left out for Gia's "figure," which required lots of tools now—bras, slips, nylons, exercise belts, Tab—and food could no longer just be eaten. It had to be planned and measured, boiled or steamed.

Metal clanged behind the house. The cereal box stuck to her skin.

"Aren't you supposed to be looking for a stupid job?" Why did she have to do everything just right, but Leo could do whatever he wanted?

Leo was under the tarp, parts scattered on a towel, his bike propped up between bricks, the dent already hammered out. He was all arms and limbs, like a metal wire twisted to pick a lock, piecing the bike back together again, the money he owed for the Salernos' fence and their father's warning already forgotten.

"This is my job." He wiped sweat from his eyes.

"But Dad said—"

"I know what he said. I have ears. I'm selling it. I have a guy."

"How do you find these people?" She tore open the cereal so fast it spilled, shoved her unwashed hand inside.

"Same way people buy your stupid killies." Gia stopped crunching. Only little kids filled up milk-bottle traps with stale bread and sold silver killies for bait. She sat under the tarp, not because she wanted to sit with Leo but because her father was still inside.

Tools dropped. Leo tightened a bolt until it wouldn't budge any farther. The disjointed sound of it was soothing, even if there wasn't anything like this she could do as well.

"Want a ride?"

"It's done?"

He kicked the bricks away and steadied the handlebars before throwing his legs over the top and revving the engine.

"You're not gonna take the fence down again?"

"There is no fence anymore."

The bike rolled forward, picking up speed as he made lopsided figure eights, wind blowing the hair off his forehead, drying sweat. It was hard to tell where the bike started and Leo ended, his back blending into the curve of it, legs parallel to pipes, only he wasn't metal. Yes, she wanted a ride. As far away as she could get.

She wondered if her father was watching, but the window was dark. Gia climbed on. Holding Leo's waist was weird even if he was part of the bike. Skinny Joseph Salerno was on the front lawn in his swimming shorts. *Go ahead,* Gia thought, *make jokes.* She wouldn't hear him anyway over the wind rushing in her ears, spiraling her hair around her face, billowing her shirt.

The bike moved before she'd settled on. There was never any warning with Leo. Houses whizzed past, the cicadas lost under the engine hum. Wind fuzzed her ears as her legs gripped metal, almost uncomfortably warm. The motion, the heat, the wind, her brother bouncing in place while everything rushed past—it was disorienting. So fast compared to the slow boat, stroke by painful stroke.

The bike stopped at a red light next to New Park Pizza, lights on, ovens warming inside.

"Turn us," he shouted.

Gia pressed her hip lower on the left, turning them onto Cross Bay Boulevard. There were just enough cars to remind them they weren't supposed to ride here. She didn't care. The bakery where Lorraine worked had a line outside the door and smelled like semolina bread. They turned toward the bait shop, where kids sold killies and hermit crabs, away from the supermarket, the bowling alley.

It was a straight shot to Rockaway. After the kiddie rides, only a few of which moved in lazy circles, the stores fell away and the scrub brush opened up, just before Broad Channel, where houses waited on stilts for the bay to wash in. The trees and low brush had been sand pelted until they lost their lushness. Trash was scattered throughout, and a stray cat slithered between the bushes with a mouse in its mouth. She hoped the mouse hadn't eaten poison that would kill the cat. The rushing of the bike made everything feel less real.

They stopped on the bridge. The cars were gone, swallowed by parking lots for Monday errands. It was only Gia and Leo, the bike and the glittering bay. Gia wished she could open her arms and step inside the bay, more than she already was.

"What a dump." Leo pulled a cigarette from his pocket, pointed to the shell of a rusted car in the marsh below. Bay water flowed through the windows. In the distance a garbage barge trudged along, seagulls swarming overhead. The lighter sparked a flame, and Leo inhaled deeply, hopped up to sit on a ledge covered in bird shit, his back to the water.

"The whole city dumps their junk right here. Lucky us."

It wasn't a dump. There was trash, yes, but it was part of it somehow. In the distance, a bayman leaned over the side of his boat with a pole and pulled up a fishing trap. Shiny things slithered over one another until he dumped them into a bucket, reset the empty trap, and chugged off. It was late for baymen. The sun was long up, and baymen in their yellow slickers preferred to be out with just fish and seabirds. Gia understood the need to be alone with the water. It filled her lungs with air.

Their ancestors had been fishermen in Sicily before they'd crossed the Atlantic, leaving behind their boats and traps for a better life, but part of them was in her blood, even if it had skipped Leo and her parents.

"Someday," Gia said, feeling bolder, "I'll make them stop dumping trash and put oysters in the water."

"Yeah? How're you gonna do that?"

"I don't know," Gia said. "But there used to be oysters as big as dinner plates. You could walk across from one side to the other on shells."

Leo squinted into the sun, tossed his cigarette over the bridge. He'd probably rag on her later, but he was OK now. He was better without everyone else around.

"Yeah," she said, making the story a fact. "Oysters change gender to spawn more babies. And they clean the water. Actually clean it. They don't just make pearls like everyone thinks . . ."

It felt good to spew out facts she'd bottled up because no one would listen. A trash barge passed beneath the bridge. Leo glazed over. Gia sped up. There was only so long Leo could be bored.

"Leo?" she worked up the nerve to ask. "What was it like? That stuff at Ray's house?"

In the sun, he had a grubby look to him, like a flag on a pole for too long, but he was amused. "You want to know?"

In one swoop, Leo was standing on the ledge, the street on one side, water on the other. The ledge was the same width as his sneaker. He walked on an angle, part of his shoe over the water. Gia's stomach squeezed into a panic. One truck would rattle the bridge, or one breeze, upsetting the tightrope walk over the water below, which wasn't very deep at all.

"Leo . . ."

"If I jumped, I'd land in that trash heap."

"Leo, get down, please."

But he wasn't listening. His face was drawn as tight as the line he was walking. She should hold the back of his shirt or something, but she was frozen near the bike, which she didn't even know how to ride. Gia squirmed as Leo balanced, arms out to either side, fighting the wind kicking up off the water.

"Leo, can we just go?" The pleading in her voice was pathetic.

He laughed, the sun blurring his face. He stood on one leg, the wind catching his shirt like a sail, and laughed as he jumped and landed with both feet on the sidewalk.

"That's what it's like," he said, pushing the hair out of his face, but it blew right back. "The realest you'll ever feel."

Gia's heart banged in her ears as Leo got on the bike and revved the engine.

"On the way back, look for Help Wanted signs." He smirked.

Gia climbed on behind Leo, just like the way they'd been born, anxious to get home without anything to explain. The bike kicked to life, but Gia was ready this time. She stretched her arms out to either side just to be reckless too. Air whooshed between her fingers, cooling the blisters, as another summer day rolled past.

The scrub brush ended abruptly as stores came into view. Leo turned into a gravel lot, tires crunching. The air stilled as the bike slowed in front of a mechanic's garage with cars on a lift. A tire bounced and rolled to a stop as a man in a greasy jumpsuit cranked a tool on another wheel.

"Hop off," Leo mumbled.

The mechanic tossed an oily bucket into the gravel as Leo rolled the bike forward. Gia cringed at the chemicals dumped on the ground under her feet, evaporating invisible plumes around her like seaweed swaying underwater. She took a few steps back, held her breath for as long as she could.

The bike gleamed. Leo had even shined it. The mechanic was her father's age. The sun had turned him the color of a catcher's mitt. She didn't know his name but knew where he lived. He heaped old things on the front porch and kept a cooler next to a plastic lawn chair, flying a torn-up skull and crossbones from a weathered flagpole. Beside him, Leo was wiry in his sweat-stained T-shirt and greasy jeans, needing a belt and a haircut, his skin different suntanned colors and scraped from taking down the fence, in a mechanic's shop piled with rusting car shells beneath a mosquito cloud. He might grow up to be this man, Gia realized, not a war hero or a Hells Angel.

The mechanic pressed the tires, bounced the handlebars, inspecting metal like a doctor telling the bike to open up and say *ah*. He shook Leo's hand with a wad of cash, and Leo walked away without the bike, gravel crunching, sunlight gleaming off his forehead. He looked less without it, more like the fifteen-year-old he actually was. It made Gia feel less too.

"You sold it? Just like that? How do we get back?"

"Walking."

"What?" The sun was so hot, the air still. Gia pulled a face, but Leo was already ahead.

"How much did you get for it?"

"Enough for two sodas. One if you're annoying."

"But really. How much?"

"I don't ask about your babysitting money."

"Is it enough to fix the fence?"

Silence. Maybe losing a bike was like losing the boat. They walked in silence; Gia stopped only once to pick up a palm-size squirrel skull from the overgrown brush, its teeth still intact. She would put it with her mother's seashell collection on the windowsill and see how long it took her to notice.

Power lines buzzed staticky and hot. Too loud. Up ahead, sparks flew from a transformer. The traffic lights went dead. Cars stopped all over the street, blared horns, daring each other to move. People came out of stores to look around. Yes, it was everywhere, not just theirs.

This was exciting. Stores would give away ice cream before it melted. Tonight, there'd be real stars usually hidden by streetlight haze. No airplanes. Everything would be quiet and dark like it had been when people had lived off eels and oysters. It was perfect, even if it meant her father would be called in to protect from looters and people who used the absence of light to do bad things.

Cars inched along Cross Bay. Up ahead, a car slowed at the traffic light before peeling through the intersection, burning rubber to make a U-turn over the grassy divider. Ray and Tommy. When everyone else was going home to wait out the chaos, Ray drove right into it.

"Hop in," Ray called, shaking the hair out of his eyes.

"And you didn't want to walk." Leo smirked, taking the front seat, Gia and Tommy the back. Leather burned the back of her legs. The car sweltered, even with the windows down, and then air rushed as Ray burned a cloud of smoke, weaving through cars. Gia gripped the door handle, and Tommy bounced into her; she counted down to home as everything rushed past. Ray turned the radio all the way up, so loud it jumbled words. Hair whipped her face, lashed her eyes. Tommy punched at the roof and yelled for Ray to go faster as Gia prayed to slow down.

At New Park, Ray slammed the car to a stop. "Under fifteen, hop out."

Gia hopped out gladly. The sidewalk was gloriously still under her feet. But Tommy simmered.

"What the hell?"

Ray didn't even turn around, just gave Tommy eyes in the rearview mirror, waiting him out until he gave up and slammed the door.

"We could swim," Gia suggested. They used to like diving for stuff in the canal. Popsicle sticks. Horseshoes. Holding their breath underwater. Racing from dock to dock. But Tommy stared after Ray's beat-up Hornet like he'd passed up a date with Jane Fonda. Was she missing something? Leo's hand was out the window as Gia's had been on the bike, wind blowing through his fingers, catching the end of a summer that fall would soon forget, as they sped off through timid cars and broken traffic lights until they were gone.

~

Gia rounded up flashlights, candles, batteries, and torches from the garage. The house sweltered. Her mother lit the barbecue and grilled all the meat in the freezer so it wouldn't go bad. They ate hamburgers without buns and hot dogs on forks before the sun set behind the canal, and then they went swimming. Even Agnes waded out to her knees and splashed water over her shoulders. The hermit crabs brushed past their feet with fuzzy shells. Gia splashed and flipped in the water, spitting it from her lips and shaking it from her ears. There were mosquitoes and fireflies, but no one minded. They walked back without towels, the lingering water keeping them cool. Firecrackers popped in the distance.

Dying coals threw off smoke behind them as a praying mantis watched them from the peony bush, still as a leaf, one leg poised in midair. She would watch it tonight in case it was mating and the female would bite the male's head off. If the moon was bright enough, she wouldn't need a flashlight.

"Can I sleep outside?"

"Yes," her mother said, damp curls coiling on either side of her face, staring into the setting sun. It surprised Gia to see her mother enjoying this night without chores or TV, eating an unbalanced meal. "Only if your brother does too."

Gia sighed. Of course. Mentioning Leo reminded Agnes that he was not there, zeroing her attention in on him again. The dreamy look fell away with it.

"Is he job searching?" She lit a cigarette with the citronella candle on the table. Straightened her shoulders. Ashes scattered in Gia's direction. A mosquito danced above the flame. Gia felt like she was being dangled above a flame too.

"I think so." Her heart sensed the lie and picked up speed.

"Where? Your father's gonna want specifics."

"Ask him. I don't know."

"He should've been home by now. Nothing's open. Maybe he found something and started working right away? That's what must've happened. Good. He'll take care of that fence. I don't like looking at it like that. Makes me feel like we've done something wrong with it staring at us till it's fixed."

Agnes's mouth closed around the cigarette in a little O. She breathed deeply and tapped it against an ashtray.

Did she really not see? Gia examined the things Agnes tried to hide: her foot grinding a circle in the grass, the way she leaned forward as she waited for someone to contradict her. Part of her knew, or she wouldn't need a cigarette to calm the unease.

"I hope it's not a restaurant. They're all owned by you-know-what. I don't want him caught up in that."

She snubbed the cigarette out for emphasis and lit another. Gia thought of the man by the swimming canal and cringed.

"He's a good kid," Agnes said to no one. "Just needs a little push."

A firefly landed on Gia's hand, spread its wings, closed them again.

"Let's check on Diane. I worry about her in this heat." Agnes pushed up from the table as Gia stacked cheeseburgers on top of one another and piled hot dogs, remembering Nonna suddenly. It was the first thing she'd eaten off the boat at Ellis Island, a hot dog.

Tinfoil rattled as they crossed the street. Lorraine was at the door before they knocked, sweaty, her hair combed back into a ponytail.

"Her blood pressure's high, and she's not in a good mood," Lorraine said. Of course, Gia thought. Why would she be, without TV? To Gia, it was horrible, constant chatter, whirling fans, commercial jingles, laugh tracks. But for Diane, it didn't matter what it was as long as it was on.

"Let me try," Agnes offered. Lorraine shrugged, and Gia thought it was brave of her mother.

"Hello, hello," she sang out, at odds with the living room two steps lower than the rest of the first floor, like Aunt Diane had weighed it down until it gave up and sank.

"He's wild," Diane said. "It's dangerous."

The edge in Aunt Diane's voice challenged the softness of her body, like Silly Putty wrapped around nails. Gia thought of the boys racing down Cross Bay, burning rubber. Did she mean them?

"What are you talking about?" Agnes forgot to exhale as she settled onto the arm of the couch.

"Did it look directly at you?" Diane's head pivoted toward Gia, her pointed finger emphasizing each word, and Gia felt stabbed through. "It'll make you sick."

Gia froze. She was right. Nonna had always said that if a praying mantis looked directly at you, it would make you sick. Diane had seen that mantis, in her head, same as she'd seen Uncle Lou's plane fall from the sky, and maybe other things, too, but no one talked about them because they were all spooked after Uncle Lou.

"Right." Agnes stood, patted Diane's shoulder while clearing away the most recent bottle, pinching it like a dead bug in a napkin, hiding her disgust with a fake cheery voice. "We'll come back another day, Diane."

Lorraine leaned against the doorway, rubbing her forehead.

"You're welcome to sleep at our house," Agnes said to Lorraine, and then, quieter, "We should go down to the VA and see if they can write the checks to you instead. She's getting out of hand."

"I hear you." Diane whirled. "There's nothing wrong with me. The world is falling apart." Diane made the sign of the cross, gathered her housedress, and settled into a charged silence.

Gia stared at her aunt, who had seen a world war and blacked out the windows when air-raid sirens had rung out, who'd welded metal at the navy yard while the men were away, sparks flying in her face as she'd pieced together machinery. But tonight, in Queens, the world was falling apart. And Gia's brother had disappeared into it, and her father was out there trying to hold it together.

Lorraine set up a bowl of cool water with a washcloth for her mother, dabbed it over her forehead. She was staying, then, in this hot house with that folded flag on the mantel staring down at them through stars and stripes. It was the saddest family Gia had ever seen: Diane, that flag, and Lorraine. Gia fought the urge to hold her mother's hand.

"Let's go," Agnes whispered.

The parakeets on the wire were in a line, swinging with the breeze. The phone was ringing in their house. Agnes hurried across the street while Gia gathered up the plates and blew out the citronella candle, the praying mantis hiding in the bush.

"Your father's not coming home tonight. They're rioting again. Burning everything in Bed-Stuy. Gia, bring the dishes and wash them before it gets too dark. And no sleeping outside. I want you in."

Whatever summer spell Agnes had been under was over. The door slammed. The rabbits shuffled. Gia locked the hutch and carried the plates inside, wondering why anyone would want to burn anything on a night as hot as this.

~

That night, a fire glowed in the distance. Smoke hung in the air, and sirens wailed far away, hopefully not where her father was, her bad feelings toward him haunting her now. Heat lightning argued in the sky. "Have you seen Leo?" her mother asked the kitchen receiver, worrying the phone cord into a tangle. No, Aunt Ida must've said, because her mother said she hadn't seen Ray either. Tommy was probably farting around at home like she was, feeling especially left out now that the sun was down and the boys weren't home. It wasn't full dark yet, but time went away with electricity.

Her mother hung up, and it was quiet again, full of a stillness that didn't extend beyond the porch. She wished her father and her brother were home. She felt less safe without them. Agnes dialed another number.

A gunshot sounded in the distance, echoing through the quiet. Gia sprang up, gathered the rabbits from the hutch. They couldn't stay there. She locked the front door and let the rabbits hop free in her room, tucking herself into the linen closet, something she hadn't done since she was little. The heat and detergent smell were almost unbearable, but there was just enough room beneath the last shelf for Gia. The chaos outside didn't fit here. It was just Gia and the dark until sometime in the night, when the power came back on and her brother tiptoed past.

"We got stuck," he told Agnes over breakfast the next morning, the half moons beneath his eyes dark as the rain clouds gathered outside, low and gray. "The cops set up a roadblock, and we couldn't get through."

"From Rockaway?" Agnes repeated. Leo nodded, twirling a sweating glass of milk between his hands. Agnes pressed her lips into a line and cooked an egg, gas burning blue beneath the pan. He didn't mention selling the bike or Ray speeding down Cross Bay.

"But I found a job," he said. "Wasn't that what you wanted me to do?"

Agnes said nothing. The clock on the wall was stuck at nine a.m. She flipped the egg as the edges curled, shut off the burner with a snap, and slid the overcooked egg onto a plate. The toaster popped. *Say it,* Gia wished. *You know he's lying.* But her mother quietly gathered her things for work, sipping the last of her coffee, waiting for Eddie to be her voice, and slipped out of the house as if she had something to apologize for and not Leo.

"What kind of job?" Gia crossed her arms over her chest.

"Working for Ray. He's got something for you too." Leo dropped his plate into the sink without washing it. "Go see him."

The rain started outside. Fast and heavy, finally breaking through the heat. The relief of it ran through her veins. She didn't understand what Ray could possibly want, but Leo was already upstairs, the shower running. A dove cooed on the windowsill. She would have to ask Ray herself.

Chapter Five

It rained for nearly two days. The thundering of water on concrete changed to water on water. The sewers spewed until it was raining from above and below. Ducks swam past in the street, where the water was deeper than parts of the bay. Gia pressed the pleats in her uniform skirt, willing them to sharpen as her mother wished. *Lazy pleats, lazy person.* School meant a schedule full of nuns, her mother's campaign to transform her intensifying. The pink razor had been repositioned in the shower, a bag of makeup left on her bed, the date of the fall dance circled on the calendar, making Gia wish she could wash out like driftwood and turn up somewhere else.

Lorraine waded over in a plaid pantsuit with plastic bags of school supplies. It was daring: a woman in a pantsuit. They divided the supplies up on the table—marble notebooks, number two pencils with perfect points, stacks of loose-leaf paper—and clipped them into last year's binders. They'd done this for as long as Gia could remember, only there weren't any crayons anymore, or markers, or stickers. It was more serious-looking stuff now.

"What is there to think about? You should go."

Part of her wanted to see streamers hanging from the gym ceiling, trellis archways and pop-up walls, a crepe-paper forest of reds, greens, and gold, nuns making popcorn and spinning cotton candy.

"What do you even *do* at a dance?"

"You eat, dance, take small sips of spiked drinks if you're lucky, talk . . ."

"Yeah, but . . ." The boy part threw her. Boys were booger-picking schoolyard fighters. With dances, they were something else, but what? Lorraine dragged her pen along a spiral notebook as Gia squirmed.

"You know, Gia, you really are pretty. You just don't know it. But it's useful."

"Useful?" A Swiss Army knife was useful. Pretty didn't come with tools.

"Yes, useful." The front door opened, and the conversation shut with it. "You'll see." Lorraine doodled her name in a new notebook, giving Gia one quick raised eyebrow, as Agnes breezed in with groceries, opened cupboards, and pulled dinner things from the refrigerator.

"Your father is coming home," Agnes sang out, unpacking groceries. "The rain finally put the fires out in Bed-Stuy, stopped the riots. You believe it started because some landlord sprayed a group of kids sitting on the stoop with a hose? Three days of riots and looting, terrifying, all because some guy didn't want kids sitting on his stoop." She shook her head.

Gia and Lorraine raised eyebrows. It was more complicated than that; people were sick of being told what to do. Ten years after Rosa Parks wouldn't give up her seat on the bus, people still couldn't sit on a stoop. It was the same for women, trapped under their bell jars, as Sister Gregory called them. She thought about Aunt Diane at the navy yard, welding along with the rest of them, sent home the day the war ended and told to learn typing. Of Lorraine, who'd be a nurse but never a doctor. Of the people who bought things on store shelves, believing they were safe, only for those same products to poison them slowly. It was unfair, and it seemed to Gia that the world was waking up slowly.

"Your brother. He's home?"

"I think so," Gia said. He'd eaten a whole box of cereal in front of the TV earlier, lifting dumbbells during commercial breaks, but she didn't know where he was now. Agnes looked between Gia and the ceiling, where Leo's bedroom would be. There would be a talk when her father got home.

"Is he sick?" Agnes scrunched her forehead. It was unusual for Leo to be home, grounded or not.

Yes, Gia thought. *He has an incurable case of the idiots.*

"And what is that you're wearing?" Agnes's already-scrunched forehead tightened as she looked at Lorraine. "It's all connected?"

Gia swallowed the giggles and wiped her face. No way that pantsuit would end up folded at the foot of her bed, which almost made her want one.

"You know, we were just discussing the dance," Lorraine said, as easily as setting out a beer can for slugs, drowning Gia in bubbles and yeast.

"Oh?" Agnes forgot the groceries. Cabinets gaped as Agnes imagined dressy pictures by the mantel, corsages, warning about curfews while Eddie glowered in his uniform to make a point, watching by the window as Gia climbed into a car in a taffeta dress.

"But she needs to learn how to dance."

You're getting the malocchio *for this,* she promised, raising her index finger and pinkie so only Lorraine could see, but it didn't matter because Lorraine had a red ribbon under her mattress, same as they all had since they were infants, thanks to Nonna.

Agnes lit up, hurried to the living room, and shoved aside the coffee table, newspapers on the floor, hands flying in every direction like on that game show with the supermarket runners filling the carts before the time ran out. It was completely mortifying.

Lorraine snapped her books shut with a glint in her eye as Agnes pulled records from sleeves. The record player spun quietly, clicking, until Agnes settled an album into place. Crackling to a start, an old, fuddy-duddy Sinatra song from family parties or New Year's Eve, when everyone wore paper hats before the ball dropped.

"Shall we?" Agnes sang.

"Shoes off," Lorraine suggested. "It's easier in socks."

Lorraine stood next to Agnes, facing Gia like captains picking teams in gym, hopeful until the options dwindled.

"Pretend there's a box on the floor. Always start with the right. Right foot, top corner," Lorraine said. "Like Twister. Your left lands lightly, like there's an ant you don't want to squash. Just trace the box."

"A small box," Agnes suggested. It *was* less awkward with smaller steps.

"Good," Lorraine said. "Now, the first two steps are slow, then quick, quick."

"We'll get to hands later." Agnes smiled, which only made Gia aware of the wet spaghetti hanging at her sides. Gia traced the box in silence. Doing this with a boy near her face? The smells alone would be overwhelming: soap, breath, sweat, aftershave. No. A panic welled up in the pit of her stomach as Lorraine prompted her to look up, but there were too many things to look at: the framed picture of Nonna and Pop Pop on their wedding day, not smiling, on the mantel; Leo in his Confirmation suit; Gia at her first Communion, hands in prayer under a lace veil; two tarnished candlesticks. Gia lost the box.

"Pick a focus point," Agnes suggested. "I always pick a brick on the wall."

Gia was sweating: on her forehead, under her arms, down her spine. Wasn't she supposed to be dry, like the magazine-ad women with powdery, fresh skin? The fireplace bricks shifted. Everything was moving too fast.

"OK, now." Agnes and Lorraine shared the same box, a confusing jumble of hands on shoulders and waists, intertwined in the air. Lorraine was taller, her lines colored in and filled out, leaving an empty space for Agnes. Gia was wispy and unfinished, too, but less so, deflating her further. They skipped around the living room as one unit, leaving a maze of footprints in the rug as Gia's knees pressed into the coffee table, waiting for the moment it clicked, like algebra, the formulas on the chalkboard finally recognizable.

They didn't hear the door over the music. Eddie framed the doorway, his uniform hat at his side like a fallen star, shoes in hand because of the high water, smelling like smoke, wavering slightly on his feet from three days without sleep, trying to hide the gash on his face by turning away as Lorraine and Agnes zipped by, a trail of perfume in their wake.

Agnes spun to a stop when she saw him; brushing hair from her face, and hustling over to lower the music, she said, "Gia's learning to dance."

Her pride was contagious. It made the house feel more alive, the floral print on the couch ready to throw back its plastic cover and grow into a jungle, covering the living room with vines, but Gia was mortified. Getting caught doing girl things was worse than rowing.

"I see," he said. The music warmed him, stripping away the things he'd seen over the past three days in layers that almost gathered around his feet. "Shouldn't the student be dancing?"

"I should get you something to eat." Agnes hurried to take his hat as Eddie rolled his sleeve past his elbow, where the anchor trailed off. That tattoo was her father through and through: frayed rope and salty metal. "And you should lie down."

He looked exhausted, but even more, he looked disappointed. It settled in the lines around his mouth and eyes, but he wouldn't talk about it, same as he didn't talk about the war or any other day at work. Those things were better left where they belonged.

"One dance." He held out his hand to Gia, and some of the disappointment fell away, a tired smile hinting at the corner of his mouth. Gia didn't want to dance, was glad the music had been turned down, but how could she say no?

"A good man asks first. You told her?" He looked at Agnes, then back to Gia. "Any boy who wants to take you to a dance has to ask me first. Understood?"

"No one has to ask you anything, you old grump," Agnes teased, plopping down on the couch, Lorraine beside her, their hair scattered, faces flushed, eyes shiny.

The attention was dizzying, even if dancing was embarrassing. Her insides were singing like she was running her finger around the rim of one of the fancy crystal glasses they used on holidays.

"A slow song, please?" Gia took her father's hand. He put his hand on her waist, their toes facing off. It was weird, her father's stubbled chin, the heat from his hand. She didn't know where to look exactly, so she looked at their feet. Agnes adjusted the stereo, clicked a new record into place, moved the needle to the right groove.

"Edelweiss," her father's favorite. She could pretend she was just brushing her teeth, her father humming down the hall.

On the first step, Gia forgot where her foot was supposed to go.

"Let my foot chase yours," he said. Gia nodded and looked down. Her father drummed his finger against hers, humming along. This time, Gia was ready. They made the box; he spun her away and back, flipping the room, then again. She was doing it. She was dancing, the surprise of it overshadowing the complicated look on Lorraine's face as Agnes whispered something into her ear, squeezed her hand. Maybe how Uncle Lou and Aunt Diane used to go dancing every Saturday night, even at the Copacabana once. The song ended, and her father gave a little bow. She lifted the hem of an imaginary dress and did her best impression of a curtsy. From the dreamy look on her mother's face, she must've done OK.

"I should start dinner," Agnes said. "And you should wash up. I'll get some peroxide."

Eddie put his arm around Gia, pulled her into a side hug, and kissed the top of her head. Then he was gone, both of them holding on to the moment a little longer in private. It felt like she'd stepped over a barrier, and it hadn't been as scary with her father. Gia and Lorraine pulled the coffee table into place and smoothed the plastic on the couch but left the record player on, music tinkling, a reminder that something special had happened.

Later at dinner, Eddie took a first bite of food, a second. "What the heck was she wearing?" he asked between bites. "Why's she dressed like a plaid mechanic?"

"It's a pantsuit," Gia argued. "They're in now."

And everything went back to normal.

~

After dinner, Gia pushed the kayak off the front porch and paddled down the street, testing every few strokes to make sure it wouldn't bottom out. Water lapped at front porches, begging to be let in; a fish swam past where cars should have been. *Water world,* she thought, smiling to herself.

Ray was on the roof above the front porch, smoking a cigarette. A curtain blew through the open window, begging at his shoulder like a cape. Even with his rolled-up pants and bare feet, he looked like a king surveying his land.

"Where's your brother?" he called.

"Grounded," she said. "Dad's home." Which meant it was enforceable.

Ray tapped the ashes from his cigarette. "Heard he got good money for the bike."

Gia nodded. A car passed where the water wasn't as deep, rocking the kayak beneath her.

"Tell him I got parts for the new one. Tommy's working on it. How about you? You want to make some money too?"

"I don't know how to fix bikes."

"Something else." Ray stubbed out the cigarette on a shingle, let it roll into the gutter.

Her brain did laps trying to figure out what Ray wanted. The neighborhood dripped. End-of-day sun peeked from behind the last storm clouds, washing out Ray's pale skin and the dark half moons under his eyes. He had the same slick daddy longlegs build as Leo, venomous but smart enough not to bite people. No one cared about a dangerous thing if it didn't threaten them.

"Just tell your friends to come see me. And make some new ones. Not the usual losers."

"How . . ."

But Ray pointed to the open window, where the vacuum revved and a shadow passed. Aunt Ida didn't wave hello. Not to Gia; she paled in comparison to beautiful Lorraine, who took such good care of Aunt Diane, or her sons, who would go to college, the first in the family, while Gia brought dead things home from the marsh. It was mutual. Being around Aunt Ida was like watching a vase too close to the edge of a shelf.

"Dock three on Friday night. Tell them to say your name."

"For what?"

"Keep it mysterious, Gia." Ray winked. "It'll work out better that way."

Three strokes turned the kayak. She paddled up the street, knowing this must have something to do with the basement and wasn't good. But money meant gas for the boat. If she saved up all year, she could be on the water every day next summer. Plus, she wanted to make her own way. Nonna had only been four years older when she'd stepped off the boat on Ellis Island and made a new life.

The water washed everything clean—all the chemicals, the grease in the street—the sun drying away whatever was left. The sparrows were safe in the newly washed trees, and Gia's lungs felt clean, too, but as she tugged the kayak onto the porch, a dead rat floated out from underneath, bloated and belly up. Sticks and a plastic bag clung to it on either side. Nonna would've called it a sign. Dead things always were. And now Gia wondered if something invisible was coming again, as it had for the sparrows.

~

That night, Gia curled up with *Silent Spring*. It was still early, but her father was sleeping. She skimmed chapters, certain she'd find a clue about the feeling she'd had since earlier, her skin coated with something she couldn't see. A silent threat. Low tide crept through her window, sulfurous and rich with plants that grew beneath the surface, as the street water rolled away with it.

Someone knocked lightly. Gia straightened her sheets and closed her book as Agnes slipped inside with a small, tired smile and settled on the foot of her bed in her outside clothes. The same blue blouse and brown skirt that touched subway seats. Low-grade nausea spread through Gia as the fabrics rubbed together, a mingling of germs beneath a tin box on her mother's lap, tied with a bow.

"Ready for school tomorrow?"

Gia shrugged.

"It's always come so easily to you." Agnes looked off through the dark window, partially blocked by Gia's pleated uniform hanging from the curtain rod. "You've probably read more books than I ever will."

It was better sometimes, with Agnes, to listen and wait for the point of this unusual visit, realizing she'd never seen her mother read a book, only the newspaper on occasion or the circulars inside. Reading was a tool like a fork or a knife.

"Eighth grade is important. It's the last one before high school. In only five years, Gia, you'll be an adult. It seems far away, but it's not. I want you to be ready. More than I was, and so . . ."

Her voice trailed off. She toyed with the navy ribbon on the tin. At least it wasn't pink.

"I want you to try." She stared at Gia intently. *Try to grow up. Be more like Lorraine.* "If I see that you're trying to become the young lady we expect you to, I will talk to your father about the boat."

Gia sat up straighter, eye level with Agnes instead of slumped into her pillows.

"I know how much it means to you, and you know how much cooperating would mean to me, so . . . there you have it." She slid the tin to Gia, nodding for her to open it.

A peace offering was always a trap. She untied the ribbon and shimmied the lid open to a watercolor set. Beyond dotting scrap paper with bingo markers, Gia had never painted.

"Since you like the water so much, I thought you might like to paint it."

The tiny brushes and pots of dry paint were an entry into sewing and decorating cakes, typing, crocheting blankets for babies, something her mother could brag about to her canasta friends. She didn't want to paint the marsh; she wanted to examine it, collect from it, experiment with it, learn how it worked, protect it. But her mother was promising the boat. Gia forced a tepid smile.

"Maybe this would be a good year to spend more time with Lorraine. She could get you a job at the bakery. It'd be fun, chatting with the girls there; they all seem nice."

Make new friends. Ray's words echoed.

Agnes shrugged as if this were a casual idea, but she'd probably already spoken to Lorraine. Gia bit her bottom lip. It didn't sound fun at all. Maybe to Agnes, who'd worked in a factory at thirteen, sewing buttons on shirts, and gone to night school for typing. She wished her mother were thirteen and could wear Gia's school uniform, do all the things she thought Gia should. Then she'd see how fun any of it actually was.

"Maybe," she said.

Agnes patted Gia's foot under the blanket. Then gave it a little squeeze, as close as either of them would get toward a hug.

"Oh." She paused by the door, light spilling onto her stockinged feet. "Next time you put a skull near my seashells, I'm docking your allowance."

For the first time that night, Gia's face lit up in a real smile. She forgot about the subway clothes as she buried giggles in the quilt.

~

A stick bounced against the screen.

"Come to the tennis courts." Tommy was red faced through the window. "Ray got bottle rockets."

"I'll get Leo," Gia said, forgetting he was grounded.

"He's already there. Lorraine too."

"Coming." Gia crept down the stairs and closed the screen door quietly. The neighborhood was still: bikes put away off front lawns, the canal rippling without moving boats, early dusk lighting with stray fireflies. They ran the whole way, feet pounding, talking between puffs. Gia could've left meatball Tommy in her dust but slowed down because he'd come to get her in the first place. That counted for something.

The park sat at the tip of the neighborhood, the farthest anyone could go before they ended up in the water. Hardly anyone used the broken picnic tables. The cracks in the tennis courts were full of weeds as tall as Gia, where tennis players should've skittered across. The guy who'd founded Howard Beach had owned a glove factory and a goat farm, had built a bunch of little houses and a big hotel in the 1800s, intending the residents to be glove-wearing, tennis-playing people, but it hadn't worked out that way.

"We got roman candles. Bottle rockets. Whistling moons," Tommy puffed just as the first whistling moon popped off up ahead, screaming into the bay. What'd he make, a list?

"Wait for us," Gia shouted. Lorraine was sitting on a picnic table behind the chain-link fence holding a sparkling roman candle in one hand and a bottle in the other, while Ray and Leo lined up more bottles on the court. Tommy and Gia walked the rest of the way across the overgrown grass, picking their way around broken bottles, stray bits of frayed tires, balloon strings.

"Let me get some." Tommy held out his hand to Lorraine. She handed him the roman candle. "Not that."

"How old are you anyway?" she teased, handing him the bottle. Tommy took a swig, fighting back a cringe before passing it to Gia.

"You even drink it?" Gia asked. "Let me smell your tongue."

"That's disgusting." Tommy backed away, swinging through the gate to the tennis courts, too full of the last night before school started and bottle rocket glow to care what Gia said.

Leo and Ray snapped a flame to each rocket, lingering longer than necessary near each one, while Tommy hung back with his red face and pudgy belly, *supervising* like Uncle Frank. He was too scared to light any himself but Gerber Baby smiling with the excitement of what other people were brave enough to do. Aunt Ida bragged about what a good engineer he'd be, designing mechanical parts, but Tommy wasn't smart like that. Never would be. The best he'd do with graph paper was color in the boxes real nice.

"Poor Tommy." Lorraine sighed.

Rockets whistled into the sky, one after another, screaming through TV dinners and last-minute summer book reports. She was grateful to step outside the wheel before it started again, so much so that she took the bottle from Lorraine and gulped a stinging mouthful to make it last longer while Lorraine's roman candle burned out in a frenzy of sparks.

"Don't you wish you could take off like that?" Lorraine traced the arc in the sky. "Look down at all this and think, *OK, doesn't matter. Fizzle, fizzle, pop. You're done.*"

She didn't. Not really. She just wanted to snap a lighter to those wicks and watch them take off.

"Again!" Gia shouted, bolder as the liquid warmed her stomach. The boys reset, frayed jeans dragging on the baked clay. Lorraine leaned over, her eyes a little glazed in the dim light, and kissed Gia's cheek.

"What's that for?"

"For being you, dummy. Just 'cause. Guess what? Ray's teaching me to drive next week."

"Yeah?"

"Yeah. Wanna come?"

"OK."

"Then I'm gonna save up for a car and take a road trip. All the way to Florida." Lorraine tipped her head back and closed her eyes, wiggling her toes in imaginary sand as a plane took off, louder than all the rockets combined. Lorraine's eyes popped open.

"I wanna go too," Gia said, wishing for orange groves and palm trees, but the plane drowned her out. The boys lit the next round, swigging from their own bottle as the sticks fizzed and took off, one after another. The quiet moment when they'd flown as high as they were going before exploding in the sky was the best.

Leo threw an empty bottle. It shattered on the tennis court. And suddenly they were all throwing bottles. Even Tommy. The bottles popped, cracked, rolled, glass scattering. Gia dug in the grass for more bottles to throw, and there were always more. Beer bottles. Forties. Coca-Cola. The court sparkled with glass, a sky of stars on the ground. They laughed as another one crashed down. No one cared about bottle deposits. Not since they were little kids and piggy bank change was exciting. There were a lot of things, Gia realized, a sudden sadness creeping into her fuzzy thoughts and frenzied laughter, that weren't exciting anymore now that she wasn't little.

Leo climbed the fence. It shook under his weight, but he climbed fast without shoes and threw a bottle from the top just as a siren whooped and a flash of blue and red lit the purple sky. They couldn't get in trouble now. Not when they were outside the world.

"Shit," Ray mumbled.

Leo jumped down, his bare feet landing on glass, but he didn't even cringe. The cops pulled to the curb. Two uniforms. No one they knew. A flashlight beam hit Gia's face, shining on the mess they'd made of the court.

"Run," Ray hissed. Gia burst through the gate, scattering away from the rest of them, arms and legs swinging.

"Stop," someone shouted. But the world zipped past, motorcycle fast. They were going for the boys, but Gia zipped past this house and that, all the way to the swimming canal, before splashing in, the water cold and sudden. What a stupid thing, running from cops, but the water hid her, far from slow Tommy, who'd cry at the station until Aunt Ida picked him up, from Ray and his smart words, or from Leo, who'd hot-wire that cop car not to get caught, but Gia had her water. She hummed quietly, trailing her fingers as her shoes weighed at her feet, feeling like a wild and dangerous creature in her own right, until the water couldn't warm her anymore and her fingertips pruned.

Only the boys hadn't gotten away. Gia hid in the rhododendron bushes in Mr. Angliotti's yard as the cop cars, two, sat dark on the street. Two porch lights snapped on, and two sets of parents waited on the porch as two boys got walked up a paved walkway, and one got walked up a path of overgrown stepping-stones. It was the distraction she needed to slip around back, her wet clothes dripping on the ground as she found new ones in her drawer. The cops were still downstairs talking to Eddie in the doorway. She caught the words *courtesy* and *bring him in* and *contraband* and *inebriated* while Leo waited at the kitchen table.

The door closed. Gia watched from the top of the stairs as Eddie scruffed Leo and prodded him up the steps while Leo tripped over himself. He stumbled to the bathroom with a dumb half smile on his face, where Eddie started the shower and shoved Leo in with his clothes on. Leo curled into himself, the smile falling away as his jeans soaked through. It was ugly.

"That's enough, Eddie. He's freezing." Agnes twisted her nightgown, working the fabric into a crumpled ball, squeezing, releasing.

"Make a pot of coffee, would you? Black."

Agnes looked between Eddie and Leo, who was curled in a ball, shivering. He didn't have much fat on him, and the cold seeped into his bones. Chicken skin, Nonna would've called it, rubbing a sun-warmed towel over them. Gia scurried back to her bedroom, but she wasn't fast enough. Agnes stared at Gia's wet hair, at the wet prints to Gia's room. For a quick second, there was hurt on her mother's face that made Gia sorry; then it hardened. She'd blown it. Any chance of her mother asking for the boat was over.

"Go to your room. I'll deal with you later."

Gia hardened too. Of course. Leo first. As always.

The unreal feeling ebbed as coffee brewed downstairs and the shower water finally stopped. Gia felt right back in the world again, with all of its sharp angles.

Chapter Six

Gia woke up with a mouthful of cotton and a headache above her right eye. It drummed through her dream about bottle rockets underwater, the muffled sound traveling for miles while her mother sat on a rock and painted the fireworks with the watercolor set, Gia's head beating in time with the ripples on the water. If that was what a few sips from that bottle could do, she did not know how Aunt Diane drank through them all day long. Her head must be close to cracking open.

Or Leo, who was down the hall brushing his teeth for school already, swishing and spitting into the bathroom sink louder than necessary while the electric mixer whirled to life in the kitchen.

"Let's go." Her father rapped on the bathroom door. "Move it along."

Both their feet pounded down the steps, and then her father was counting in the yard, up to fifty and over again. Gia sat up. Her alarm was set to go off in two minutes, but she silenced it early. No ringing. No, thank you.

Her door opened, and her mother rattled in with a glass of water and a cupped hand, her mouth set in a thin line. She charged around the room, kicking dirty clothes on the floor into a pile. This was a crackdown if ever she'd seen one.

"Up. Now." The cup of water was in Gia's face, along with two aspirin that stuck to Gia's dry tongue, releasing an acrid taste worse than the rock in Ray's basement. She would absolutely not swallow these chemicals. Not a chance. "You're not off to a very good start."

"It's one minute to seven, and I was already up."

Her mother crossed her arms and clucked her tongue, an old habit, borrowed from Nonna. Gia's head hurt too much to care. The police hadn't even taken her home. She'd come home all on her own, wet, but that wasn't even unusual.

"I want all these clothes picked up and put in the wash. It smells like a pet store in here. No more wet clothes on the floor. Be down to breakfast in fifteen minutes."

The teakettle whistled on the stove downstairs, and her mother hurried off. Gia blinked away the sun as a new round of counting started from the yard. Leo was doing push-ups while Eddie stood over him, sipping from a coffee mug in his favorite black-and-white tracksuit. From high up, his scalp was visible through his hair, and it creeped her out to see the lumps in his skull. Leo's T-shirt was plastered to his back. His arms wobbled, but when he finished, Eddie demanded fifty more until Leo puked in the grass.

The whole thing felt like an episode of *The Twilight Zone*.

Gia made her bed, put her uniform on, everything she would've done anyway without being told. She even opened the bag of makeup and did what she could. The concealer erased the dark circles under her eyes, but the eye shadow made her look punched, so she wiped it off and rolled lip gloss on until it was sticky enough to catch bugs, pleased with herself for trying. She took an osprey feather from her drawer and put it in her pocket for good luck.

Downstairs, her mother put two pancakes on everyone's plate without any syrup and drank coffee by the kitchen sink, staring past the seashell collection on the windowsill to the house across the street, where the Salerno kids were taking first-day-of-school pictures in front of a hedge. Gia hadn't done that since third grade.

"You see?" her mother said when Leo came back inside dripping sweat into a puddle on the floor. "That's what we should be doing today. Nice pictures. Not having our kids dragged home like criminals for making trouble in the park."

"But I wasn't dragged home," Gia protested. "I didn't even—"

"Not another word." Agnes cut her off. "Not one. You hear me? I've had enough of both of you. And wash your damn plates."

She slammed the mug down on the counter. Coffee sloshed over the side, but her mother didn't wipe it up, nor did she sit down and eat her pancakes. She grabbed her things by the door and headed off to the train, an umbrella dangling from her wrist even though it was sunny, as Mrs. Salerno shouted "cheese."

Gia's face burned. Why was she being lumped in with Leo? If this was because she wasn't excited about the stupid watercolor set, then fine, let Agnes throw a hissy fit. And she wouldn't eat the pancakes either. She stabbed a fork through one just to ruin it, then squeezed a stream of maple syrup into her mouth.

"Let me get some." Leo reached for the bottle, and Gia handed it over. He tipped his head back and squeezed, closing his eyes while it pooled on his tongue. They'd done this as kids, sneaking snacks from the cabinets and doling them out in the backyard, Leo's room, or down by the canal: Oreos for a Hershey's bar, Halloween candy for a soda, the trade mattering less than the fact that they'd gotten away with it. They were in on the same secret again, them versus their parents, the warm haze of last night snatched away. It made Gia want to do it again, sneak another few minutes of real living.

They walked to school togetherish, keeping their distance from one another as school came into view. There wasn't anyone Gia was particularly excited to see, so when Leo split off for the boys, Gia joined Lorraine's huddle outside the high school entrance. At least she could hide a little longer before being on her own in eighth grade.

"I heard there's a thing on Friday night. One last float before the boats come out of the water." The girl was chewing gum, cracking it loudly, blowing bubbles, and swallowing them back like a lizard rolling out its tongue. She was a hostess at the clam bar with Ray and liked to flirt with him even though she had more pimples than a toad, but she curled her hair and rolled a tube over her lips until they were mirror shiny. Alessandra. Gia wondered if Agnes would prefer a daughter like her instead.

"Are you going?" Lorraine asked.

"Maybe." Alessandra shrugged. Ray's words about being mysterious filtered back to Gia. She obviously wanted to but wouldn't admit it. "Depends who else is."

It was already hot. The makeup was sticky, like flour stuck to a rolling pin. She waited for someone to make a joke about it, but no one did. The bells rang. People filed through open doors, where nuns waited in habits at the top of the steps, the breeze rustling the dark fabric, guarding a tomb. Sister Gregory wasn't there.

"There's another thing on Friday." Gia copied Alessandra's shrug. "At the dock."

"Says who?" the other girl asked. Gia didn't know her name. In her uniform, she could have been any of them. Lorraine turned to Gia, the surprise sharp in her eyebrows.

"Heard it around." Gia shrugged again.

"How old are you? Ten?" Alessandra threw her head back and laughed, the bones under her skin catching the sun. Gia turned red. She shoved her hands in her pockets and fingered the osprey feather. She'd never be cool or mysterious. Stupid Ray. Stupid. Stupid. Stupid.

"It's Ray's thing," Lorraine added. "You'll hear about it. It's getting around."

The snickering stopped. Neither of these girls was as popular as Ray, no matter how much they curled their eyelashes. Alessandra looked between Gia and Lorraine. The other girl inched closer. The circle closed as the nuns rang the bells again.

"I heard about that," the other one whispered. "What's it all about?"

The girls were hooked now. Gia's heart kicked up. Maybe it wasn't so hard after all.

"Dock three on Friday night," Gia said. "Find out for yourself."

Lorraine winked at Gia. "I'll catch up with you," she said to Alessandra and the other girl, waving. To Gia, she said, "C'mon, I'll walk you in."

They fell into step for the short distance between the high school and the middle school.

"Ray talked to you too, huh?"

"Yep." Gia nodded. "He said he'd cut me in if I told people."

"Did he say how much?" Lorraine's arms swung a little at her sides.

"No, but I'm gonna use it for boat money. For gas."

"Always ask for details," Lorraine said. "Because you know as well as I do that Ray knows math, and if you're working for him, you should know what you're selling. Any idea why he wants people at the dock on Friday?"

Gia shrugged and stared at the school steps. First her parents and now Lorraine. Maybe she wasn't so smart after all. Deep down she knew Aunt Ida's shadow in the window wasn't why Ray hadn't told her. Suddenly she was struck by how artificial everything was here: starched shirts and skirts, makeup, the sticky lip gloss, the way people talked to each other without saying what they really meant. It immobilized her, reminded her of the sparrows on Mr. Angliotti's lawn again, made her wish for the simplicity of the marsh.

"You remember how Uncle Frank taught Ray to play chess, and then Ray 'taught' us so he always won?"

Gia nodded. Anger stacking as the pile of pieces next to the board grew, at Ray's smug smile as he slid his pawns around and made them queens.

"Remember that about Ray. It always sounds better than it is. Plus he's counting on people not knowing any better. So be careful, Gia. If you need money, you can work at the bakery with me."

"My mom talked to you?"

"She did." Lorraine smiled. It sounded like joining the Lollipop Guild coming from Agnes, but from Lorraine, it wasn't so bad.

"Would that be OK?"

"Only if you take me for a ride in your boat with all that gas money." Gia smiled so big. Like she'd swallowed the whole sun.

"I'll bait your hooks too," Gia gushed, knowing Lorraine hated putting the hook through fish eyes, even if they were dead. They could bring snacks and cold sodas in a Styrofoam cooler and hide in the bay until the sun went down.

The bells rang again. The people outside thinned out.

"Go be a good student," Lorraine said. "I'll talk to my boss today."

Lorraine walked the other way, head down, hair swinging, her knapsack slung off one shoulder. Her blouse was perfectly tucked in, her arms and legs summer tanned, glowing. She tipped her head back as she walked up the stairs, catching the sun one last time before slipping inside. But if Lorraine was right about Ray, and she probably was, then why was he teaching her how to drive? Especially when her father would have taught her in an empty parking lot in the old LeBaron.

Gia tried to walk like Lorraine, as best as she could. The only part she didn't feel self-conscious about was letting the sun turn colors under her eyelids. Black, yellow, red, and black again before she blinked the sun away and found her place indoors.

～

The dock behind the clam bar had one rotten bulkhead and warped planks, and no one used it except clam shuckers for cigarette breaks. The fish smell could make anyone nuts, according to Ray. If Gia sat at the tip of her dock, she could see the clam shack farther down the canal. Tonight, it was hopping. Dinghies pulled up, flashed lights, and Ray came out of the kitchen, drying his hands on an apron, leaned down to greet the boats, handed them something from his pocket, and waved them off.

When the dinner rush started, Tommy set up shop instead, flipping peanut shells into the water, legs dangling, so small Gia could only see the top of his head, the clam bar's floodlight giving him a halo. Leo was there, too, sipping from a straw, jumping on the loose planks in the dock until they popped free.

Gia picked her way over splintered wood and frayed ropes tying off boats and crab traps, as dogs barked from fenced yards. She was curious how it worked and figured Tommy could use the company, like with the bikes sometimes, when she'd pass him parts as he worked so he didn't have to hold metal bolts between his teeth.

"Gia," Leo sang. "Gia, G-G-Gia . . . Do wah diddy diddy dum diddy Gia." Leo shook his legs like Elvis, his bony knees popping through his jeans. There was sweat on his nose and his hair was damp, his face flushed, but not from dancing. If her father didn't like how he'd looked the other night, he should see this. Gia ignored him.

"Hey," she said. "I'm going to New Park. Wanna come?"

Leo sang louder, so loud Ray threw the screen door open and banged his fists together. That shut him right up.

"Can't," Tommy said. "Got business." A boat light shone on the water, bright on the inky black. There was no moon, just enough light to make out two shapes in the boat, then two boys in leather jackets, beer cans rolling on the bottom of the boat. They didn't live here, but they knew Tommy.

One leaned forward, wobbling to catch the dock and playfully slap Tommy's hand. "How's it going, man?"

"Grooving." He rocked back on his heels. Ew. Gia rolled her eyes.

"Who's your lady friend?" The kid smirked, not mean, just lollipop-after-a-tetanus-shot slimy. Gia took stock of her bare feet and frayed jeans, an old sweater. She wasn't anybody's lady friend. Gross.

"My cousin." Tommy smirked back, and then she was forgotten as money slipped into Tommy's pocket, something else passed between them, and the boat kicked off the dock.

Leo unzipped his fly and peed into the water, making a show of it. Gia turned away, a mild disgust furrowing her brow. What the hell was wrong with him, and why didn't it bother Tommy?

"What are you giving them? And what's wrong with him?" Gia hissed as another boat chugged up the canal.

"Shhh," Tommy hissed back, but he couldn't meet her eye.

"Is it the basement thing?"

"Gia," Tommy warned.

The screen door of the kitchen slapped shut. Ray came down the little hill in his dirty T-shirt and white pants.

"All good, man?"

"Yeah," Tommy said.

"Hey, kid." Ray turned to Gia. "Go home, a'right? This isn't girl business."

Gia opened her mouth and closed it.

"We got it figured out, but you did good. A couple of your friends came by tonight, so . . ." Tommy counted out bills and handed them to Gia. She stuffed them in her pocket. Since when did a family thing not include her?

"Go bowling or something. Catch a flick. There's more coming." Ray nodded toward home, then to Leo. "And shut him up, would you? He's gonna get the whole thing shut down."

Leo picked up a plank and flung it into the water, where it floated with a nail sticking through it. Why couldn't he just tell Leo himself?

"Come on, Leo," she said. "Let's go."

"If she says go, we go," he sang. "If she says go go go . . ."

"Shut it."

She looked between Ray's sharp cheekbones and Tommy's round zeppole face. Tommy stared off at the canal, waiting for the next boat, a can of Tab at his feet. Since when did he drink Tab? Or wear jeans instead of sweatpants? A new white T-shirt. He was trying, Gia realized, to be a different person, much like her with the makeup on her face, only Tommy seemed to enjoy the new version of himself, which made it seem more permanent.

She flipped Ray the finger before huffing back the way she'd come as Ray called something Gia didn't catch. Leo slurped from the straw, too close to the dock edge. *Oh well,* Gia thought. *Let him fall in. Can't be worse than the shower.* But he didn't fall in, not when it was more annoying to follow right on her heels.

Up ahead, Crazy Louann was pedaling down the block, ratty bicycle streamers trailing as she meowed and scattered cat food from the basket with three plastic flowers. Her gray-streaked hair stuck out in every direction, and she'd wrapped herself in mismatched scarves, though it was hot. She was all fabric and wild violet eyes, and it was impossible to tell how old Louann was because she'd always been here doing exactly this. It creeped out Gia to watch the cats trot from bushes and smack their teeth on crunchy bits in the street before slithering off again to cooler bushes.

Leo was on the lawn, barefoot like she was, wiggling his toes in the grass, watching Louann's bicycle tires spin.

"Wow," he said, reaching out to where they'd been, raking his fingers through something imaginary in the air. "Wow."

He looked past Gia without really seeing her and meowed softly. The cats were coming now, gathering around the scattered food, the streetlight shining on their matted fur, chunks missing from fights, skinny, gangly things with shadows of rib cages, snatching bits of food. Leo's head darted in every direction, to the bushes, to the trees, to cars, to every place the cats were collecting from, pooling in the street, lured out by Crazy Louann, only it had never been a thing of wonder before. Never had it been something to stop and look at and wow over. Gia stared at her brother, who would've laughed at Louann before because they all had. It was a joke, always, *So-and-so wants to be just like Louann when she grows up,* because nobody did, but now Leo was meowing softly in the street, watching the cats gather, dart away. He sank down to the grass and watched.

When they were kids, her father had told them to stay away from raccoons in the daytime because they had rabies, even if they weren't foaming at the mouth or walking funny or doing anything odd. *Don't poke it with sticks. Don't provoke it. Don't ride your bike past it. Just go home.* Gia stared at her brother now, sitting in the grass, meowing at Louann and her cats, and did just that: she went home, feeling as if she'd walked through a spiderweb and needed to wash the whole thing off—Leo, Ray, Tommy, the boats in the canal—knowing it wouldn't change Leo in the grass or Tommy pulling another boat into the dock.

Inside, Agnes was polishing silverware at the table, rubbing furiously at a fork. Her father was on tour, wouldn't be home until morning. Gia paused in the doorway, opened her mouth, closed it, backed up a little farther from the silver polish. Not that she wanted to snitch, but just so her mother might see that she, Gia, had been good this week with the makeup, every day, hanging her clothes.

"Remember magic?" Agnes smiled, held up a fork, the tarnish transformed into shiny silver in one slow swipe. Gia used to think it was magic. Now she knew better.

"Would you like to join me?" Agnes gestured toward another chair, Gia's usual spot. She was still in her work clothes, a pink blouse, pearl earrings. It was so lonely, polishing silver on a Friday night, nearly repulsive.

"There's something . . ." Gia looked toward the door. "On the lawn."

Agnes pushed back the chair, curious and worried. It could've been a dead cat or a new car with a bow on it, and Gia felt a little bad leaving Agnes to figure it out alone.

Upstairs, a note fluttered on Gia's door. She peeled back the tape and unfolded it.

Lou said yes. See you tomorrow at seven a.m. I'll train you. —Lorraine

Gia smiled, imagining the two of them in the warm cocoon of the bakery, surrounded by sweets. It was official. She had a job, a real one, like her father and mother. Now she could say things like, *I can't. I have work.*

See, Leo? she thought smugly. *See how easy?*

In her room, she pulled the money out of her pocket. Two twenties were folded neatly together. Forty dollars just like that. More than she'd ever make at the bakery. More than she got on her birthday or Christmas, but it felt wrong. The tree across the street rustled in the breeze, shaking loose a yellow leaf, reminding Gia again of the sparrows scattered on the lawn. She shoved the money in her drawer and closed it tightly, hoping it wouldn't feel as gross in the morning.

"Go to bed." Agnes walked Leo up the stairs, pointed toward his room at the end of the hall. "You'll feel better in the morning."

Agnes crossed her arms as Leo did as he was told.

"Is he drunk?" Agnes whispered. It surprised Gia that her mother was genuinely confused. Shouldn't she know?

"I don't know," Gia said. It was true. Agnes nodded, looking at Leo's closed door, at the humming coming from inside, before smiling weakly and closing Gia's door.

"Good night," she said. But her mother was still in the hallway, standing guard because Leo was supposed to be grounded, but now this. She must've given up at some point, because the silverware was packed away by morning, and the smell of polish lingered in the kitchen, holding back the tarnish for the time being.

Chapter Seven

"And no matter what"—Lorraine dropped her voice to a whisper as the bakery door swung open—"pull back the sample tray when Cheap Joe comes in here, 'cause he'll clear the whole plate and not buy a single thing. Drives Lou nuts."

Lorraine snatched the tray off the counter and handed it to Gia, who busied herself with moving the day-old butter cookies around, sweeping crumbs off the plate, refilling it, while Joe flipped pages in a newspaper.

Big Louis had mirrors everywhere, which made the whole place feel like a spy movie. She'd catch herself tying a bakery box or sliding a new tray into the display window and think, *So that's what I look like.* So serious. Like she was wiring a bomb. It was distracting, this new information about herself.

"So vain," Lorraine teased.

"I can't help it." Gia laughed.

"You get used to it. Big Lou does it so no one steals."

Lorraine made the bakery look easy. She knew where everything was, what the busy times were, when fresh trays would come up from the basement; she counted change so fast it made Gia dizzy, and she knew what to box up just by who came in the door. When it was quiet, she hopped up on the counter and ate whatever she wanted after pulling off the plastic gloves that made Gia's hands feel like slugs in baby powder, even though Big Lou said no one could eat on the job.

"Just tell him your blood sugar's low or you're feeling faint. He's too scared of women's bodies to call you on it," Lorraine said between bites of a fresh chocolate éclair, handing one to Gia. And they were perfect. The cream so fresh it was still warm. Gia ate the first one slowly, then gobbled a second before the door opened again.

"See?" Lorraine hopped down as Cheap Joe finished the newspaper and headed for the counter. "You're learning.

"And the other thing about him," Lorraine whispered under her breath, "is that he likes to haze the new girls. So get ready."

"Any day-old bread?" Joe asked in a stained flannel shirt that made Gia hot just looking at it in the mirror. Joe was older than anyone Gia knew. Old and gray and talked loud enough to drown out the jets taking off from JFK.

"We don't sell anything that isn't fresh, Joe, you know that," Lorraine called.

But Cheap Joe wasn't looking at Lorraine.

"Hey, you," he called over the counter. "I'm gonna give you my order. You gotta get the whole thing right, no mistakes, and no writing it down, or it's on the house."

"That's your rule, Joe. Try telling that to Lou, and see how fast the door hits you on the way out." Lorraine waved her hand, waving off his nonsense. "But go ahead. This one's smart. Make it extra hard. And if she gets it right, maybe you'll even tip us for once."

Cheap Joe laughed, a deep belly chuckle, one eye squinting more than the other. Gia wondered when he'd last washed that shirt as he rattled off a bunch of biscotti that sounded exactly the same to Gia. Almond this. Chocolate almond that. Hazelnut. Anisette. All before Gia had even folded the box or put on a fresh pair of gloves, but she filled it anyway and put it in front of Cheap Joe to inspect.

"You missed the—"

"Nope." Gia cut him off and tied the box shut. "I didn't miss anything, 'cause I'll bet you can't even remember what you said. They're all good, and you know it."

Lorraine's eyes twinkled in a laugh, but she held it back until Cheap Joe laughed and took out his wallet, paid for all the cookies, and even threw a few coins in the tip jar as Gia put the sloppily tied box into a bag.

"See you next week," he called out as the door chimed, smiling the whole way out.

"See?" Lorraine said, crossing her arms over her apron. "It's not hard."

"She's cute, your cousin," another counter girl said to Lorraine. "Like a mini Audrey Hepburn."

"Right?" Lorraine said. "I wish she'd let me give her bangs."

The girls chattered. An oven door opened and closed while cookies cooled on racks and people all over the neighborhood ate their treats with tea and coffee, alone in their quiet moments, or carried cakes to relatives' houses, and Gia was a part of it all just by being here. Gia smiled, and it glinted back in a hundred mirror angles, herself to infinity, as another mixer whirled to life in the basement and a few stray seagulls raced for the bay.

~

The parking lot behind Pathmark was empty except for one lonely car in the corner and the last employee, pushing a line of shopping carts back to the store. The streetlights made everything a hazy orange. When the carts were back in front of the store, the guy lit a cigarette, skulked back to his car in the dark corner, and sped off as Lorraine and Ray changed seats. Everyone made a big show of buckling up; they never did the rest of the time, but Lorraine had never driven before.

Gia was squashed in the middle between Leo and Tommy because she was the smallest and both of them had to sit with their legs wide open. Tommy wouldn't stop humming the stupid Oscar Mayer Wiener song under his breath because he thought it was hilarious.

"Would you shut the hell up?" Leo snapped finally, reaching past Gia to knock Tommy's head.

"Shut the hell up with what?" Tommy swiped back.

"Knock it off—I'm in the middle, and you *know* exactly what, you dumb moron," Gia said nastily.

"It stinks in here," Ray announced as he slid into the passenger side.

"Course it does. Look who's here," Lorraine said. "What'd we take them for?"

"Because who'd want to miss this?" Leo asked. Lorraine met his eye through the rearview mirror. "The day Lorraine killed the Hornet."

"The Hornet's on its last leg anyway. She'd be doing me a favor," Ray mumbled, taking a half-empty bottle of rum from the glove compartment and passing it around. Even Gia took a sip. Lorraine waved it away, too focused on where everything was, snapping the headlights on and off and then the windshield wipers, adjusting the mirrors, turning the radio off, giving them a smile in the rearview mirror when she was good to go.

"OK, we're gonna do this slow and easy," Ray said. Lorraine was so small in the front seat, the wheel enormous. Ray took off his sweatshirt and rolled it into a donut for Lorraine to sit on, boosting her a little higher, and checked her foot on the brake.

"All of you in the back, keep your mouths shut so she can focus. If you get annoying, you can sit on the curb, you hear?"

Leo snorted, took a swig from the bottle. "What? Like lawn gnomes?"

"Yeah, but dumber," Tommy mumbled.

"Ten and two," Ray told Lorraine. "No one drives like that, but that's how you learn."

Everyone shut up as she put her hands on the wheel.

"OK," he said. "So the motor's gonna spin, but you need to transfer that energy from the motor to the wheels. That's RPM for those of you in the back with half a brain. That's where the transmission comes in. The gears have to come up to speed slowly, which is what you need the clutch for. The clutch eases gears and works them up to speed without grinding . . ."

Ray went on and on. The only one who didn't look dead bored was Lorraine, but that was because she was about to do the fun part and the rest of them were shoved in the back, listening to Ray drone. *Blah, blah, blah. Don't burn out the clutch.*

"Can we just move yet? C'mon." Gia crossed her arms over her sticky T-shirt.

"Yeah, move it." Leo passed Gia the bottle of rum, stuck out his tongue.

"A'right, first thing," Ray said to Lorraine. "You're in neutral, so nothing's doing. Put your left foot on the brake—good. Now take your right foot, and push the clutch all the way down."

Ray changed the gear into first.

"Don't worry about the gears right now; just move your feet the way I tell you. Now, left foot off the brake, and let your right foot up slowly. Very slowly. OK, now add a little gas."

The car crept forward, and Gia squealed a little bit, bouncing in her seat, because Lorraine was doing it—she was driving! As soon as Lorraine could really drive, they could do girls' trips to Manhattan or Long Island and get egg creams and real bagels from Brooklyn. Or maybe even Florida like Lorraine wanted, where they'd get tons of pecan logs without sharing with the boys.

"Try a little faster," Ray said, ready on the gear-shifting thing.

"She sees the pole, right?" Tommy said.

"Yes, Tommy, I see the damn pole." Lorraine eased the gas, but the car shot forward. The car slammed to a stop. Lorraine squealed. Leo cracked up.

"OK, that's OK," Ray said. "You stalled. That's what it feels like. Let's try it again."

"Who taught you all this?" Gia asked, forgetting to be quiet. "Oh, sorry."

"Your father," Ray said without looking up, his hand still on the gear switch. When? Where? Gia had so many more questions now, but Ray's tone implied it wasn't time to ask.

They were quiet as Lorraine practiced with the brake and the clutch, Ray shifting gears, the engine churning away inside, occasionally stalling. The whole thing was actually rather boring. Leo nudged at Gia's leg, at Tommy's, pointed to his face, held up a finger that told them to wait for it. The car was dead silent beyond the hum of the motor, until Leo opened his mouth wide and let out a yodel that startled Lorraine and stopped the car dead, shooting them all forward.

Ray whirled, red faced and spitting, "Out! You're gonna make her burn out the engine. Damn morons."

They spilled out. Even Gia was laughing. They walked faster than the car had even been moving toward the curb and settled down, same as in the car, with Gia in the middle.

"You want?" Tommy asked Leo, holding out pieces of paper with yellow smiley faces.

"What is that?" Gia asked.

"Not for you." Leo took one and put it on his tongue. "You wouldn't like it."

"He's right," Tommy said, ripping a square for himself. "Unless you want to try it."

"But what is it?"

"Acid," Tommy said. "Makes you see stuff. Colors, sounds."

"Monsters," Leo added.

"No, thank you," Gia said. That did not sound fun, but these two idiots had the smiley faces on their tongues now. Between this and the stuff in the basement, Gia wondered sadly why they couldn't just be together anymore without needing to add something to it, if this was how it would always be. It was lonely being the odd one out.

The Hornet stopped, started, bounced forward, like a bumper car in a jam.

"She's not very good at this, is she?" Gia said.

"No shit," Leo said. And suddenly they were hysterical, even Gia, rocking back and forth, faces red, kicking at the pavement until her sides hurt and the car came to a final stop. Ray and Lorraine switched sides, waving for them to hop back in. Poor Lorraine. Good thing for automatics.

Up ahead, a car bounced into the parking lot, coming in fast and pulling a donut that left tire marks on the concrete. This was the lot for doing donuts in the snow, every so often sliding into one of the light poles if they hit the ice wrong. A smoking car in the snow would end things for the day, and everyone would go back to snowball fights on the block, sleds on the side of the highway.

"Is something burning?" Gia asked.

"Yeah, dummy. Look at the rubber." Leo passed her the rum. It was sweet and warm on her tongue, not unlike a flat Coca-Cola.

"Not the rubber, idiot. Something else." Gia looked around. "Yeah, look." She hit his arm, pointing back toward Cross Bay, where a thick plume of smoke rose in the air, not like the slow gray smoke when a pope died but fast and heavy.

"Something's on fire," she said. The boys turned to look. The car at the other side of the parking lot stopped, honked.

"Leo," Tommy said, blinking real fast, his voice suddenly serious. Gia wasn't sure if he was seeing something that wasn't there or if the car had spooked him.

"Oh shit," Leo said, standing, dusting the curb from his jeans. Ray looked up from the driver's side, standing over the open door.

"Who's that?" Gia whispered. The car was dark except for two headlights on the pavement.

"Antonio," Tommy whispered back. And someone else. Gia forced back a shudder. It was the same man from the canal. What was he doing here? The two men got out of the car and leaned against it as the boys walked toward them, and they did look like boys in comparison, playing at Hells Angels with their mismatched heights and slouchy T-shirts, compared to Antonio's crisp shirt, rolled-up sleeves, shiny shoes, hair gleaming in the streetlight.

Gia got in the back seat, safer with the car armor around her, but they were trapped regardless because Lorraine could not drive this car if need be. Lorraine was quiet in the front seat, watching the boys huddle in a circle, as Antonio threw his arm around Ray and laughed at something he said. So quiet Gia slid over the seat and sat as close to Lorraine as she could.

"What are they doing?" Gia whispered. The air freshener on the rearview mirror stank of lemon. Gia snatched it down and flung it in the glove compartment.

"I don't know," Lorraine whispered. "But I wish we weren't here for it."

"I won't talk back this time," Gia promised.

"Good," Lorraine said, but the word fell flat because the boys, all of them, were coming toward the car now, spread out in the empty parking lot, looking like the cover of an album with the lights making shadows on their faces. Antonio gestured for Lorraine to roll down the window, and she did, slowly cranking in circles as Ray slid into the driver's side, Leo and Tommy in the back.

Antonio leaned into the open window, filling the space with the brightness of his shirt, the smell of Old Spice aftershave, two tan arms crossed on the ledge. He was dark angles up close, harsh stubble on his cheeks and chin, cigarettes and peppermint gum.

"Hey," he said, nodding at Lorraine. She gave the tiniest smile. "What do you say you and me go for dinner one night? Get to know each other a little better."

"Ray," Gia whispered, hoping to distract from whatever was about to happen. "Something's on fire."

"Oh, you saw that?" Antonio smirked, amused, pointing off to where the smoke was still rising on Cross Bay, where sirens were now whirling in the background. "Perceptive, this one," he said to the other guy, who Gia couldn't see over the car frame. Just shirt and a leather belt. "You gotta watch that," he said. "Too much noticing isn't a good thing, you know what I mean?"

Gia looked at her lap, running her thumbs in circles. *Shut up, shut up, shut up.*

"I'm teasing," he said. "Hey, kid, it's all right. I'm only teasing. Lighten up."

Gia stared at him, wondering if he'd just started that fire in his nice shoes and clean white shirt. If he had punched through the glass of some store and poured lighter fluid on everything inside, struck a match like her father did to light the barbecue, then just walked right out, driven over here, and asked Lorraine on a date, all in ten minutes. Was that even possible?

Antonio turned back to Lorraine.

"So Lorraine, lovely Lorraine, what do you say?"

Lorraine straightened her skirt, smoothed a crease in the red fabric.

"OK," she said.

"OK, she says." Antonio smiled, pushed a strand of Lorraine's dark hair behind her ear, thumbed her chin to lift her face a little higher, practically breathing right on her. Gia was disgusted. He couldn't just touch her like that, like they'd known each other forever. He didn't even notice that Lorraine was barely breathing, her eyes on her lap, digging her thumbnail into the fleshy spot of her hand so hard it left a half moon.

"Set it up," he said, pointing at Ray, before turning back to Lorraine. "Wear something pretty."

He flipped his keys to the other guy, and the two of them walked back to their car on the other side of the lot. Ray looked at Lorraine, but she stared into her lap, silent as hell, so quiet it was more unnerving than Antonio had been in the window, and they weren't even done with him. It was only just starting.

Ray reached over Gia's lap for Lorraine's hand, squeezed it, and drove off.

The car ride home was silent. They drove past what was left of the bagel shop, firefighters spraying powerful water into the busted-out glass.

"They're missing more than the hole in the middle now," Leo joked, but no one laughed.

Ray parked, and everyone hopped out. Lorraine slammed her door extra hard.

"I hope it's worth it," she threw over her shoulder before turning toward her house, where the porch light was off and Aunt Diane's TV shows flickered inside.

Chapter Eight

"It's kind of peach." Lorraine held the nail polish bottle up to the sun. "Or pinkish."

They were sitting on the porch with a bottle of Cutex and cotton swabs between them, filing their toenails. School was two weeks in, but it wasn't part of the regular routine yet. The afternoons were still endless, the sun burning and burning.

"I drew blood today," Lorraine said. "They let me do it alone. It was a weird feeling, tapping into a vein. All I kept thinking about was the blood flowing through, you know? How important it is, carrying oxygen and stuff people need to every part of their body. Like really need. Not just think they do like clothes or cars. I did a good one too. No bruising after."

"It wasn't gross?" Gia asked. "All that blood spraying around?"

"Don't be dramatic. And I put an IV in too. She looked so much better in an hour. It was amazing."

"Like finding a baby bird and putting it back in its nest?"

"Sure," Lorraine said. "I guess it's kind of like that."

If it lives, Gia thought but didn't say. Same as the old people Lorraine worked with.

"And you're being ridiculous." Lorraine rolled her eyes as Gia adjusted the swimming clip on her nose to keep the nail polish stink out. Nail polish was pretty, but it was made of chemicals. But at least painting toes meant she didn't have to help with dinner. "Remind me I have your envelope from Lou inside. It's light 'cause you only did one shift. It gets better."

"OK." Gia sighed. The two twenties from Ray were under her mattress, the weight pressing them crisp and new. It'd been so easy. The next Friday the dock had been much the same, only Leo had done jumping jacks for hours. *Of course it's good stuff,* Ray had said. *Look at him go.*

Gia opened the bottle of base coat as Ray came out. Summer had changed him. He walked taller, his hands in his new jeans' pockets, dye turning his skin blue, strutting past the trash cans lined on the curb as if giving them all the finger. He took his time walking. Endless time. Endless opportunity. And word was out. Everyone whispered about him in the hallway.

"Here comes the mayor," Gia mumbled. Lorraine snickered. Across the street, Leo climbed through his window onto the oak tree with tools, legs dangling over either side of the branch, and started sawing.

"Are we driving?" Lorraine put two hands on an imaginary steering wheel, pressed her toes to a pedal. "Yes? Yes?"

"Friday at eight," Ray said. "He's picking you up Friday at eight, so be ready."

Lorraine stared at Ray. Everything about her was still, even her chest, where her breath should've been.

"Who?" Gia blurted, looking from him to Lorraine. But she already knew. She was nauseous all over again, her clothes suddenly transparent. Gia tugged at her shorts, covering her skin, the memory of that day at the canal making her blood cold. What was worth that?

Ray rocked from heel to toe in a pair of shoes so new the leather stank through her nose clip. He had the look he always had when he built a row of hotels on Boardwalk: the son with the future everyone had sailed across the ocean for. But there was no board to flip here, no fit to throw. It burned quietly instead.

"Ray." Lorraine's voice had a quiet, pleading panic.

"It's done. One date. It's good for all of us, Lorraine."

Moron. He'd peed his pants once when a dog had barked too close to him. Who did he think he was now?

Lorraine huffed. She rarely cried, not even the time the car door had slammed on her finger. She'd just wrapped her good hand around the hurting one and pulled it to her chest, soothed by her own heartbeat instead of someone else to make it better. Now, she tipped her head back to the sky and closed her eyes, the sun filling her with courage.

"Even you're not that stupid." Her voice came out choked. Lorraine was on her feet. The front door slammed behind her. Ray looked between Gia and the door, still smug but wavering under the surface. The silence was worse for Ray than anything she could say.

Agnes was on the front lawn now, barefoot, staring at Leo in the tree.

"What the hell are you doing?"

"It's scraping the friggin' window."

"Let your father do that on the weekend." Agnes paced, her skirt blowing around her knees, like a balloon that a little child had let go by mistake, zigzagging in the sky. The sawing continued. Ray watched Leo the same way her father and Uncle Frank scoped out horses bucking at the gates before putting money down at Aqueduct. She couldn't blame Ray for not wanting to pick up garbage cans or supervise any more than she wanted to make Bundt cakes. She didn't care about homes or lawns or dream about raising kids any more than Ray did. They were alike in that way, and yet . . .

"Where's the rest of the money you owe me?" Asking felt greasy, but her boat depended on it. And she didn't trust he'd remember on his own.

Ray unfolded five twenties from his pocket but didn't let go.

"Keep her company on Friday, a'right? She'll be fine. It's not as big a deal as she thinks."

Gia snatched the money from his hand. She would've done it anyway, but now he'd think it was his idea. Great. She stuffed the bills in her pocket.

Agnes went inside just as the branch snapped and Leo fell with it. Gia's breath caught, but Leo was up again, cursing softly, dragging the branch to the curb. Only her brother could fall out of a tree and keep going. Ray was the same. Her father, too, but not Tommy or Uncle Frank. Certainly not the women. It made for good soldiers. Or Hells Angels.

Ray was gone. Somewhere in the commotion, he'd slithered off. She checked her pocket, but the money hadn't gone with him.

Across the canal, tarps flapped over hollow windows. The insulation was up, making the houses look like trash bags. It was interesting to see a house constructed, all the guts concealed within to make it work. There were a lot of ugly things hidden inside a house.

~

Lorraine didn't come around. She left for school with her head down and skipped out early, picking up frozen dinners for Aunt Diane before heading to the hospital with her nursing books. She took extra shifts at the bakery but didn't look up when Gia passed by, just busied herself with tying boxes and restocking trays. Even at night, the light in her bedroom was always off.

"What's with her?" her mother asked as she parked and shut off the engine. Lorraine walked ahead on the sidewalk, not turning to see whose car it was.

"Don't know," Gia lied.

"Full sentences, please," Agnes huffed, annoyed. "Maybe I should talk to her."

"Just leave her alone. She's mad at Ray."

"Over what?"

Gia shrugged. That was already saying too much.

"You just said you didn't know, but you do. Why should I believe you now?"

Gia shrugged again, but this time, instead of being annoyed, Agnes held up two hands and wiggled her fingers, threatening a tickle. This had worked when Gia was eight, but now the idea of her mother's hands so close to her new, growing parts made Gia flinch. Her mother looked almost desperate for Gia to be a foot shorter, kicking the seat, begging not to be tickled but really wishing it, her hands and face sticky with secret ice cream they'd picked up on the way home. Just girls. Even her mother realized it was ridiculous and sighed, dropping her hands to her lap.

"I'll just pop over real quick. Take these in, would you?"

The car door opened and closed. Her mother swished along the sidewalk, catching up to Lorraine. Through the windshield, the two of them looked like an episode of *Leave It to Beaver*.

The grocery bags slumped as cold things sweated inside. Gia left them in a heap on the kitchen table, flung the keys on the counter. She had a new Agatha Christie novel in her backpack, and those were always fun, even with the long, improbable whodunit explanation at the end, but she liked looking for clues. She always wondered what her father would think of one, if it was anything like what he did all day. She spread out on her bed and cracked the cover, smelled the pages, proud to be the first person to check it out of the library. The first! So when a pebble hit her window, and then a stick, Gia ignored them until the third stone shook the window. It would break glass. She threw the window open. It was Ray.

He held up a brown bag and raised an eyebrow. "Come down for a sec."

Gia rolled her eyes and slammed the window. Was this what it would be like if boys came around for her? Throwing things at her window, their faces tipped back and triangular, and she, from above, holding the power to open the window or leave it shut. It was nice to hold the upper hand.

"Is that Ray out there?" her mother called from the kitchen, clicking the stove on and pouring oil into a pan.

"Yes," Gia mumbled.

"For you?" The optimism in her mother's voice was terrible, as if Gia's status had miraculously gone up overnight, a leaf turned, the *It's a Wonderful Life* miracle she'd been praying for transpiring on the front lawn in a shopping bag. Cue the snow. Gia ignored her.

Ray was under the branch Leo had lopped off, the poor tree unbalanced now. Raw. He smiled and held out the bag. A black dress and a shoebox were tucked inside.

"Oh hell no." It might as well be a bag of barnacles.

"Watch your mouth, would you?" His impatience only made her more irritated. "Just take it to her."

"Bring it yourself."

But Ray just stood there holding the bag to his stomach, the way they used to scoop T-shirts into baskets and fill them with sandbar clams or plastic Easter eggs, desperate to find every last one.

"What do you want, Gia?"

Grass scratched her ankles. Her mother was watching from the kitchen window, washing vegetables, as Gia squirmed like an earthworm cut in two. No one had ever asked her what she wanted. Not about the food on her plate, the clothes that showed up in plastic bags from Lorraine's house, or what she wanted to be when she grew up. Not even what flavor ice cream she wanted from the supermarket.

"You want to live on this block your whole life?" he pushed on. The bag crinkled. "One day, your parents will move to the apartment like Nonna and Pop Pop, and you'll live in the main house with your husband and kids, using the same ironing board your mother does, making the same sauce on Sundays. Doesn't matter if you finish school, Gia, because your husband works. Maybe you'll drive; maybe you won't. A new washing machine or a lawn sprinkler will be your Christmas gifts. You'll sit around making snacks for little parties like my mom . . ." He gestured toward the front porch, where the rabbits were huddled in the cage. "Play canasta with your church friends. Sound good, Gia?"

Gia stared at Ray, her insides squeezing over each other like eels in a trap.

"Because I don't, Gia. I don't want that. And everyone on this block, your parents, mine, even Aunt Diane, that's all they want from us. And this"—he shook the bag, but he was still holding it close to his stomach, so close it breathed when he did—"is the only way I know how to change that. So . . ."

He stared up at the parakeets on the wire. Always swinging. Always flitting, no matter what was happening underneath. A mosquito landed on Gia's arm, but she didn't swat it away. Instead, she wished she could trade places with it: stick her straw through someone's skin and steal tiny bits of blood, fly away with a bloated belly, lay eggs in a bottle cap of rainwater instead of making choices like this.

"We're never gonna come up any other way, Gia, not how I see it. Not if your brother ships off to Vietnam, or me, or Tommy. I know what Antonio is. I also get what he can do for us. Do you see that? Look at his life, Gia. He has options."

"But you have options too." Gia kicked at the dirt. More than she had. The whole world was one big smoking advertisement for men in bright rooms with chairs tipped back, making important choices. Women were lucky if they could smile in the corner with their tight pencil skirts, tottering around in toothpick heels, one button too many undone on a blouse. That wasn't her. She was stuck, same as him, under this broken tree, parakeets laughing overhead. Unless the world changed. Or they changed it. She took the bag and held it to her own stomach, where it pressed against her insides and made it harder to breathe.

"Thank you," Ray said. He ruffled her hair. He'd done that to Tommy when they were little and Tommy's legs had pumped four times as hard to keep up with Ray on their bikes, or when Tommy had shared the extra Halloween candy people had dumped in his pumpkin because he was smaller, rounder, but it was a first for Gia.

"Hey," he called back, halfway to the curb. "Everyone's looking at the shadows on the wall. We see the fire."

You and I, he meant, his arms swinging freely without the burden of Lorraine's outfit. The sun gave his hair a red glow. His sneakers silent on the sidewalk.

Gia lingered in the yard, unsure what to do next now that every choice mattered more. Onions fried on the stove inside. The radio was on, her mother humming along, sweating as heat filled the kitchen. She tucked the bag into the hallway closet as quietly as she could, behind old baseball bats and shoes they'd outgrown a long time ago, then walked to the dock. She climbed into the boat and untied it, pushed off, the metal seats burning against her skin as Gia rowed to the end of the canal and back. The boat cut through the calm water like a needle as she settled into a rhythm, turning at the end of the canal, starting again.

She would be ready next time, her muscles stronger, eager, practiced, instead of the doubled-over thing she'd been last time. She could do anything her brother could, even Ray. The muscles in her arms woke up. It was easier when it was just her and the water. The boat buoyed under her weight. Water lapped the sides of the boat, cheering her on. The sun was red in the sky, lower on the horizon. All the colors of the sun were trapped in it, waiting for the right time of day, the right atmosphere, just like her.

Chapter Nine

The radio was a lonely, low hum in Lorraine's room, while the curling iron heated in the corner, the hallway heavy with shower steam. A sweating glass of ice ran rivers over the dresser's edge. After Pop Pop had died, Nonna had picked a brown suit, a freshly ironed shirt, and clean socks from the closet and carried them over her arm as if Pop Pop had just slipped out, leaving his clothes behind. Gia shook the memory as she smoothed the dress on the bed, took the shoes from the bag, snipped tags on the costume Ray had bought for Lorraine.

The shower ran and ran, thousands of pinpricks raining down like a meteor shower, emptying the thoughts in Lorraine's head. The women in her family went to water for comfort.

"Oh," Lorraine said when she saw Gia on the window seat, the dress on the bed.

Gia made to leave, embarrassed by the flushed skin above the towel. She could wait in the hallway, across the street, but Lorraine pushed the dress aside and sat down. Wrinkles! Gia panicked as Lorraine dipped a cotton ball into cream and made circles on her face. The dress looked like some exhausted person who'd flopped down on the mattress.

"Maybe it won't be so bad." Ray's words tumbled from her lips. The wrong ones. Lorraine's hands moved in fast, nervous circles, making her skin shiny, though her mind was heavy underneath. Lorraine swallowed a lump in her throat, a muscle twitching at its base, betraying the expressionless look Gia interpreted as *Whose side are you on?* Silence. Gia stared out the window. Clothes and towels shuffled behind her. Had Lorraine ever been mad at her for more than a few minutes?

But knowing someone your entire life meant there was nothing they could do that you wouldn't get over, because there were too many memories intertwined to ever live without them.

Lorraine zipped the dress by herself. It was black and smart with an Audrey Hepburn neckline. The shoes were black leather with a pointy toe, a leather sliver missing under the ankle. Everything fit just right, like the plastic shoes they used to slip on Barbie feet, the outfits they'd Velcro shut, smashing Barbie's and Ken's mouths together as their plastic eyes stared into one another's. Lorraine ignored her. It was uncomfortable, but it was too awkward to leave, so Gia curled into herself.

"Listen," Lorraine said finally, fastening a thin chain with a single pearl around her neck. "Why don't you stay here, and if I'm not home by midnight, tell your dad, OK?"

Gia's heartbeat flapped in her chest, worse than when she went over the handlebars, worse than the time her sled had flashed down the hill on the side of the highway and skidded under the metal divider, where a truck had smashed it to bits. Only once there was air in her lungs again, her chest pounding in her snowsuit, Lorraine and Leo tiny at the top of the hill, did she realize she'd jumped.

"Why are you scared?" Gia didn't want to know, just like she hadn't watched as cars had swerved around the sled. It was easier to stare at the sky. To hear it smash outside herself.

"Scared?" Lorraine's voice was brittle. "I'm not scared, Gia. I'm just not stupid. If you really can't figure it out, then I'm not going to explain it."

"But what if he's right?" Gia blurted. "What if this is the only way for all of us?"

The only adventure women ever had in movies was falling in love. It didn't matter what they did before or after; it was just about meeting *him*. It never showed them sitting at the table with a checkbook afterward, arguing about whether the butcher overcharged them for a pound of pork chops or how much to put in the church collection envelopes. But that wouldn't happen if they came up. They could live anywhere, go to Florida just because and have their own sticky pecan logs under palm trees, fill canals if they wanted, drive shiny cars and ride around in boats on Mondays, all week, read books all day and never need shorthand. What if he was right and this was how to do it?

Lorraine lingered by the door. It was easy to forget she was only seventeen. She was so much like the movie stars with black dresses and clutch bags with shiny chains, sipping from cocktail glasses, slipping into glamorous yellow taxis, but Lorraine didn't have a driver's license or a high school diploma, couldn't vote or buy cigarettes, didn't have a father. Tonight, she looked more like a sleepy-eyed kid asking when her parents were coming home, needing to wake up with everything right again.

"Just be glad it's not you."

The door closed. What did that mean? Her shoes made a snapping sound on the steps like branches breaking on a bed of leaves until the quiet echoed. Gia didn't want to touch anything. It was too private to be here alone.

A dad should've walked Lorraine to the car or demanded that her date ring the bell. But Lorraine was already waiting in a circle of streetlight, rolling a pebble under her toe. Her head lifted when the car pulled up. She opened the door for herself and hesitated, turning back to look at her bedroom window, her face blank, just splashes of makeup for lips and eyes, before slipping inside. The door closed soundlessly. The car drove away. The whole thing felt final now, stamped in time.

Gia couldn't sit still, so she collected bottles and cans in a trash bag, tossed expired food from the fridge, scrubbed the counters, swept, washed the bathroom towels, wiped down the bathroom mirror until her face was uncomfortably vivid, swirled the toilet brush in the bowl.

Only Lorraine would notice. Poor Lorraine. No one noticed when she cleaned. Or Agnes. Maybe Agnes didn't even want to scrub toilets but was stuck with it. She felt a sudden appreciation for her mother, who never left moldy food in the fridge, who didn't sit around like Aunt Diane.

Nine o'clock. Maybe the bread basket had been cleared and their dinners were steaming and pretty—eggplant parmesan or fettucine Alfredo. Stuffed shells or lasagna.

Aunt Diane shifted in the recliner. The TV volume lowered. Gia froze.

"Lorraine! Lorraine!" she called out, then shifted again and went quiet.

Something in her voice made Gia panic, but it was too early. Lorraine had said midnight. Gia went back upstairs and flipped through one of the nursing books next to the bed, but there were too many drawings of people without skin, exposing the puzzle of guts inside. It unnerved her that the drawings had faces, oblivious to the fact that their insides were exposed.

Diane called out again. This time, a sob caught in her throat, broke through Gia's patience. She couldn't take it. Diane had known when Lou was in trouble, and now she was crying for Lorraine. Something was wrong.

She could call the restaurant. Make sure they were there. Only she didn't know which one. She grabbed the phone book and dialed the fanciest first.

The phone filled with plates and voices, music lost in restaurant rush. She asked for Lorraine, and the phones dropped noisily as one gum-cracking hostess after the next "looked" while Gia wrapped the phone cord around her wrist until the veins throbbed under her skin, which made her queasier than she already felt, as they all reported back that Lorraine wasn't there.

"Did you even look or just put the phone down for a cigarette?" she snapped at the last tight-pants, clicky-heels-wearing hostess, probably counting down the hours until she could pop a cap off a beer bottle and chain-smoke in a car going nowhere. It was infuriating.

The hostess hung up. The silence echoed. It was time to tell Ray.

The Jimmy Dean Show blared, but the living room was empty. Gia stared at the abandoned chair. It spooked her worse than she already was. She slammed the door and jumped down the steps.

The houses were dark, even her own. Everyone was at the movies or bowling. The emptiness made her feel more alone. The canal was full. High tide. The temperature dropped, and the leaves turned over. Rain. She ran to Ray's, holding her breath past the tree stump in Mr. Angliotti's yard where the sparrows had fallen. It felt important to move fast.

Aunt Ida's back door was open. Music snaked from the basement. The kitchen was hazy with cigarette smoke and stale beer, dishes drying on a towel. She took the basement stairs two at a time because she couldn't fall. Not when she was this angry.

"She's not home." The words burst out before the bottom step. "Something's wrong."

She expected Ray, Tommy, and Leo to stare at her dumb faced, but it was just Ray and a bunch of strange guys in greasy T-shirts. Some of the bravery huffed out of her.

"She's not home," she said again, ignoring these other idiots.

"Gentlemen, this creature is my cousin." Ray smiled, inviting his friends in on a joke as sweat beaded on her forehead.

"Maybe she's having a nice time." He smirked, another meaning lurking in his words. The guys laughed, and it was a horrible, forced sound.

"I wish *I* was having a nice time," one said, bursting out in smoky hysterics.

She glared at Ray and his stupid curly hair. She wanted to destroy him. Everything he was built on. She mustered the *malocchio*, summoning up all the hate she felt and shooting it toward him, hoping it was stronger than his stupid gold horn or red ribbon. Gia wouldn't get any help here. She needed her dad.

She pulled at a curl on Ray's head. It sprang back as it always did.

"When we were kids, he used to scrunch up his nose and squeal like a pig when we pulled his curls because they look like pig butts. Remember, *Ray*?" she hissed. He slapped her hand away, but his friends were laughing, hooting it up. Gia was giddy as she thundered up the steps, Ray at her heels.

"I'm telling my *dad*," she shouted, but Ray was on her now. His long legs closing the gap between them. She was almost at the curb when he grabbed her arm, squashed it in his whole hand, worse than her father's blood pressure machine.

"Let go, asshole!"

"Stop." He squeezed tighter. Gia tugged, trapped. He might let up if she stopped, but she couldn't stay stuck on this disgusting chemical lawn while Lorraine needed help. She could see her house: if she couldn't pull free, she could pull him with her.

"Listen," he said. "You're not telling your father anything."

Her arm was numb. She wished it would snap off like a lizard tail. She was out of time.

"You're a waste." She spit Uncle Frank's words from long ago, her voice rising. "You're a waste! You're a waste!"

There was a hysteria in it, a chant. The more she screamed it, the truer it got. Even his own father had seen it. They were nothing to him, and he should be nothing to them.

"Lower your voice," Ray hissed, but she couldn't hold it back now. It rose from her throat like a ribbon of smoke toward the sky. Waste, waste, waste. Like all the thrown-away garbage on the street his father carted off. A big nothing.

Ray's hand shot out and slapped her, making her eyes sting with tears, making her nose run. She touched her nose gently. There was no blood on her hand, just the web of lines it had always been: life lines, love lines, health, blood, rooted to her past, present, and future—until her palm flashed out and smashed the underpart of Ray's nose. He dropped her arm, and Gia broke free. Blood ran down his face. Their blood. It felt like a spell. She promised herself that she would take a lemon to Mass on Christmas Eve and pierce it with needles, because he was her enemy. The idea beat through her head in a frenzy as she ran, the air rushing her face as clouds rolled over the moon and the first raindrops splashed against the sidewalk where they used to have lemonade stands and ride bikes and shovel for money when the snow dumped down in heaps. Gia pushed faster, farther from Ray and whatever game they were playing now.

"Bitch!" Ray screamed. It echoed through the tunnel of houses, but Gia didn't stop. She pushed through the front door, past her mother in the living room, who tried to warn her that her father was sleeping, but that was the whole point. It was time for everyone to wake up.

~

Bucketloads of water dumped in every direction. The windshield wipers couldn't keep up. Gia slumped and pulled her knees to her chest as her father drove even more slowly. They would never find her in this. The fight ebbed out of Gia as time stretched on. It felt hopeless now. *I'm sorry,* she prayed to Lorraine, wherever she was.

The lines were white and yellow in the headlights, the only thing they could see ahead of them, dotting a path to nowhere.

"Let's head back." He leaned into the wheel. "She might be back."

"Fine," Gia mumbled.

"Hey," he said. "You did the right thing."

But it didn't feel like the right thing. Not even close. Believing Ray was like swallowing a mouthful of vinegar and trying to keep it down.

The ride back was slow, even after the rain let up. On their block, water glittered in the streetlight.

"Shit," he mumbled. He reversed to drier ground, parked, locked the doors. "Hop on." He lowered to one knee so she could climb on his back, and Gia did because it was late and she was tired and the night was not over, and she had failed so badly it made her afraid of whatever was under the dark water. On the surface, it reflected houses and cars. Underneath was different.

Her father sloshed through, soaking his pants and shoes. Gia stared into the water, at her own distorted face, tracing layers of fault: Had she not thrown a fit and gone swimming, Antonio wouldn't have seen Lorraine. Had she not been jealous of her mother adoring Lorraine, she would not have sided with Ray. Had she not wanted her boat, she would have told Ray to piss off. Three deadly sins. She was a bad person at her core, like a shell dropped from a seagull's beak, rotting in the sun. And yet she was being carried on her father's back. Safe. Accounted for. With food in her belly and a warm bed to sleep in, things her parents had worked for and she'd taken for granted. *Just be glad it isn't you.* She wrapped her arms tighter around her father to keep from slipping any deeper into the terrible thing she'd become.

But when they rounded the corner, a small shape walked along the sidewalk ahead, shoes in hand, head down, the curls lost, following the streetlights. One flickered and went out. Lorraine was lost in the dark.

Her father slowed down, almost to a stop, water rippling against his ankles.

In the dim light, a bruise was darkening on Lorraine's upper arm. One of her shoes fell and disappeared under the water, but Lorraine didn't notice. Her hair hung around her face. She looked down a few steps later, stopped, noticing there was only one shoe now, and let the other fall. It plunked into the water. When they were kids, they had stabbed toothpicks with newspaper sails into watermelon rinds and launched them off the front porch. Only the boats had floated. The shoes sank. Lorraine opened and closed her hands, walked to her front porch, where Aunt Diane was waiting, leaning her weight on the railing to hold herself up. They went inside without closing the front door. Everything dripped with a sadness so strong there was no name for it. Not like the smell of rain.

"Go get your mother," Eddie whispered. There was no room to be jealous; she raced upstairs and shook her mother's shoulder, watched as her mother waded across the street in her nightgown like a ghost in the streetlight, as Lorraine had been.

They waited on the porch, her and her father. He lit a cigarette, and she flicked the ashes, waiting for Agnes to come out. But she didn't. Nor did the light in Lorraine's room turn on. The water in the street rolled away, and somehow, Gia woke up in her own bed the next morning, where she balled the sheets under her nose and breathed in the clean laundry smell, wishing last night had been a dream.

Downstairs there were pancakes cooking, heavy with butter and syrup, though the sun was not up.

"Morning," her father said, alone in the kitchen, pushing aside his coffee mug and folding the newspaper into an imperfect rectangle. He looked every bit as black and white as the newspaper print, his face covered in stubble, freshly splashed with cold water he hadn't bothered to towel off, his anchor tattoo tethering him to the table.

"We need to talk."

Gia couldn't ask if Lorraine was OK because she already knew. She poured a glass of water because it was comforting to hold between her hands and waited for the questions to come.

Chapter Ten

Eddie got ready for his usual tour on Saturday, but he paused by the door as he strapped his holster around his waist, grabbed his star-pointed hat from the coat tree.

"Did I ever show you this?" he said, pulling two yellowed pictures from the inside liner. One was of Agnes with the same green tint all the old photos had, leaning on a railing at the beach in a sundress. Rockaway maybe. He told Gia he'd taken it all the way to the South Pacific in the lining of another hat.

The other was of her and Leo bobbing behind the boat in floaties because they couldn't swim yet. Leo was missing his front teeth. Gia's hair was in a ratty wet ponytail at the top of her head, water sparkling around them. Knowing he carried them with him was like being scooped out of that water, teeth chattering, and wrapped in a sun-warmed towel.

"What are you going to do, Dad?"

She'd told him everything, and yet the morning had passed with Eddie in the kitchen, cracking eggs into a bowl, holding one up for her to see. "Look at that," he'd said of the two yolks from the same egg. "Twins."

He slipped the pictures back into the lining of his hat. He'd shaved, and his skin was fresh and pink, offsetting the unusual coldness in his movements, the calm that made Gia afraid there was a more dangerous plan brewing than just the schoolyard fights that usually settled someone being wronged.

"Do you know why we moved here?" he asked instead. Gia stared. "Because we wanted to see the sky and smell the ocean instead of rooftops and garbage, that's why. Because we felt alive here."

And nothing would threaten that. Fear fanned through her in waves that left her nauseous. Gia was afraid for any perp he chased down an alley today or any doors he kicked down, because they would all be the Ray he couldn't catch.

"Let's go. I'll drop you at the bakery."

The bakery. How could she still go after everything? She stared at her father with her same frozen face, her bare feet stuck to the linoleum, sweating off a faintly metallic smell.

"You gave your word," he said. "That's all anybody has in the world."

The shame of believing Ray's words washed over her again. She changed. The short ride was silent minus a flock of laughing gulls calling in the distance as Gia wished for the bay and her boat, the steady chop of water. Mr. Angliotti bent for a newspaper near the tree stump. It felt stupid now, hunting for chemicals, when there were so many more invisible things to be afraid of. She hopped out just as Big Louis was unlocking the metal gate over the bakery's front window.

"She's sick," Gia lied. "I'll cover for her."

Louis was already sweating yellow stains through his T-shirt. Unlike her father, he hadn't shaved, and stubble collected on each of his chins, making dark shadows. A bit of butter stuck to the corner of his mouth. Gia pushed away her disgust.

"What good are you? You don't know nothing yet." But he let her in when the gate rolled open with a clang and showed her the register, assuming she knew enough about cookies not to screw up orders too badly even if she wasn't tall enough to see over the glass display case. And then the other girls filed in, and Gia drifted into a powdered sugar background, filling boxes, refilling trays, her hands drying in the plastic sanitary gloves, the whole thing a kind of penance without Lorraine that she didn't even deserve.

"Oh, you're home." Agnes sat up, forcing a brightness she didn't feel, brushing away the damp streaks on her face. "How was it?"

"Fine," Gia lied. Her fingertips burned from bakery string, but it was honest work, unlike the money under her mattress. She would stuff it in the poor box at church. Or give it to Lorraine. Fill up the freezer with Aunt Diane's TV dinners. A pot of chicken broth boiled on the stove.

"I'm going to take this over . . ." Agnes trailed off, shuffling away.

"Is she . . ."

"She will be. Just give her a few days. And not a word, do you understand? Not to anyone. Especially not Ray." She spit his name with such hate and followed it with the sign of the cross. Gia took one small step forward and wrapped her arms around her mother's waist. Agnes held her back, rested her head against Gia's, until the pot splashed a few warning drops over the rim and forced them apart.

~

That night, Gia couldn't sleep. She curled up on the couch in the dark and watched Lorraine's house across the street in case Antonio came back. Or even Ray. She had one of Leo's old baseball bats until her mother came in and took it away.

"Think about it," she said. "If they see someone small like you coming and snatch this bat, you just gave them your own beating weapon."

She was right. Gia said nothing as Agnes stuffed it back in the closet, wondering how many fights her mother had seen growing up in the Lower East Side. Together they sat on either end of the couch, but Lorraine's house was quiet all night.

Until sometime after midnight. Agnes had dozed off, breathing deeply, the house settling around them. Even Gia opened and closed her eyes in fits and starts until the two shapes rounded the corner, zigzagged down the street.

"Mom." Gia nudged Agnes, her foot icy against Agnes's warm calf. Her mother shot up, fumbling in the pocket of her robe without taking her eyes off the window.

"Get down," Agnes whispered. The two shapes were still small in the window. One of them stopped, hoisted the other. One walked while the other dragged along beside. Was this what always happened late at night, and she'd just never noticed?

"Mom," Gia whispered. The object in Agnes's hand slowly took shape. The barrel, the click as it loaded. She'd only seen it once or twice, her father's off-duty gun, and both times he'd made a point of unloading it in front of her, dropping the bullets out and snapping it shut while Gia sat on her hands. She didn't even know where they hid it, only that it was not a toy and she was never to touch it. But now it was awkward in Agnes's small hand, pointed at the window, as the veins in her mother's neck throbbed in the dim light.

"Your father knows I have it," Agnes whispered back. "If anything happens, you run. Understood?"

Gia went cold. Her whole body. Straight through the frozen canal. She would not run. She would take the bat from the closet again. Or would she? Would she leave her mother with two men and an off-duty gun like she'd let Lorraine leave for that date? It was sickening to be unsure if she'd do the right thing when it mattered, but the two shapes were coming up the walkway now, and the off duty went under the couch because Leo's arm was around Tommy's shoulders, his legs jelly, as Tommy dragged him up the sidewalk.

"Call your father," Agnes whispered, tightening her robe. "And not a word about the gun."

Agnes opened the front door, and Tommy stopped for a moment, caught, unable to look Agnes in the eye as she positioned Leo's other arm around her shoulders. How many times had Agnes dabbed at one of

Tommy's scraped knees, peeled the backing off a Band-Aid, or handed him slices of cake with an extra frosting flower, a candle of his own to blow out even if it wasn't his birthday? And now he couldn't look at her.

"What'd he take?" Agnes asked, but as soon as Leo's weight came off Tommy's shoulders, he turned for home, walking quickly down the front walk.

"Fifteen minutes," Eddie promised over the phone. "Get him in bed."

Agnes struggled under Leo's dead weight, so Gia took the other side. He stank. Sweat. Piss. Alcohol. Something else. Gia wished she had her nose clip, a white suit like the workers when they'd taken the tree down and picked up the sparrows, in case they could catch what Leo had by touching him. His breath near her face was repulsive. She stared at the steps as they lumbered up, dumped him onto his bed. Gia scrubbed her face in the bathroom, her arms, her neck. She wet her hair and scraped at her scalp, praying whatever it was hadn't already seeped through her skin.

Eddie thundered up the steps. There was a shuffle in Leo's room, a clink of metal on metal.

"He's not a criminal, Eddie. He's your son," Agnes protested, her mouth open in the doorway.

"I'll deal with him in the morning," he said, taking off down the steps again and back to his cruiser at the curb. It was still running. He was still on shift, Gia realized, and he'd just cuffed a passed-out Leo to the radiator. The car pulled away. Gia locked the doors, curled into a ball on the couch, too exhausted to watch Lorraine's house any longer, and fell asleep to her mother pacing on the floor above until Leo woke up and banged the cuffs against the radiator. Gia couldn't take it and called her father at the station again while Agnes pleaded with Leo that they didn't have the key. Could he just stop yelling until Eddie came home? Whatever he needed, she would bring it to him if he would just stop.

"I'm off in an hour," Eddie said. "Tell her to put the radio on and give him a bucket. Wait downstairs at Nonna's."

"Mom." Gia carried a new bucket upstairs, set up the radio on the floor in Leo's room. Agnes was sitting against the wall. There were fresh tears on her cheeks. Her eyes were puffy. And she was tired. They both were. It sat on Gia's forehead, the need for sleep, and made Leo banging on the radiator, the cuff cutting at his wrist, less real.

"Gia, just get me a pin," Leo pleaded.

"Dad's coming home in an hour," Gia said, tuning the radio, avoiding her brother's eye. "Just knock it off. Mom, come on." She slid the bucket closer to Leo. She did not want to be near him, did not want to look at his dirty clothes. She was embarrassed and disgusted, wished they could air this room out and air him away with it, clean up the mess of clothes on the floor, the crumpled sheets, the dust on the shelves, all of the broken parts he kept scattered around, the dirty plates and glasses. It was disrespectful after how hard their parents worked, her mother typing all day, her father working nights and days in danger, just for them to live here, and this was how Leo used it. Agnes was up, avoiding the pinups on the wall. It was uncomfortable, her mother in her bathrobe in front of those women in sheer fabrics, throwing their heads back with waves of glossy hair. Agnes must've caught Gia staring because she turned suddenly and ripped one in half, the pins popping out of the wall, and crumpled it into the garbage can, then another. She stripped the sheets off the bed and scooped the clothes on the floor into the hamper. Opened the window.

"Keep your mouth shut," she told him, pointing to the open window as a trickle of cool air circled the room. "No one needs to know our business." Then she lit two cigarettes and passed one to Leo, who shut up and smoked in silence until Agnes slammed the window and waited downstairs at the kitchen table with the off-duty gun in her pocket again.

"Unlock him." Agnes was at the door as soon as Eddie came in.

"Let me change, Agnes." He sighed heavily, undoing his uniform. "And put some coffee on. I'm taking him for a ride."

"Where?" Agnes lit another cigarette, struggling to snap the lighter into cooperating. "Where are you taking him?"

Eddie didn't answer. He filled a glass of water and drank it. Then another. Agnes was all nerves. The newspaper thudded on the porch, and Agnes shot her hand into her pocket, pulled out the gun.

"Jesus." Eddie snatched it, gave Agnes a look that stopped Gia cold, emptied the barrel.

"Take her with you," Agnes challenged him. "Wherever you're taking him, take her too. They both go, or he doesn't."

"Agnes."

But Agnes was already filling the percolator with water, washing the thermos.

"I'll go." Gia sat up taller so both feet would touch the floor and she wouldn't look as small as she felt. "I'll help."

Eddie sighed and looked at Gia for a long time before tucking the off duty into his waistband, the bullets in his pocket.

"Fine," he said, taking the stairs slowly.

Agnes waited until he was at the top before turning to Gia.

"Watch," she said. "Make sure he doesn't hurt your brother."

"But h—"

"He won't do anything if you're watching."

Agnes poured milk into the thermos as the percolator bubbled. Upstairs, closets opened and closed to throw them off about the hiding spot, because he came down without the gun, towing Leo behind him. There was a reddish-purple mark on his wrist from the cuffs that wouldn't have been so bad if he hadn't kept tugging at them. He always made things worse. But he looked thoroughly ragged, especially beside Eddie. Even without sleep and with twenty years between them, Eddie looked less gray than Leo. Less weathered.

"What the hell?" Leo protested.

"Get in the car." Eddie grabbed the thermos, and Gia skittered off behind him, giving Agnes one last look.

In the car, Leo slumped in the front seat. Eddie nudged him. Told him to sit up like a man. Forced a few sips of coffee into his mouth, making Leo cough. Eddie wiped the thermos with his sleeve before sipping from the other side. Gia wondered if her father had the same low-grade disgust she felt toward Leo now that he wouldn't even sip from the same container anymore.

The road was empty. The green lights clicked in such a way that Eddie barely had to slow for the reds before the lights turned and they flew on, all the way to Rockaway. Eddie made a left under the A train, though it wasn't running. The tracks sat over them, dark and metallic, blocking a starless sky, making it impossible to imagine the ocean on one side of the peninsula, the bay on the other.

Eddie killed the lights and coasted to a stop, turned to Gia in the back seat.

"Wait here. And don't open the doors. Not for nothing. If anyone bothers you, keep your hand on the horn, and I'll come back."

Watch. She couldn't watch if she wasn't going, but she didn't want to get out of the car here. There were only a few sparse buildings with broken windows hiding behind overgrown grass. Trash skittered down the sidewalk and pooled at the curbs. In between, there were shapes that could've been trash bags or slumped people. She wanted to stay in the car with the disgusting pine tree and wait till it was over, but that wasn't the deal. And another part of her imagined a face through the glass while she was in here alone, scrambling over the front seat for the horn to blare into the silence, waking up unseen things. She was sorry she'd come. It was brave in the kitchen, but here it was just stupid. When her father opened the car door, she opened hers too. He didn't stop her, just pushed Leo along and told Gia to stay close.

Between buildings, cardboard boxes were draped with tarps. Upside-down buckets dotted the sidewalk. It smelled like piss, unwashed bodies.

People lived in those boxes, Gia realized. One crawled out, shoeless, his feet so filthy and scarred that Gia wanted to vomit, but she pressed into her father's side, his belt digging into her ribs, and hung on to the back of his shirt, as Eddie pushed Leo forward, away from him, closer to the boxes and the makeshift tents, on his own.

"Take a good look, Leo, 'cause this is where you're heading."

Leo wiggled his jaw. His hands opened and closed. Almost the same way he got ready to fight in the lot behind the rectory, though it didn't look like there was much fight in him now, more like he wanted to run away from this place fast. Inside one of the boxes, a baby cried, and someone yelled for it to shut up. Gia pulled at her father's shirt harder, rolling the fabric into a ball in her fist, because she didn't want to see or hear any more, even as Eddie toed at the needles on the ground, at the bottle caps and debris.

"The rate you're going, this is where you're heading. If this is what you want, we'll shake hands right now, and you can stay here. Speed the whole thing up and keep us out of it."

Leo opened his mouth. Closed it. He was rigid now where he'd been loose limbed before.

"Because if you keep using, this is it. There's kids younger than you in here, so don't think you're an exception because you're fifteen and come from a nice family. Doesn't matter, Leo, doesn't matter. And don't think you can control it, because you can't. You'll run out of second chances, and this'll be it."

Eddie nudged him forward. "Go ahead. That's what you want, isn't it? C'mon, Gia. Let's let him think about it."

Eddie turned for the car and put his arm around Gia, walking quickly, like he couldn't wait to shake this place off, Leo at his heels.

"Watch where you step," he said, looking at Gia's thin Keds. He opened the door for her, and Gia was thankful for the seats, the familiar smell. Her mouth was so dry. She wished for just a little bit of water, though the thought of putting anything in her stomach was sickening.

"Not you." Eddie turned to Leo. "We're not done."

She almost felt bad for him, but part of her was glad to see him twitch, to call his bluff and prove he wasn't such a tough guy after all.

"Lay down," Eddie said. "If anyone bothers you, hit the horn."

He slammed the door and locked it. Gia peeked for long enough to see Eddie and Leo going deeper into the city of boxes, Eddie plowing forward while Leo followed close behind, but Eddie pushed him away. *Stand on your own,* he must've told him. Gia had a hard time pairing up the kid who wanted to go to Vietnam and blow things up with the one gravitating back toward their father. Gia tucked her head into her arms and closed her eyes, imagining her bed, the macramé owl on the wall, her poster of the World's Fair that Eddie had taken them to, dragging them by their collars past the admissions line and setting them loose with a couple of bucks and instructions to meet back at the car by ten p.m. How had it changed from money at the World's Fair for belgian waffles with whipped cream and strawberries to a walk through this place?

"I'll stop," Leo was saying outside the car. "I'll quit it. I swear. Just . . ."

The pleading in his voice was terrible. Gia pressed her hands over her ears. If her father was really going to leave him here, she did not want to see. Her father's voice was low and measured, and it made Leo's rise. No more drugs and no more stealing. No more Ray or Tommy. He'd make new friends. Do his homework and go to school. Get that job he was supposed to. He would not even drink. Eventually, Eddie opened the car, and they both slipped back inside.

"Sit up," Eddie said, and Leo slid into the right shape. There were tears on his face, and he was sniffling. She'd never seen her brother scared, but this was it. Gia felt mildly amused that her father had broken him down, tactically, like a sting operation after months of planning when police finally stormed a card table on a regular night and the whole crime ring came down with it. Hadn't he said that once? One of the few times he'd talked about work.

"I'll be good," Leo promised, again and again, convincing himself as much as Eddie as the sun broke over the subway tracks and the first train of the day rattled past with its headlights on, outshining the sun.

"We'll see," Eddie said. "If this gets the better of you, I promise there will not be a funeral. We'll bury you in a pine box."

And for the rest of the ride, everyone was silent.

~

By Sunday afternoon, everyone knew.

"Act like everything's normal," Agnes told Gia as she pressed change into her hand and sent her to the grocery store for eggs. "Don't say anything."

But it was clear in the way people stopped talking when Gia cut through the church crowd lingering on the sidewalk that something had changed. Or at the grocery store when the aisle cleared and Gia was alone with the milk and butter, the refrigeration of the shelves soaking through her clothes, or when Mrs. Salerno whispered something into Flora's ear on the checkout line and sent her away before Gia could wait behind them. They were dirty now because of whatever Ray had set in motion on Friday night, so much so that the cashier waved Gia through without ringing up the eggs or Snickers bar. Gia threw the money down on the belt and stormed out, eating the Snickers bar in three angry bites.

Ray's new '64 Dodge Charger was the same color as a night sky, split down the middle with a white stripe. He pulled up as Eddie arranged tables on the lawn, as Aunt Ida opened the lid on her pistachio cake. Eddie gripped a folding chair tighter, looking off at Lorraine's dark house instead of Ray's new car.

The car was out of place on the block. It was too new, too perfectly waxed. Little kids wouldn't hop in and out of the back seat for school or church. It wouldn't carry groceries. It would drive real slow, revving at stoplights, hinting at how fast it could go if every cylinder fired. It made the promise of school and hard work for a good life laughable. It gave Gia the creeps.

Everyone stopped. Aunt Ida clapped her hands, smiling as big as the White Rock fairy if she'd just seen something unbelievable in her puddle, while Uncle Frank swung his arm over his head for everyone to follow, bellowing for the ladies to come see.

"Would you look at this?" Uncle Frank bent so close to the hood that his round face reflected back. "What a beauty."

Ray's arm dangled from the driver's side, one eyebrow raised, absorbing the attention the same way little kids shouted for their parents to watch them cannonball.

Her father circled the car, noting the custom finishes. *The Art of War* and *Republic* were dog-eared on the leather back seat, meant to be noticed.

Ray looked at her through the side mirror, asking a silent question, but she couldn't look at him. Even being near him betrayed Lorraine again. Was she watching from her window? Gia waited, prayed, for her father to do something. Her father, who chased perps up dark staircases, who tackled men twice his size to the ground and put them in cuffs, who ran into the places other people were scared to go but still brought home salted street pretzels and woke them up so they could eat them warm from paper bags in their beds. Her father, who'd seen Lorraine wading home that night. Gia tightened her grip on the handful of silverware she was holding. She would key this car, leave a thick gash in the new paint like the one he'd left on Lorraine.

Leo asked how fast it went, but he was off, dazed, his voice floating down from some other place. Gia looked away in disgust. Again? How could these people be family, any of them? She wanted to pick up Buster and press his warm body against her face just to feel his honest heartbeat, breathe in the good of him, but she was too angry.

"Everyone'll see you coming," Agnes said, but her voice was steel. She dried her hands on a shabby dish towel. Everyone *should* see him coming, was what she meant, and run. Gia buzzed, bracing for whatever came next. Finally.

Eddie snapped up from the other side of the car. He stared at Agnes, his hands in his pockets, inspecting every dirt particle and fabric fiber until it clicked. Silent words flew over the midnight roof between them.

"How'd you pay for this?" Eddie circled back. "Hard-earned clam-shucking money?"

The mood shifted. The new toy forgotten. Eddie was ready to pull Ray through the window, hold his head to the ground, and make him talk.

Ray's eyes narrowed. Or maybe Gia only imagined it as he tipped his head to one side, pretending not to understand long enough for Uncle Frank to save the day.

"Hey." Uncle Frank crossed his arms over his stomach, squishing the fat against the organs inside, making Gia sick. "What are you implying?"

"It's a question," Eddie asked.

"What kind of a question?" Uncle Frank's face reddened. "You're saying no son of a garbageman could ever make good on a car like this, is that it? You want brass tacks? Maybe the paper trail would be proof for Mr. Officer that everything's above the table?" He pointed a finger at his son. "He earned it. Fair."

"Why don't you ask Lorraine?" Agnes flung the dish towel into the dirt. "Ask her about Ray's 'good, honest work.'"

But Agnes might as well be a mosquito buzzing in the distance to Uncle Frank.

Aunt Ida stepped closer to Uncle Frank, but she was watching her sister, pressing her fingers to her lip, confusion playing over her face. Gia almost felt sorry for her.

The tarps on the new houses flapped angrily in the distance. Ray had gone silent. Leo slunk back to the sidewalk, stared at the sky, where a plane passed, rattling everything on the ground. The air was thick with everything no one said.

"Agnes," Aunt Ida begged. But Agnes stared at the ground, where tears were falling softly into the dark earth. They used to cut earthworms in half, Gia remembered suddenly, with sticks, collecting the pile on the ground and watching them wriggle. "Do you think they'd know each other," Leo once asked of the two separate pieces of the same worm, "if they saw each other again?"

Just like Agnes and Aunt Diane and Aunt Ida used to hang laundry on the roof of the Lower East Side, sleeping up there on nights it was too hot, praying for rain to splash down and break the heat, or opened fresh bars of soap on Christmas Day and tucked them in drawers to scent the clothes they shared while Nonna cooked on the woodstove. Now they had their own homes, their own kids, the language of their childhood forgotten except for the memories they'd rewritten and shared with their children, whether they were true or not.

Lorraine's front door opened. Aunt Diane hobbled onto the porch, her housedress grotesque in the sun. Had she sensed the break between them the same way she'd dreamed the night Lou had fallen from the sky? The same way she'd known something was wrong with Lorraine?

Eddie whirled on Ray. "You want to fool them? Fool them. They don't deserve it. Stay away from my children. Stay away from Lorraine. You'll live with what you did for the rest of your life."

Ray stared straight ahead. He could have pressed down on the gas and revved that magnificent engine, leaving them in the dust, but he'd hollowed out like a cicada shell clinging to bark, the real him somewhere else, and Gia was disgusted with the mute thing he'd become. She scratched the handful of utensils across the car hard enough to leave a long gash, but silently enough for no one to notice. It was satisfying, but not enough. She wanted to hurt him worse.

"Ida, get your things." Uncle Frank directed his wife toward the house before turning toward Eddie. "Keep your smut to yourself. Go on." He tapped the roof of the car. Ray drove away, and Uncle Frank shoved off to his shabby convertible. At least Tommy had the sense not to show up today.

"Worry about your own," Frank threw over his shoulder, the smugness in his voice an arrow landing on Leo at the curb, who'd folded in half, dangling like a rag doll.

But Eddie stared him down, holding his ground. "You should ask more questions before your kids end up in cement shoes."

Aunt Ida hesitated, looking between Frank and Agnes before slipping into the car and driving down the block.

"Get him off the damn lawn," Eddie hissed, his back to Leo, putting a wall between them, before turning toward the house and slamming the door.

Aunt Diane and Agnes looked at each other for a very long time without speaking.

Without being asked, Gia folded the tables, carried the cake inside. It unnerved her that Aunt Diane was still outside, staring. She could not remember a time Aunt Diane had ever spoken to her. The dish towel was still curled on the lawn as Agnes prodded Leo toward the house. She couldn't think with Aunt Diane leaning on the porch railing like that, looking right through her at everything Gia had failed to do.

~

By Wednesday, nothing had happened.

"We should talk to them," Agnes said over coffee, over dinner, on the porch at night with a cigarette burning, so often that Gia wished Agnes would just put her shoes on and go. Eddie didn't stop her. He just said nothing, which was exactly, Gia figured, what talking to them would change.

Lorraine did not go to school or leave her house, which was maybe better because Gia didn't know what to say to her. Or what to do. The only thing she could think of was covering Lorraine's shifts at the bakery until she was ready to go back.

"Again?" Big Louis said when Gia came in. He was huffing like a truck without a muffler as the fan ruffled papers on his desk, but he must've felt sorry later, because he came back with a box of warm S cookies for Lorraine. "Settles the stomach," he said. "With a glass of milk." There was a five-dollar bill taped to the bottom of the box. That was one nice thing about being the boss, handing out however much money you wanted.

On Thursday, Our Lady of Grace called Agnes at work to say that Leo was in an unusual state and could they please pick him up at once. "Call him a cab," Agnes told Sister Kathleen. "I'll mail them a check." Sister Kathleen walked Leo out to the car and closed the door behind him, hoped he'd feel better soon, and Leo had the driver make the first correct turn toward their house before taking him the rest of the way to Coney Island, where he ordered hamburgers and french fries on the boardwalk, skipped out on the bill, jumped a fence into a vacant lot, and cut his arm on a piece of rebar before the cops cuffed him.

"It's bad enough your father has to pick him up after his tour and take Leo for a tetanus shot on the way home. Make dinner, would you? I don't want them waiting around to eat. I'll be home in an hour."

Gia dumped a packet of hot dogs into a saucepan, cranked the can opener on a sauerkraut lid, boiled water for frozen pierogi, and set the table, all before her father walked in with Leo and the phone started ringing.

"Get that, would you?" he called from the hallway. His voice was hoarse. Either he was sick or he'd been yelling all the way home. "And go to your room."

Gia snapped the phone up as her father's shoe hit the floor in the hallway and he hung his empty holster in the closet.

"Hello?"

"Sergeant Martino, please."

"Dad?" The station. Gia pressed the receiver into her shoulder. He'd just gotten home and had to go back again? Agnes would flip. Plus they'd have to deal with Leo alone then. And maybe it was selfish, but dealing with Leo felt like a job for her father, same as mowing the lawn, cleaning gutters, or working under a car hood.

Her father took the phone and stretched the cord to the hallway. He was closer to the door and the front porch, farther from her, farther from Leo, like all he needed was the word to clear out of here in a second. "Yes, everything's all right. No, it won't happen again." Gia caught bits and pieces as she pulled the hot dog buns apart and put them on a plate, set the table with ketchup and mustard, folded paper napkins into triangles. Something was wrong. She kept her head down when her father put the phone back in the cradle, poured a glass of water, and washed his hands in the kitchen sink, just before Agnes walked in.

"Dinner's ready," Gia said, putting a hot dog in a bun for her father, which he ate without a plate, in several small, deliberate bites that gave away the fact that he was not happy with whatever that phone call had been.

"Get your brother," he said. "Then everyone can sit down."

Gia walked all the way upstairs to get him. Leo was on the foot of his bed, rocking quietly back and forth, his hands pressed to either side of his head, his foot beating against the floor. The moon was low outside the window. Was he crying?

"Leo?" Gia said softly, afraid to cross the line into his room for reasons she didn't understand. His room was as messy as always, clothes and shoes kicked around, unfinished things scattered. He didn't hear her the first time. She tried again, but not before realizing that he was really alone now. No Ray or Tommy. No school or other friends, really. Even her parents were angry with him. Maybe she should try a little harder.

She sat beside him on the bed, careful not to startle him. When he still didn't look up, she put one hand on his knee, softly, like he was one of her rabbits.

But it spooked him. He jumped up, squared off.

"Get out," he screamed. Gia opened her mouth, but there were no words, just hurt, bruising the good in her. She was off the bed in a second, by the door in another.

"Dinner's ready," was all she'd had to say, so she dropped those two words and took off. The door slammed. Drawers opened and closed. She had a pretty good idea of what he was rummaging for. She slid into her seat at the table still shaking, avoided his eye when he slid into his usual spot a few minutes later, noticeably calmer.

"The captain called tonight," Eddie said. "To strongly encourage me to get my son under control. Because in case you're not aware, it's an election year, and Wagner's on his way out. You know what the new guy's slogan is, Leo? 'He's fresh, and everyone else is tired.' Any idea what that means?"

Leo shrugged and stuffed a hot dog into his mouth, ketchup dripping down his chin. *I made that stupid hot dog,* Gia thought, bitter that all he had to do was open his mouth and chew when it was time to eat, but she'd made the whole meal. After school. After she hadn't skipped out on classes and spent the whole dumb day at Coney Island like he had.

Eddie slapped the fork out of Leo's hand. It clattered to the floor. Leo stared with his mouth open, hot dog and all, bouncing his knee under the table.

"It means the new guy won't turn a blind eye, Leo. So when I'm leaving tours to pick you up in whatever state you're in, it won't go unnoticed. And if you think I worked my whole life to have you ruin my reputation—"

"What are you talking about?" Agnes cut in. "What happened?"

"I'm on desk, Agnes, all because—"

Gia quietly pushed back her chair, because Leo was standing at one end of the table shouting now, and her father was at the other. She wasn't hungry anymore. And all her effort felt poured down the drain, so she picked up her backpack and a blanket from the living room and closed the front door quietly behind her, aware as she passed this house and that one that her neighbors were sitting down to dinner about now, passing the salt, passing the pepper, talking about what TV program to watch that evening after homework was finished and the dishes were put away. Was there room for one more? If she slipped into one of those houses and poured herself a glass of milk, pulled out a seat at the table, passed biscuits, and smiled at stories about people's days, would anyone mind that she didn't belong? Probably.

It was the first time she missed Aunt Ida and Uncle Frank in all of this. They wouldn't have blinked if she'd stayed for dinner. Not that they'd ever really asked her to. Not that Tommy or Ray sought her out enough for that to happen. But it was her best shot, and now it was gone, so she walked to the dock and slipped into the boat, made a pillow of her backpack, and spread the blanket over her so she could look at the first few stars, bright enough to shine through city haze, wishing she were one of them, because stars couldn't hear the yelling that happened on Earth. They just kept shining.

The canal smelled of motor oil, and Gia imagined rainbow sheens gliding quietly past. Chemicals. She laughed at the irony of it, how much she'd wanted to keep them out of her body while Leo welcomed them in, how she'd been afraid of powders and invisible vapors, and yet they'd been here all along, unavoidable. Again, she envied the stars, too far away for people to poison.

When enough time had passed and it was too cold, Gia made for home just in time to see her father round the corner toward the swimming canal in his jogging suit, only he wasn't running, just walking fast with his head down, darting toward Charles Park, which was odd. But Gia didn't have the energy to follow him, not when all she wanted was quiet and maybe a hot dog if there were any left, because she was cold and hungry and she couldn't be a star in the sky, not tonight, and not ever.

~

On Sunday, the tables and chairs weren't put out. It was too chilly to leave the front door open, so they turned the porch light on. It was barely visible in the early-afternoon sun, confused whether anyone was really welcome. Agnes pushed the couches back and vacuumed underneath. The kitchen table had been polished with lemon chemicals, stray shoes tucked behind the door, junk mail into a basket. Agnes wrapped prosciutto around sesame breadsticks and put them on a plate with melon slices and provolone cubes because no one knew what else to do on Sunday.

Gia swept the front porch and changed the straw in the rabbit hutch. Buster had already doubled in size, his real fur growing in over the fuzz, hopping around on his sturdier legs with the others. The cold tasted like fall, and it lit her up inside, a fresh start. She picked around the yard for leaves to press between book pages, but she couldn't think right on the ground. From the garage roof, she could climb the oak tree, see above the whole neighborhood. Maybe that would help her understand how to talk to Lorraine, who was still hiding, or what to do if she saw Tommy or Ray around or where Leo was all the time. Her foot was on the window ledge when the front door opened. Her mother had taken off her apron and checked the street, her watch. It was late. The melon had probably sweat all over the salty prosciutto.

The chipped paint was rough under Gia's fingertips, probably full of lead. *No one's coming, Mom,* she wanted to say. *You know this.*

But what were they doing? They had come here after church for as long as Gia remembered. She wondered if they were sorry now, licking their wounds and lumping around without her father's barbecues, if Aunt Ida was sorry she'd missed a week with her sister.

Grass crunched under her feet, dry from the sudden chill. The block smelled like meatballs and gravy. Yeast. It carried on the cold. Aunt Ida's walkway was newly lined with flaming mums, a cornucopia of dried flowers on the door. The windows were closed, but the house had a warmth to it, a full feeling. The radio was on. Shadows moved across the streakless, perfect windows.

She crept closer. Two tall candles burned on the dining room table, which was piled with linguini and clam sauce, sliced semolina bread, lemon wedges so vivid they made Gia's mouth pucker. A bakery cake was on the sideboard, a sparkly cake knife at the ready. Gia wondered if she'd had the nerve to buy that from her bakery, from Lorraine's. Aunt Ida shuffled about the kitchen, a flash of apron, an open oven. Gia felt slapped. The house hummed with music; Uncle Frank laughed as Aunt Ida called everyone to the table. Why had they never been invited to something so nice?

The back door opened, and Tommy dumped bottles into the trash. She stood in full view, a cat cornering a mouse.

He smiled sadly, shrugged, embarrassed. It was so honest it made her feel like the mouse instead of the cat. He put the lid on the can and went back inside. Behind her, the canal rolled quietly past, carrying debris in clumps. Ray's new car was parked in the driveway, the scratches buffed but still visible. They were sitting down now as if everything were fine.

She stormed off toward the street, weighing options: ring and run, tell her parents, scratch Ray's car again, something to prove they hadn't gotten away with it. The whole stupid family. That was it, she realized, the reason she couldn't bring herself to see Lorraine yet—because she hadn't done anything to make it right.

At the edge of the lawn was a baseball. It was perfect, just right for her palm, even though the chemicals Aunt Ida sprayed made Gia's skin tingle. She lined up with the dining room window, released. Glass shattered, but Gia was already running, fighting the urge to look as voices spilled and chairs pushed back, springing up from their charter plates and napkin rings, like on New Year's. Ringing in Sundays alone. *Sweep glass,* she thought. *Scrape linguini into the trash and order Chinese food, morons; see what it's like to have something taken from you.*

Mr. Angliotti dumped a pot of pasta water near the rosebush, steam rising from the ground. He waved. To him, she was Gia playing in the street, same as always, not Gia who'd just broken a window on purpose, who'd scratched a car, who had a brother who dangled in half. She waved back, playing the everything-is-normal game they played now.

"*The Ed Sullivan Show* is on," her father said. "Bring the prosciutto in here."

Her mother tucked her feet beneath her. Her father settled onto the couch, handing Agnes one of Nonna's crocheted blankets as Gia carried the tray over with a breadstick in her mouth. No one corrected her as she slid in beside her parents, as crumbs sprinkled Nonna's blankets, or asked where Leo was. This was nice, Gia thought, better than napkin rings and linguini. Her father popped open a beer, passed it to Agnes over Gia's lap, the air sweet with cold yeast. Gia smirked, hoping Aunt Ida was still crawling around on the ground for glass slivers while Uncle Frank duct-taped a garbage bag to the window, worrying over how much it would cost to repair, and Gia promised herself it wouldn't be the last thing she did to hurt them.

Her father was watching her instead of the screen. Gia smiled at him. He raised one eyebrow, but she couldn't tell him. She only knew that he'd approve. As he spread the blanket over her folded knees, she took that as a sign that he wouldn't have done anything differently.

~

On Monday, Lorraine left for school, the bruises yellowed. She'd twisted her hair into a knot as compact as a fist at the base of her neck instead of the soft tangle it usually was. For all the creams that could cover dark circles or imperfect skin, there must be something to cover the bruises, only Lorraine didn't bother.

"Walk with her," Agnes whispered above her coffee cup. Gia hesitated by the rabbit hutch, holding lettuce leaves, pretending they needed her to feed them the rest of the strawberries and apple peels, knowing she was being a coward.

"Go." Agnes looked at Gia directly this time. *Be my girl,* the look said. *My brave girl.*

"Lorraine!" Aunt Diane followed her to the porch, leaned over the railing, and whispered something, pointing her finger at Lorraine and then down the block, looking up long enough to lock eyes with Gia, nod an approval, a hello. It could've meant anything. Gia swallowed back a lump. Would it have been different if it were Gia? Would she have fought him off, gone for his nose with the heel of her hand, used her fishing knife? All those years of fighting with Leo, wiggling out of headlocks and buckling the backs of his knees, suddenly useful.

She fell into step beside Lorraine, who smelled like soap but not perfume, no makeup. It made her look older, and maybe she was now. Gia felt older too. Up ahead, Ray's new car backed out of the driveway, the engine cutting through her nerves.

"I keyed it." Gia worked up her voice. "Real good. They buffed it, but it was too deep."

Lorraine stared straight ahead.

"And I threw a rock through the window on Sunday, but no one knows it was me." She cleared her throat. These offerings weren't enough, dropped at Lorraine's feet. "I'll hurt him more," Gia promised. "I don't know how yet, but I'll figure it out. And . . ." They passed the stump on Mr. Angliotti's lawn. The rings were fresh circles. How old was that tree, and why did it have to come down? What had it done wrong? They punished all the wrong things.

When they were kids, Nonna used to rub honey on their scraped knees and elbows, singing to them in Italian the whole way through. "It fix you," Nonna had said in English. Gia wished for that honey now, or anything really, that could fix the inside things and that lasted longer than honey.

"And I'm sorry," Gia said, her voice breaking. "I really am."

"I know." Lorraine sighed, staring off at the parakeets.

"We'll get him for this," Gia said as the car turned the corner. He didn't even stop, adding to Gia's urge to crush him. "I don't know how, but . . ."

"Why?" Lorraine said, her eyes vacant. "There's too many people to blame here, Gia. What's the point?"

The rest of the walk was silent until their schools loomed before them, dividing them in the only way they ever were.

"Gia." Lorraine stopped before they split off. "It's not your fault."

Lorraine's voice broke and her face crumpled, but when Gia stepped forward, Lorraine waved her away, rearranging her face, forcing a smile.

"It's not yours either," Gia said. Lorraine nodded but didn't believe it. Not yet. The sun shifted behind a cloud, leaving the world gray. Maybe she never would.

Lorraine closed her hand into a fist, turned for school, nodded at one of the nuns on the top step, and then she was gone.

But up ahead, Leo rounded the corner, heading for the lot behind the rectory in regular clothes. No, Gia thought. This was ridiculous. He couldn't keep missing school. Couldn't keep doing whatever he wanted, filling his body up with poison. Ray had ruined enough for them. He couldn't win with Leo either.

"Leo!" Gia called out. "This isn't right. You can't . . ."

He turned to face her, and her voice trailed off. He was already wild eyed.

"This isn't real." He pointed at the school behind them. "None of this. None of what we were taught. It doesn't matter, Gia. It doesn't matter."

He kicked at the dirt with his toe, working it into a dust cloud that blurred his face. Gia swallowed. What did she even know about anything anymore? Why was she more right than him? He walked away, kicking up more dust in his wake, and Gia let him go, stood in the middle of that empty lot and watched him because she didn't know what else to do.

He turned back and smiled at her. Or maybe he was only squinting at the sun. But it reminded her of following him into the grocery store and down the aisle with the candy bins, him climbing shelves, grabbing handfuls of gummy sharks and Chuckles and Baby Ruths, and shoving them into her backpack while she pretended to look at the shelves. Who would ever doubt a little kid? And they hadn't. Gia and Leo walked out every time and split handfuls in the parking lot, gummy sharks turning her mouth blue on the walk home.

And he was right. School couldn't teach her anything, nothing that applied to what had happened to Lorraine or even Leo, but she didn't know what to do instead, so she followed the ringing bells and smiled apologetically as the nuns reminded her not to be late while her brother disappeared into a cloud of dust.

Chapter Eleven

On a Tuesday night, Agnes found a needle in Leo's desk next to a brand-new notebook with only his name written in shaky pencil on the front. He said it was Lorraine's from nursing school, which was a lie, and then didn't come home for three days. Gia wondered if it would be better to let him see Ray and Tommy again—if, bad as he was, they'd been keeping him from getting worse. But Ray drove around in his new car with Tommy in the passenger seat. They'd moved away from the docks and had new spots now, which must be going well, because Aunt Ida's house had gotten repainted and a new set of air conditioners installed, so they couldn't be missing Leo much, which only made Gia more annoyed.

That week, Gia slid her hand between the mattress and the box spring to put her bakery money with the rest of the folded bills, including Ray's, but it was only smooth and cool. She lifted the mattress, but there was only the thin lining. She checked under the bed in case it had fluttered away, knowing it was gone. And it had to be Leo. And she felt sick, wondering if he'd taken it all at once or in little bits, knowing she wouldn't notice either way or didn't care. It was almost a relief not to worry over what to use it for that was worth what she'd done to get it in the first place. She could start over, and her honest money wouldn't mix with Ray's, but the shock of it surprised her, stinging through her skin and up her spine like a man-of-war in the ocean, her stupidity for not seeing it coming squeezing at her chest until it was hard to breathe and all she could do was curl up on the slanted mattress and promise not to let it happen again.

The secret of her brother made Gia painfully careful of everything. It made the whole world look different—house numbers were suddenly important, the call of crows cut through street noise, and subtle smells like shampoo or soap as people passed on the sidewalk were sharp in Gia's nose—because she was always *ready*, even if the purpose was unclear.

It was exhausting to be on alert all the time. At school, she put her head down on her desk and asked for passes to the nurse just to lie down for a little while. Ten minutes of sleep on the nurse's cot was more than she got at home, where every creak in the hallway sparked her awake. Sometimes she skipped gym and slept on the exercise mats piled in the locker room. They were greasy and stamped with shoe prints but far from anywhere Leo was. The nurse sent a note home recommending a test for mono, but they all knew it wasn't the kissing disease. That note ended up in the trash.

And word got around. Big Louis at the bakery took Gia off the register.

"Bag it up and give it to Regina to ring in," he huffed on his way down the basement steps one day, hauling a bag of flour that leaked from the seams, clouding his face, and Gia knew why. It didn't matter how honest she was or that she'd never stolen or done drugs herself, because it was in her blood, same as Leo, and it could pop out at any time. She wondered, too, if Big Louis was right, and it haunted her that they might be the same, she and Leo, the same way they hated escarole or raisins in braciola or had slightly webbed toes. If it could run in Gia like it ran in Leo, all she needed were the right things to unlock it.

So Gia turned down aspirin for headaches and Alka-Seltzer for her stomach, because they were chemicals. She didn't know where the line was anymore.

Her parents whispered about options at the kitchen table and a plan starting "soon": cold turkey, halfway houses, a trip, a place called Brother Island. That meant a lot of brothers needed sending off, which gave Gia a guilty relief that they were not the only ones. Brother Island was closed forever, her father said, because locking people up and making them quit didn't work. There were other places and programs.

But he should be home, Agnes argued. They would fix this themselves.

"What's the difference?" he asked Agnes one night. "If he's locked up either way?"

But *there* it would just happen, whatever it was, and they'd see Leo when it was over. Here, it would be two doors down from her room, without doctors or nurses or hospital things. He would be away like all the contaminated sunflower fields and orange groves in her book had been. Not here. This was too big for an eighth grader, like the sparrows falling from the tree.

"Stop comparing him to the kids you see on the street," Agnes snapped, pausing to finish the rest of the amaretto in her glass, an old bottle that could've been Nonna and Pop Pop's, a gift forgotten in the hutch, dusted off and poured into a glass with ice. "You can't write off your own son."

The clock ticked between them. Eddie lit a cigarette but didn't smoke it. It sat in the ashtray, burning. Agnes took another sip from the empty glass.

"What if we just gave him little amounts at a time? Control how much he takes?"

Eddie slammed a fist down and stormed out the front door in a huff with a new pack of smokes, Leo's cue the kitchen was safe.

"I need money," he said as Gia swiped a butter knife of peanut butter over toast.

"For what?" Agnes refilled the glass as an ice cube melted on the table.

"Don't give him money," Gia snapped, remembering those kids under the train tracks and their burning trash, unwashed bodies, and soggy clothes.

"Shut up," Leo snapped back. "Shut the hell up."

"Hey!" Agnes stood, rattling the Tiffany lamp above the table so the dust shook free. "Watch your mouth."

But Gia'd had it. The butter knife flew, hit him in his sweat-stained T-shirt, leaving a smear of peanut butter. Gia braced as Leo charged forward until Agnes jumped between them.

"Enough! Enough! Here . . ." She unfolded a five-dollar bill from her purse. Leo glared at the crumpled bill, clearly disappointed, before storming out.

"Not a word." Agnes rubbed her forehead. "Just be glad he won't steal it from you later."

But he couldn't. Not when her bakery money was in a Maxwell House can in Lorraine's kitchen cupboard, all the way in the back. She wasn't that stupid anymore. Even if Agnes was.

Gia stormed out, too, forgetting about her peanut butter toast, and headed for the dock. October had emptied the boats from the canal. Barnacles had already been scraped from the hulls, motors winterized, boats packaged under snow-proof tarps. There was nothing sadder than a boat out of water, the stillness of it, eerie in the same way Nonna had been at her wake, when Gia had been convinced she was still breathing. Their boat was one of the forgotten few still bobbing in the water.

They weren't doing enough. Even Gia could see that, and she was only thirteen. They were thinking like adults, running over the same ideas old people always did. Timothy Leary was wrong about LSD, but he wasn't wrong about people opening their minds. Maybe it was like the person who'd invented the felt tip pen or the time Leo had added the Möbius strip to the lawn mower. One small change could make all the difference. Gia stared at the sky, where the constellations were changing with the seasons, knowing her brother was sinking. *Let him sink,* she thought bitterly, but no. Her mother was right. He was still in there somewhere. And he didn't deserve that place under the train or being buried in a pine box, no matter what her father threatened.

~

Brother Island was a kidney-shaped splotch on a nautical map of the Hudson. Too far to swim to the Bronx or Queens. Without a boat, you'd be *Gilligan's Island* stuck. The encyclopedia said it had been a hospital for smallpox and tuberculosis once, a swamp of trapped germs. It was disgusting, all that death and sick gobbled up by water lapping at the shore.

"Dad?" she asked one night, slicing a cucumber at the counter while her mother washed lettuce in the sink. "What happens at Brother Island now that it's abandoned?"

"Crime," he said without looking up from the Aqueduct race scores.

"How do you know about that place?" Agnes left the water running in the sink, her hands in the lettuce, looking like she'd hopped off a merry-go-round too fast.

"Heard you talking about it." Gia shrugged, knowing her mother was wondering what else Gia had heard. Agnes snapped the water off and dried her hands with a dish towel that left little fibers on her skin.

"But why?" Gia tried to sound casual, kept chopping. A cucumber slice rolled off the cutting board and dropped to the floor.

"Because people do whatever they want when no one's watching."

"But not everyone." Gia searched for the right words. Her father understood crime. Were the two so different, crime and drugs, when they were both illegal? Why Leo and not her? "Some people make the right choice even if there's a bad option."

"Some," he said, but the optimism fell flat. *Some* people won the lottery. *Some* people were rich. *Some* people went to college.

"Well, with the island, why did it work for some people and not others?"

"'Cause." Her father rubbed his eyes. "You can take the junk away, but the need for it sticks. The second they get off that island, they go right back to it."

The old stories about her father clicked together: Chin-ups off the fire escapes on the Lower East Side to bulk up before the draft, faking his papers to enlist before he was old enough, lining up next to a high school pool for the sink-or-float test. Later, he'd been a navy machine gunner, even though he hadn't finished eighth grade, but people listened to him anyway. He had a habit of picking things up around the house—a wire hanger, an empty bottle—and saying things like, *Someone could get hurt on this.* His quiet calm made people like Uncle Frank nervous because he didn't air his thoughts all over the place, but he was missing the point.

"Why would it work here versus Brother Island if the need sticks?"

The question hung in the kitchen like cigarette smoke around a light, clouding the plan.

"Your brother has an *obligation* to do right by us," Agnes snapped. "None of the boys on that island had any reason to get better. Why should they if their families abandoned them?"

The last sentence cut through the haze of Gia's question.

"But there were doctors and scientists," Gia argued. "And they couldn't—"

"It's different." Agnes gathered the floating lettuce into a bowl, splashing water all over the counter.

If scientists sent things into space and built submarines and bombs, how could they fail a bunch of boys on an island? Gia opened her mouth, but her father shook his head. *Drop it.*

Dinner was silent, the table set for Leo even though he wasn't there. Her father ate only a handful of bites before gathering his keys and a thermos of hot water with lemon.

"I'm gonna take a ride," he said. "See if I can find him."

Agnes let out a breath, the relief clear. She'd been waiting for Eddie to suggest this all night. Gia cleared plates and scraped the uneaten food into the trash while her mother stared at Leo's empty seat, his clean plate, holding an invisible conversation.

"Leave it," Agnes said as Gia cleared Leo's place. "He'll eat when he gets home."

Gia bit back the words on the tip of her tongue: that he did not care about chicken and mashed potatoes or eating with his family or school or even motorcycles or anything unless it could be snorted, smoked, or injected. She left her mother in the kitchen with a glass of water sweating a river over the edge of the table.

~

That night, Gia lay awake. Maybe quitting cold turkey would work; maybe not. She traced the shape of Brother Island in her mind. A kidney, like a Florida pool or a bean. The hospital on Brother Island was a big stone thing. Maybe any hidden place would work. Slowly other shapes formed in her mind like smudges on a warming car window. Pumpkin Patch. West Marsh. Salt. Garbage barges dumped in the bay because trash washed out to sea. The marsh was an in-between place for fresh water and salt, absorbing storms, filtering pollution.

They were wrong, Gia realized, the doctors, nurses, scientists, her parents—because at the stone hospital on Brother Island or his bedroom, he would have everything he needed to survive, just not the drugs. He would crave what he couldn't have, but without food, water, and shelter, maybe the missing part wouldn't seem as important and the marsh could work its magic. It was closer to the edge Leo lived on.

At some point that night, her father came home and closed the door quietly behind him, but there was only one set of shoes on the stairs in the morning.

But at breakfast, her mother let out a small cry in the kitchen because Nonna's silverware was gone, every last teaspoon with curved roses. Gia felt sorry for Agnes, who'd polished and set it out on holidays like Nonna had. Now it had been stolen by someone who should've inherited it and set it on his family table one day. Agnes closed the cabinet door and went to work, walking the long way toward the train to avoid Aunt Ida's house.

"I will fix this," Gia promised everyone, veering off on her way to school and doubling back for the house. Leo was right about nothing being important at school anymore, not when everything was falling apart. She would make her own Brother Island. She would make him fight to be alive where there was no silverware to steal or drugs to change his brain. Where there was no one left to hurt but himself.

~

First, she needed a place.

Second: the boat needed to be empty, like always, so Leo wouldn't suspect, which meant she'd have to take the boat out alone. The thought gave her a fluttery feeling not unlike what she imagined girls felt when some boy asked them out and they stood in a gaggle flapping with excitement.

And she'd have to get Leo in the boat. Her parents would need an explanation without enough information to ruin everything. She would figure that out later, but for the next few days, Gia slipped things away unnoticed—saltine packets, canteens of water, flashlights, clothes, the old camping gear from the garage—while her parents prepared for their own experiment. She stashed everything in the boat, a little at a time.

He'd have everything he needed at first; then she'd cut back. The more he lived without, the more he'd fight to live.

It was during one of her trips from the grocery store to the boat, transporting chips and Moon Pies, that she realized she'd missed the dance. Her mother hadn't noticed the circle on the calendar as she'd folded clean towels and carried them to the linen closet, nor had her father as he'd pulled Leo's furniture from the wall and felt the edges for hiding spots.

The neighborhood felt like Halloween: costumes and makeup, flashes of taffeta sparkling in the early-evening light, Flora Salerno posing in front of the rhododendron bush for her mother's Kodak with some poor schlub in a suit. It was only when Gia rounded the corner that she realized the boy in the navy suit and neatly combed hair slipping a corsage of pink tea roses onto Flora's thin wrist was Tommy.

And yet she had passed right by, unnoticed, as invisible as a gnat, barely recognizing someone she'd opened presents with on Christmas morning for as long as she could remember, sat side by side with at midnight Mass, dipping their fingers in wax melting from slender candles and drawing like with crayons on the back of the pew. He'd once given her a rock for her birthday because it looked like a dolphin—did she see? The tail here, the fin here, a long pointed nose. And she had seen. It was in her room somewhere, along with the cotton candy they'd tried to save but forgotten about until they'd found it months later, pink and crystallized into a kind of fascinating coral. But they were unstuck now, and it was hard to believe it could happen so fast, that it could happen at all.

Gia rolled the grocery bag into the others. There was still sun in the sky, enough for a few hours. She couldn't go home, not when everyone in the world, even Tommy, was at the dance, couldn't go home and accept she'd become invisible. Her throat squeezed at the memory of Lorraine pushing back the coffee table, how easily she'd laughed then, how pretty she was with her long dark hair around her face. Now she was a shadow of her other self. Slowly, Gia uncleated the ropes, nudged her shoes between the supplies at the bottom of the boat, lowered the outboard, and motored off into the great big welcoming bay, laughing at Tommy dressed in his penguin suit and the thought of him dancing with stupid bug-eyed Flora while nuns measured the distance between them with rulers. Salt spray sparkled in Gia's hair, her own galaxy of stars, the boat rising and falling out of tune with Gia's breath, crashing her teeth into each other. She was a flying fish, jumping waves and changing direction, water soaking her clothes. She wasn't forgotten or out of place here. She was Gia. *G-I-A*. Three proud letters just like three proud elements: water, air, and fire. She was all three, born again on the water in a wild world of marshes.

And there it was: her island. It was just right for a tent, for the experiment that would save her brother, her parents. She killed the engine and tugged the boat forward, knowing she'd find it again as she had tonight, because the marsh would lead her right to it, whisper her closer and call her home as many times as it took.

~

That night, Leo stole meat from the supermarket and got caught on the way out. He slugged the store manager and left him with a black eye and a broken rib. Eddie was on tour, but he came straight home in his cruiser, lights and sirens blaring, threw Leo in the slammer for the night a few precincts over, and came home with the hundred dollars of frozen meat Leo had stuffed under his shirt and a receipt that made Agnes cringe.

"Paid in full." Eddie sighed. "Party's over."

The preparation was quick: Eddie nailed fabric to the windows in Leo's room to block the light; Leo's stash was flushed, minus the little bits Agnes kept to dole out later if need be; they equipped the room with clean towels, an ice bucket, a washcloth, a chair for sitting watch, and a pitcher of water sweating on the nightstand; and Eddie took a quick nap before getting ready to pick Leo up again at the station. It was so hospital-like that Gia was thankful to snatch her things and head out.

"Dad?" Gia asked as Eddie pulled back Leo's bed and ran his hand under the headboard before doing the same to the dresser and Leo's desk. "What happens exactly?"

"What happens with what?"

"With whatever you're doing tonight."

Eddie paused and sat on the floor. "Remember when you got the flu a year or two ago? It's like that, but worse. The worst flu you could ever get."

Gia sat beside him, resisting the urge to put her head on his shoulder because she was too old for that baby stuff now, and he was busy. She only had a few minutes at most before he started working again.

"Is it true that heroin comes from a flower? The same one they give out on Veterans Day?"

"Almost," he said.

"And is it true that it used to be medicine?"

He nodded and rubbed his hand over his cheek where stubble was growing in, making his whole face darker. So science and doctors were wrong. It was disappointing. How could regular people get it right if people as smart as doctors or scientists were wrong?

"Will it work?" she asked. "Whatever you're doing in here?"

Her father was quiet for a long time, staring at the scuff marks on the ceiling where Leo had bounced a rubber ball too many times.

"Come on," he said. "If I sit for too long, I'll lose the nerve."

~

From Lorraine's front porch, Gia's house was dark except for one missed light in Nonna's old apartment. She wanted to be *away* before Eddie pulled up again.

"Can I stay over? The exterminator's coming."

It was a stupid lie. Why would one come on a Friday night? And there wasn't a truck out front. It was the first time Gia had been back *since*, and now she wasn't sure she could sit in Lorraine's room again, same as usual, without thinking of that stupid dress on the bed. Those shoes stacked neatly. She was thankful when Lorraine took her purse from the hall closet.

"Fine, but I was about to go out."

"Can I come?"

Lorraine hesitated. *Out* used to mean makeup and hair spray, perfume and small purses, but Lorraine was skinnier now, the bones in her face more defined, the rest of her hidden in a baggy flannel shirt that might've been Uncle Louie's once. She looked like she was ready for the flu, not a night out. Guilt washed through Gia again. Maybe it would be better to hide in Nonna's apartment for the weekend instead.

"I guess, but it's not your thing."

"Why?" Gia anchored her toes in her sneakers, forcing back the sting, because she couldn't go home.

"It's hard to explain."

"Fine," Gia said. Anything was better than staying here alone again with Aunt Diane, who called out quietly for Louis.

Lorraine took the glass from Aunt Diane's hand and put it on the coffee table. "No, Mom, it's me, Lorraine." She closed the blinds and shut off the lamp, spread a blanket over her mother. This dance between them was so personal that Gia inched closer to the porch, a new sadness sitting in the pit of her chest at how lonely it was.

The air was refreshing. A yellow leaf drifted toward the ground. People were eating dinner. TVs and radios humming along. A new wash of people came off the train. It was Friday. Tomorrow they'd sleep in and mow lawns after bagels and coffee, but tonight was for bowling or movies, dinner out. Gia had forgotten what Fridays used to be like now that her parents dreaded them for Leo. They turned onto Cross Bay Boulevard and waited for a bus toward Rockaway, which made Gia even more curious about where they were going.

A car sped past, full of teenagers, with the windows rolled down. A boy leaned out, pumping his fist and screaming into the race of wind. A few months ago, she'd been with Ray, Leo, and Tommy, doing the same thing. Now everything was different.

"Is this OK?" Gia asked about her outfit, hoping for a clue about where they were going and wanting to break the silence that used to be comfortable but wasn't anymore.

Lorraine shrugged. "It doesn't really matter."

Gia smoothed her pants and tucked in her shirt, pushed her hair behind her ears as the bus pulled up.

The sun was setting as Broad Channel came into view. The houses jutted into the water on stilts, everyone inside probably fishing from their living room windows. Crab traps were tied to the moorings, and everyone had little fishing skiffs meant for early morning before the water got crowded. They got off at the next stop. Lorraine turned a corner at the Legion Club and kept going, past an empty lot with a chain-link fence and stacks of old tires. Never once had Gia been inside any of these houses.

Lorraine turned down a walkway to a single-story house hidden behind shrubs, and Gia was disappointed it wasn't on stilts. There wasn't a front porch, just a faded red door with chipped paint and a wind chime made of beach bottles. The stoop was a mosaic of broken plates, uneven under Gia's sneakers. Inside, a pile of shoes was gathered by the door. The air was spicy, like the buckets of cinnamon pine cones outside the supermarket in October.

The orange light at the end of the hall drew them forward. Lorraine pushed aside the beaded curtain and stepped into a room of pillows. A side table had metal pots, bowls of rice, and stacks of flatbread; the floor was littered with tambourines and bells, and a tiny accordion sat next to a table of plants with long, viny arms growing over everything.

Lorraine picked a spot in the corner, but Gia could not move. Where the hell were they? And how, how, had Lorraine found this place? It was unnerving how comfortable Lorraine was, crossing her legs on the pillows and closing her eyes in a room full of strangers where Gia was easily the youngest and everyone else was the same age as their parents, or at least older than Lorraine.

One of them stepped forward, a woman wrapped in fabric.

"Welcome." She smiled, holding Gia by the elbow so she couldn't dart, smelling like a spice rack. The whole thing was kind of welcoming in an unexpected way, more than Aunt Ida's or even Lorraine's. The woman didn't ask Gia's name or why she was there, just led her to a pile of pillows next to Lorraine and told Gia to make herself comfortable.

There was too much happening: People whispered softly, someone poured water from a pitcher, and a stick of incense curled a smoke ribbon into the thick air, making her faintly nauseous. A woman had a small dog wrapped to her chest with a scarf. Gia pulled at the tassel on her pillow, where a parade of blocky elephants was crossing. The room was not full, but it closed in as everyone found their places, forming a circle that, like it or not, Gia was part of. The boys would've had a field day, ripping into this whole place. *Lorraine found a cult.* She could almost hear them snickering. For a second, she missed them terribly. Even Ray.

"Lorraine?" she whispered. "What is this?"

Lorraine's eyes stayed closed. "Pretend it's church."

But it was not church. That was wrong to say. There was no priest or altar or Communion wafers or red prayer candles or holy water. This was not where they'd made their first Communions or penance. It didn't have nuns. Our Lady of Grace would not approve of this place. It seemed like everything they warned against. False idols and all that. Gia worried about her soul, surprised any of what she'd learned in religion had stuck. There was still time to sneak out. She could catch the bus back to Howard Beach and sleep in the boat if she had to because maybe Lorraine had lost her mind. Maybe she was more broken than anyone thought, which made a hard lump form in Gia's throat as she looked at her cross-legged cousin on a pile of pillows, so different from the person Gia had known her entire life.

A bell chimed at the front of the room, startling Gia.

"Let's begin." The same rag doll woman settled onto her own pillow. The accordion hummed to life with a few sad notes that made the room vibrate through the smoke, swirling together two competing senses, smell and sound. It coursed through her, waking up the little atoms that made Gia until she no longer cared what this place was, whether it was allowed or not. It was just music, same as anything on the radio, and her body was singing, weightless, so unlike what she felt at home lately.

"From the outside," the woman said, chanting along with the accordion, long slow notes, "we may look like different people. Different hair, different eyes, different skin. Different wants, different needs. But we are all the same."

A tiny sound came from Lorraine. Gia knew she shouldn't, but she peeked, and a small tear was rolling silently down Lorraine's face. Before, Gia would've put her hand over Lorraine's. Now, a sickening guilt plastered itself in Gia's head and made her hands immobile, made her close her eyes to block Lorraine, pretending she had not seen. So much for not being a coward, Gia thought.

"And in the forest or the park, just as trees may look like another at first, on closer inspection the differences become clear. Different leaves, different bark, different branches, different seasons to wake and slumber."

Gia cringed. It was hard to pretend this was church if they were going to use different stories. But the woman went on, lowering her voice, and it was surprising that that quiet woman could be so powerful behind an accordion.

"But they are all one, their roots connecting to the earth, drawing from the same abundance of nutrients, and if one tree calls out its need, another answers. One tree will not drink more than another if there is a drought, just as trees know not to grow into the space another needs."

She should have told her parents sooner. Right after the basement. After Leo had sold the bike. After the first time he'd skipped school. She wrapped her arms around herself, laced her fingers, pretending it was Lorraine's hand covering hers. The woman was still talking, and Gia tried not to listen because it had already woken up something unexpected.

"And we are not so different from the trees if we can learn to hear those around us and trust that we will be heard, that our roots anchor us not only to the earth but to each other."

The accordion played for a while without words.

"If we can learn to hear those around us."

Her voice rang out, repeating it again and again to make it more important. She thought of Crazy Louann calling out for her cats, how they came to her. Her mother sitting at the foot of Leo's bed, keeping watch. Her father on the porch at night with his smokes. Her longing for the water.

The room was chanting, repeating a name. Someone had a tambourine, and whenever it seemed the chanting would end, it started again. It was worse than reading the saints at Easter vigil, Leo and Gia elbowing each other in the pew, only this was pleasant. She opened her eyes to see what everyone was doing. Singing. Even Lorraine. It was a little embarrassing, all those voices.

Finally the accordion stopped. The singing stopped. But the music was stuck in her bones, lingering like water after a swim or sun after the beach. She felt lighter, the way she was supposed to feel after confession or church but never did. Here, no one asked her to confess anything or apologize for not being good enough. It just filled her up with strange music and a poem.

With her eyes closed and her head tilted back, Lorraine looked almost herself again. She lay back on her pillows, her arms fanned above her head, as if she were floating in the canal.

But when she opened her eyes, the heaviness settled around them again. Gia wished she could keep that music in Lorraine a little longer, bring some of the happiness back.

"Imagine my dad at this place." In his uniform on pillows covered in elephants, struggling to keep his eyes closed in a room full of strangers, commenting on how close the incense was to the table edge. What if someone bumped it? They'd burn the whole place down. And he would definitely never pick up a tambourine unless it was bagged as evidence.

Lorraine's mouth hinted at a smile, but it was only a hint. "The exterminator's not really coming tonight, is he?"

"No," Gia said, shedding the lie more easily than she'd planned to. "It's Leo."

Lorraine stared at the ceiling, where the incense had left a gray film.

"But it's a secret," Gia said, rushing on.

Lorraine nodded. Gia lay back, too, closing her eyes on the pillow as someone snuffed out the incense and people piled their pillows in a corner, walking barefoot on a shiny wood floor.

"Come on, let's eat," Lorraine said. "There's some kind of curry tonight."

Gia had no idea what a curry was, but she followed Lorraine to the metal bowls, where the covers were lifted and steam spiraled above, surrounding Gia like music, her body singing in the newness of it all. She could understand why Lorraine liked this place, weird as it was. Here, she wasn't just Gia from Queens but a star in the universe, burning alongside billions of others, and all was right.

~

Lorraine was asleep, but Gia tossed in her cot until she gave up and sat by the window. Her house felt far away. The spicy bean thing she'd eaten earlier rolled in her stomach, sending angry heat waves through her. She wanted to run or jump or climb to burn it off. The best she could do was bounce her knee.

Her house was dark. No sign of whatever was going on inside. The street was quiet too. Everyone was inside, asleep, or waiting it out. Was the worst over yet, or had it even started? What would the worst flu even be? Chills that blankets couldn't stop, sweating through them, nauseous at the memory of food, an eye-burning fever, body aches that made it painful to roll or stay still, forgetting what good felt like, what life had been like before, only sick.

Just let it work, she prayed. *Whatever they're doing. Just let it work.*

She was ready for everything to go back to normal, though it startled her that she couldn't remember what that was anymore.

A lighter flared. Someone was on the porch, pacing by the bunny hutch. A cigarette burned orange, lowered, lifted. It was not her family, because the front door was closed, the porch light off. It was someone looking for Leo. Gia's breath fogged the glass, making it harder to see.

The cigarette flipped off the porch. So rude. A shape crossed the yard until it was under Leo's window, kicking around for a stone or a stick. Ray. Gia's stomach clenched.

This was his fault. Everything. Why wasn't he locked in his room with the worst sick of his life? He threw something at Leo's window, but the light stayed off, the window closed.

Piss off, Gia prayed, but Ray threw another stone. Then another. There was something desperate in his pacing, off balance.

"Wake up, Dad," Gia whispered. He had to tell Ray to get lost, because if Leo knew Ray was outside, he'd go nuts. There was no movement in the house, but Ray was not leaving. Another stone arched toward the window.

That was it. Gia's insides burned. She grabbed something heavy and hard from the dresser. Her feet flew down the stairs; the front door swung behind her.

"Hey." She charged across the street. "Piss off."

Ray's eyes went wide. He threw his hands up, but Gia couldn't stop. Not when Leo was unrecognizable, her parents barely sleeping, skipping showers and meals, while Ray was fine with his pockets full of cash and his new car and big, stolen dreams.

"Listen, you don't understand," Ray said, rushed. "This thing, it's bigger now. It's bigger than me. I stopped, Gia. He's gotta stop too. He's not getting it from me anymore, OK? That's not what this is about anymore."

Lies, lies, lies. The thing in Gia's hand cracked against Ray's head. He staggered, wiped at his eyes. It smelled suddenly of Lorraine's perfume. Gia crouched as if on the back of Leo's bike to kick down garbage cans and nailed Ray's stomach; he doubled over, wheezing.

He held up one hand to stop her, wheezed something about Antonio, but Gia didn't care.

"Hit me again," she taunted. Slapping girls. Pathetic. She aimed for his face. Gia was out of breath, her vision blurry, but she shoved him down, jumped on his back, pummeled with her fists. His nose was bleeding. It was on her hands, her face, but she hit harder, the bones in her hands screaming, swelling every time they smashed into his skin and the bones underneath. Ray was catching his breath, screaming something, muffled from where his head was hiding in his arms. Lorraine's perfume was in her nose, her mouth. She spit and pummeled, her fists coming down slower now, running out of fight. She pulled at clumps of his hair.

There were hands on her shoulders, lifting from under her arms, shouting, "Enough." But Gia kept kicking, throwing her legs in the air until Ray skittered away. His car peeled off without headlights.

She stopped, suddenly exhausted. Lorraine's broken perfume was in the grass. That beautiful bottle. Lorraine had saved up to buy it, and now it was ruined. Gia sat in the grass and tried to piece it back together again, but it was hard to see, and her hands were shaking and swollen. There was blood under her fingernails, and even if she fixed it, the perfume couldn't go back inside. The smell of it was everywhere. Gia sobbed. A piece of glass sliced her hand, and a line of red welled up.

"Gia." Her father lifted her face. She had to look at him. The sadness there was too much, so she focused on his tattoo instead. She used to pretend the ink rope tied them together, drawing a rope down her own arm in blue pen, and she wished she still believed that. He kissed her forehead, and Gia threw her arms around him. He picked her up. Not as easily as he used to, but Gia didn't let go even though she was too tall, too old.

"He's gonna ruin everything," Gia sobbed.

"I know, Gia. I know."

His voice broke, and it was terrible, like the sound of feral cats calling for missing kittens. Her father rocked until Gia felt ridiculous for being held like a baby in the front yard. The light was on across the street. Aunt Diane was at the window.

He carried Gia to the porch and told her to stay put. He was in his pajamas, barefoot. Gia felt a new wash of tears spring up and wrapped her arms around herself as her father gathered blankets from inside. *Do you see?* she thought to Aunt Diane. *I'm trying.* Aunt Diane disappeared from the window. The light clicked off, and then her father was back.

"Don't worry about this. We'll get Lorraine a new one."

"But it's expensive."

"So what? I'd buy ten bottles to see you crack him again."

Gia laughed. The relief of it made her even more exhausted.

"You're not mad?"

"Mad? No. Proud, maybe. You hope a girl could hold her own if she had to. Just don't seek it out, a'right?"

He was quiet for a while as the sky lightened around them in a hazy purple, the trees still black.

"Did I ever tell you about your aunt Em?"

Gia stilled. He never talked about his family. "They're gone," was all he said. There were no pictures, no stories, just quiet moments on birthdays and holidays when her father was thinking of them, and Gia always knew.

"Well, she was tough as nails. Could scare anyone off the block with a look and wasn't afraid of dumping water on their heads if she had to. I was more scared of Em as a kid than I was of my parents. She was a field nurse . . ."

The way he paused told Gia she hadn't come back.

"You take after her," he said and smiled so sadly his eyes were wet at the corners. "When people are gone, you know you won't see them again, but sometimes you catch pieces in other people, and it takes the air out of your lungs. And you . . ."

He pressed his hands to his face and wiped away whatever feelings were bubbling underneath, but Gia let them rise, wishing he'd tell her more about Aunt Em, because her heart felt full with her, with the idea that she might've taken after someone she'd never met, that it might explain all the things about herself she didn't see in her parents or Leo or her cousins.

"Come on," he said, snapping back to himself. "Let's get some ice on your hands."

They went inside. Her father closed the door quietly, but instead of going to the kitchen, they made their way slowly up the steps to the second floor, avoiding the creaky spots, then tiptoed down the hallway to Leo's closed door. It was quiet. Still. The room smelled faintly of vomit, strongly of sweat. *A filter,* Gia thought. *A marsh is a filter.* Her mother was in a chair at the foot of the bed, resting her face on her arms, her hair messy around her. Leo was curled on his side, mumbling slightly, the blankets kicked away, his forehead dotted with sweat, his eyes lined with dark circles, pale, but sleeping. He did not look comfortable, but he did not look extremely uncomfortable either. It equaled what Gia had expected. If anything, it calmed her.

Her father led them back downstairs, poured Gia a glass of milk with a straw, and put a bag of frozen peas on her hands. He took cookies from the jar and put them on the table without a plate or a napkin, but neither touched them.

"It's easy to blame Ray," he said. "But your brother made some shit choices."

Crumbs dotted the table like a constellation on a wooden sky, the swirling wood grain slightly nauseating. Something had to be at fault, a first event all the others could be traced back to. Creation. Illness. Everything had a timeline. A cause and effect.

"I'll take care of Ray." Her father nodded, as if deciding for himself. "No more fights, OK?"

"How?" Gia rested her head on crisscrossed arms, her fists and fingers pulsing, knocking through her skin for a second fight, but underneath the throbbing, she was satisfied. She'd done her part, made the right choice by taking action, so what was her father's plan? She wanted details. A path. Logic. Because she'd gotten lucky this time.

Her father ran his fingers through her hair, and Gia closed her eyes, knowing words weren't coming. He wouldn't tell her, which meant it was better if she didn't know. Instead, she was thankful to be home, where the refrigerator hum and the clock tick and the rattling pipes recharged her.

"C'mon." He stood and stretched his arms over his head. "Let's get you to bed."

But instead of walking Gia upstairs, he crossed the street with her to Lorraine's, where her father hugged her on the porch and waited until Gia waved at the window before going inside. Lorraine was still asleep as if nothing had ever happened. If not for her sore muscles and the missing perfume, Gia would doubt it too.

As she lay awake, scenes from the fight flickered in her head: grass stains on her knees, a bottle cap in the grass, Ray's rib against her calf, the keys in his back pocket rubbing her leg, one of Ray's eyes staring up at the sky like a fish in a bucket of ice. She'd seen enough fights in the lot behind the rectory to know when it was a good one and when it wasn't, but she wasn't sure what this was. There were some fights where kids went cold, stopped moving, hoping their fighter would give up and end it, but that wasn't it. Or it was a poor match and the whole thing was over real quick. Only Ray had not fought back. Not even a little. That one staring eye haunted her now: waiting it out like he'd wanted to get beaten, deserved it, taking his penance. It didn't seem brave anymore to beat on someone who wasn't hitting back.

And it wasn't enough penance, if that was what he thought it was. In Gia's court, he still had a million Hail Marys to go.

Chapter Twelve

On Sunday, Gia rang her own front bell because the door was locked. The back door was too. She tore off the bread crusts she'd brought for the rabbits because no one would remember to feed them and rang the bell again. Then she gathered the newspaper on the lawn, tried the bell again. And again. Agnes finally answered, her hair greasy, blinking back the sun on the porch as if she'd woken up on the moon, holding a metal bowl she must've just rinsed in the sink, and Gia fought the urge to straighten the bathrobe Agnes had thrown over her clothes so sloppily it dragged on the floor, collecting dust at the hem.

"Can I come in? I need some clothes."

Agnes rubbed her forehead so hard it left a red mark. "Now's not a good time, Gia."

"But I need my uniform for school."

"Lorraine must have an old one."

But she didn't. It didn't make sense. If she had an old uniform, it would've crossed the street a long time ago. Plus, anything in Lorraine's closet wouldn't fit right, and she couldn't go to school with a million safety pins digging into her waist. The stairs to Gia's room were right over Agnes's shoulders, shadowy without the lights on. It would take less than a minute.

"But why can't I just go upstairs and—"

"Do me a favor and ask Lorraine, please," Agnes snapped. "I don't have time for this."

The door swung shut. Gia stared at the spot where her mother had been and knew it must not be going well, but it hurt. More than Gia wanted to admit, so she kicked a pebble down the sidewalk for a while and swallowed the lump in her throat, knowing Lorraine was at her new church, or whatever it was, and it was only Aunt Diane in her armchair. She kicked pebbles as far down as almost to Ray's house before turning around and starting over.

"Something bothering you?" Mr. Angliotti asked as he pulled a trash can to the curb.

"No," Gia lied.

"Kicking rocks for fun, then?"

"Something like that," Gia mumbled, because she didn't belong anywhere at the moment, and no one minded her one way or the other. It was lonely.

"Navy yard's closing in '66." He sighed, staring off toward a moon sliver in the sky. "End of an era."

Not for her. Or Lorraine. Or Leo, Ray, or Tommy. They'd never stepped foot in the navy yard. It was a weird thing to tell a kid. Gia waited for him to say more, but it seemed he'd run out of words and waved goodbye.

It was getting dark, and she couldn't kick pebbles all night, so she went back to Lorraine's and took a deep breath before walking toward the armchair and turning the TV down.

"The navy yard's closing," Gia said. "In 1966."

Aunt Diane stared at her from the chair, but there weren't any bottles tonight, just a bag of potato chips.

"I thought you might like to know because you used to work there."

Aunt Diane nodded.

"Yeah, so . . ." What a stupid idea. She'd never been lonely enough to talk to Aunt Diane. Even Crazy Louann would've been better, but here she was.

"You know what the funny thing about metal is?" Aunt Diane asked.

Gia only stared, her back to the flag on the mantel and the pictures of Uncle Lou.

"It looks solid until you blast heat on it. Then it does whatever you want." Aunt Diane's mouth twisted into a kind of smile, but a painful one.

"Like ice," Gia said, thinking of icicles thick as carrots hanging from the garage, or icebergs strong enough to rip ships in half, even though they were only water.

"Sit. It's the Sunday Night Movie," Aunt Diane said, pointing at the other chair. "Turn the volume up."

Together they watched a movie about building a railroad until Gia fell asleep and woke up to her uniform hanging from the coat tree in the hallway. Her mother had even pressed the pleats until they were stiff, tucked a peanut butter sandwich in waxed paper into the pocket. Her mother hadn't made her lunch in years. She unwrapped it and ate the whole thing in tiny bites even though the bread was a little stale, because her mother had made it just for her and it tasted like home, even if Lorraine was upstairs humming the same three lines again and again, burning incense that smelled like the heart of a faraway forest. For a minute, Gia was home again.

~

A week later, Gia washed the sheets and tidied Lorraine's room, not that Lorraine was there much anymore. If she wasn't at the chanting place, she was at the hospital for her nursing classes or the bakery, where she'd told Big Louis to shut his mouth and not make any comments about where she'd been if he really wanted her to come back. Well, actually, she hadn't said that. She'd asked Gia to. Thankfully, Big Louis had just laughed and waved her away. "Sure, she's welcome back here. Sure."

But not for long, Lorraine had told Gia one night, because she couldn't stand knowing that the bakery used so many eggs anymore. Or butter. Or milk. They stole those things from animals.

"But we like cookies," Gia had insisted.

"We did." Lorraine had sighed and flipped the light switch off. "And I'm sure chickens would like their babies. Cows would rather give their milk to their calves. It's unnatural. Taking things that aren't freely given."

"So what do you eat instead?" Gia had asked in the darkness, but Lorraine had only mumbled a half-hearted good night.

The next day, Eddie rang the bell for Gia. They'd been in the living room, she and Aunt Diane, Gia reading and Diane half-awake. She kind of liked the TV now. The noise emptied her head.

"Come home," he said. He'd taken a shower and shaved and was wearing clean clothes wrinkled from being in the drawer for too long, but the half circles under his eyes were puffy, and his limbs hung around him like clothes on a laundry line after an unexpected storm. He looked exhausted, and it made Gia wonder what her father had looked like when he'd come home from the South Pacific, if he still dreamed about torpedoes in the middle of the night when his room was as dark as an ocean without a moon. "It's OK now."

But Gia didn't trust it. The dark shade her father had tacked to Leo's window was down now, the window cracked. All the windows were open, but it didn't have that summer-day feeling to it, more like they were airing out the plague.

"And your mother could use your help."

Two kids rode by on bikes, dressed in bedsheets with cut-out eyes, pillowcases wrapped around their wrists.

"Dad?" Gia said. "Is it Halloween already?"

He looked as surprised by the ghosts on their bikes, pedaling, laughing under their sheets, pillowcases swinging, as she did, and Gia's throat tightened because she'd missed it, hadn't even realized it was already the end of October, and she would not be wrapping herself in toilet paper this year to make herself a mummy or going door-to-door with Tommy and Leo because Ray and Lorraine were too old now. They all were.

"I'll pick up some candy," he said. "Come on. You can get your stuff later, but come see your brother first."

She didn't want to. Not really. But she followed him across the street. The rabbits were huddled together because it was chilly in the shade. Inside, her mother was curled into a ball on the couch. She opened her eyes when the door opened. But closed them when she saw it was only Gia and Eddie. Everything was a mess. The trash had not been taken out. There were dishes in the sink and fruit flies hovering where a bunch of bananas had browned on the counter. The steps upstairs were littered with shoes and clothes. Gia was glad the windows were open because it felt like the house was closing in around her.

"We had to give him little amounts at a time because quitting cold wasn't working. So we'll cut him off little by little," Eddie said.

Those sounded more like her mother's words, but Gia stayed quiet.

"Leo," Eddie called from the bottom of the stairs. "Come see your sister."

There was a shuffle, and like a good prisoner, Leo appeared at the top of the stairs. They used to play jail as kids, taking turns being a prisoner or a jailer, rubbing dirt on their clothes and going barefoot as the prisoner, the jailer handing them small cups of tap water and one piece of sliced bread through the banister bars, occasionally announcing that someone was free to go. The prisoners played rummy on the steps and made up stories about what they'd done to end up in jail while the jailer chewed on candy cigarettes.

"Hey," he said.

"Hey," she answered, trying to match the kid at the top of the stairs in a sweaty pair of pajamas holding a bottle of Coke with the number one fighter in the neighborhood. He now looked like the fight had been kicked out of him.

For now. It was obvious to Gia that all he needed was the chance to spring himself from the banister jail, and he'd be back in business.

And that was all there was to say. Leo went back to his room. Eddie went for bagels and orange juice while Gia cleaned up at Aunt Diane's, then at her own house, until the dishes disappeared from the sink and the fruit flies scattered. They ordered Chinese food that night and ate from take-out containers in silence until Gia turned on the TV just for noise, the whole house feeling like a truce no one trusted as kids skipped past outside, spraying shaving cream on bushes, smacking cars with tube socks full of baby powder.

There were bags of candy by the front door, but no one rang the bell.

~

Leo didn't go to school. He walked as far as the corner in his uniform, the tie loose around his neck and thrown over one shoulder, one sleeve rolled up, the cuff of the other balled up in his fist, his pants bagged around the knee, like he was one of the drunks leaving the bar by the train station. Agnes that morning had wet her fingers to push the hair out of his eyes, as if smoothing stray hair into place would correct the disheveled heap her son had become. His knee had bounced under the table as he forced down spoonfuls of cereal just to be let out of the house.

It was unnerving watching him wiggle his jaw, face twitching. You could, Gia realized, physically see the chemicals being released, coursing through him like a roller coaster on a track, surging, spiking, dropping, coasting, arms up in the air, people screaming and white-knuckling the bar, or when it whooshed to a stop after a few last uneventful dips and rolls, her brother hopping off before the bars were up, racing back for the next go.

Except that when he veered off at the corner, Gia followed, ignoring Aunt Diane in her plastic lawn chair on the porch, who was watching the parakeets heavy on the wire. She'd never ditched school before, and now, in her pleated skirt and knee-high socks, she might as well be a crumpled can on a fence waiting for a BB shot. The neighborhood emptied as school started, the commuting crowd already at their desks. Lawn-care crews revved leaf blowers, and housewives took short rides to the supermarket before rushing home for morning soaps as chicken marinated for dinner. She wondered if this normal, calm life was really so bad after all, if it was not preferable to following your doped-up brother and trying not to be seen. Up ahead, a meter reader rang a bell, and Gia walked around the far side of the truck because it was better not to be spotted. Less risky.

Truant. That was what her father called the kids he picked up for ditching school and brought home again. It was strange then that kids would do anything but go to school, and now here she was, on the outside of everything too.

Leo lit a cigarette and tossed it aside after only a few breaths. He was unraveling. Walking faster. Limbs jaunty. Gia squashed the cigarette under her toe to put it out, keeping her eyes on his back. He crossed the footbridge into Hamilton Beach, past the weeds, then into them, his head barely visible above the mess of brown sticks. She hesitated at the weed line, thinking of the trash inside, the weeds scratching at her legs, thorns, burrs clinging to her skirt. Or long snakes opening their mouths to swallow frogs or mice whole, snapping at the bones, strangling them in a coil, the shape bulging through their skin as the animal died slowly inside. She pressed her fist to her mouth and bit down, leaving teeth marks to offset the scream in her chest, her stomach rising and pulsing as unfairness burned in her chest; her brain was calculating fear to keep her safe, while her brother's, well, he might as well be a zombie.

One step. Then two. Just go. She imagined the kidney-shaped island on the Hudson, the tent on her real island, and then she imagined Thanksgiving: her father with a full plate instead of only buttered noodles, the cells in his stomach healing when he slept through the night. No more circling the neighborhood. No more missing money. Her mother carrying piles of warm, folded towels to the linen closet instead of ice buckets and vomit bins to Leo's room. And Leo. She couldn't exactly remember what she wanted him to be anymore, but it wasn't this.

Following someone through dry weeds was tricky. Branches snapped and rustled through the path he'd cleared. She stopped every few feet to stand on tiptoes and find his head above the weeds, the path back. He stopped. The weeds thinned, and an old tree house came into view: a rickety plywood thing stained with mold, littered with empty beer cans, the labels weathered. It had fallen at some point or been dragged here, and now it was spray painted with swooping tags, and bits of clothes and chip bags were scattered around. Leo ducked through the cut-out door, kicking bottles and cans as he shuffled, and then it was quiet.

Above her, the sky was a perfect blue. A seagull flapped toward the water with a shell in its mouth and released it into the weeds, where it dropped soundlessly. She'd forgotten about snakes and now worried that someone else would come here, some other beer-drinking spray painter. Birds called out from trees overhead, announcing their presence—or someone else's. It was time to go.

This time she didn't care if her feet made a sound on the sticks and trash. It stank of piss and wasted time, people, the same way a doctor's office stank of germs after the last patient. She fought back the nausea rising in her throat, the sudden urge to be home again at the kitchen table, listening to spoons ding against cereal bowls and Rice Krispies snapping in milk, to wash this place off with enough soap to leave a shield on her skin. *Soon,* her brain promised.

"Leo." He was sitting against the wall, his clothes touching the crumpled tissues and napkins on the floor inside, the strap still around the pulsing blue vein in his arm. His eyes opened and settled on her. He didn't ask why she was here or why she wasn't in school. For a second, Gia wondered whether she was real, in this disgusting place, or if Leo saw something different.

"Leo, I want to take the boat out. Dad said I can't go without you."

"Yeah," he said.

"Right now." She glanced behind her, terrified the weeds would rustle and another pair of feet would crash through, but it was quiet. Just the wind. Birds. The call of traffic in the distance.

"The boat's ready. I just need you to come with me."

Her heart pounded in her ears. The whole plan depended on getting him to the island. Leo fumbled in the dirt for solid ground. So slow, clumsy. His eyes stretched to their widest with the effort of making the world make physical sense. It was irritating. Gia crossed her arms and waited for him to get it together, realizing the walk to the boat would be slow and labored, making it more likely someone would see them.

"Come on," she said, following the path back the way they'd come, the urge to reach the street as strong as the need to breathe.

Leo ran his hands over the same weeds Gia tried not to touch.

"To the boat," she said. "For a ride. It's a nice day. The sun is out. I cleaned the boat up real nice and brought Moon Pies and Oatmeal Pies, you know, the ones with the cream in the middle? I couldn't find pumpkin faces."

The ones they used to smash into balls and pop into their mouths whole, cinnamon melting on their tongues with the taste of fall and leaves and Halloween and fresh notebooks. The memory was so surprising she tripped a little on the uneven path.

The sound of her own voice was soothing, if too loud. She didn't have to turn back to make sure he was there. He was crashing through, breaking sticks underfoot, making a trail even the dumbest tracker could follow.

"I have candy too. Snickers and Milky Ways. You like those, right? Milky Ways?"

Leo made a sound Gia guessed was a yes.

"And Kit Kats. And Oreos. And Fritos." The sidewalk was up ahead. Gia could've kissed it, scooped a handful of it and let it run between her fingers as the wind took it. That was how beautiful that sparkling concrete was, crackled and riddled with mugwort and lady's thumb, paths leading to houses and people. She walked faster to leave this place behind; a part of her felt unclean for knowing it existed. It ruined the world a little. How could she ever listen to music and flip through magazines, talking about this movie or that one, knowing disgusting places like this existed? A washed-out sun was scribbled on the concrete in sidewalk chalk. A child's drawing, done where his mother could see him from the kitchen window, and just a little farther into the weeds, that place. She thought of Lorraine suddenly and whatever had happened to her that night, how little Lorraine left the house now, and Gia understood. Gia swallowed the lump in her throat.

"I know how to do everything on the boat. You don't have to help. You can just enjoy the sun and the water and the seagulls, the breeze. If we're lucky, maybe we'll see osprey."

Please, she prayed to her marsh, thinking of light sparkling on the water, the marsh grass green and tall and reaching for the sun, anchored into the soft earth with a web of roots, *wash it away.*

They crossed the footbridge. Leo stopped, put his hands on the concrete wall, and heaved over the side. Nothing came up, but the retching cut through Gia, echoed through the quiet canal. He leaned over a little farther, and for the first time, Gia wondered if she was making a terrible mistake, if he could fend for himself. She imagined the tide washing in while he was in his tent. Had she put it too close to the water? Or a storm surging through the thin tent walls, floating everything inside, sinking the island. Was there even enough high ground that wouldn't flood completely? And if that happened, they wouldn't be able to take the boat out and get there in time to help. What would her mother say then?

Gia's breath caught in her throat. She couldn't breathe. Her head lifted from her shoulders, and everything broke into salt and pepper. She put her hand on the same warm concrete wall to steady her, but it was sticky with bird shit and made her skin feel inside out, like rubbery chicken skin pulled off a thigh. Leo retched. It floated in the canal below. They were contaminated, him and her. Their whole family. That was what people thought of the two kids on the footbridge, two contaminants meant to be kept away from.

"Come on," she called, losing her nerve. If they didn't get to the boat soon, she wasn't sure she could do it at all.

At the dock, Gia dipped her hands in the canal as Leo climbed into the boat. It wasn't clean water, but it was cold, washing that place off, chilling the blood at the pulse point in her wrists until her head cleared and the frazzled feeling passed. She untied the rope from the dock, coiled it into the boat. Someone was walking a dog on the other side of the canal, smoking a cigarette in a housedress and rollers. Gia shoved off the dock, started the motor. There weren't any other boats, so she cut out of the canal faster than usual because they had to get to the island. Leo sat between the metal seats, threw his arms out to either side, like the crucifix on the wall above her parents' bed. Only Leo was not a saint. And he deserved this island. And she was finally fixing something her parents couldn't, or Leo, or Ray, or anyone, because he'd done enough to hurt them and couldn't help himself. She hardened. Like eels or crabs or anything else dumb enough to take bait from a trap. Those were the ones that didn't deserve to pass on their genes. They were not the strongest or the smartest or the most adaptive.

Waves crashed at the boat. It bounced over whitecaps. Her father would've turned back, but Gia revved the motor. Leo looked green. Even Gia's stomach rolled, but she was too determined. Laughing gulls screeched overhead. The water was a dull gray. A pencil-point color. Her island came into view. The tent was still there, the flap zipped as she'd left it, bottles of water piled behind. Her heart was pounding. This was the part she hadn't planned: getting Leo off the boat. She coasted to a stop and let the boat drift, rubbed her temples, wishing he were small enough for seagulls to scoop up and carry off, dropping him at shore.

"Let's take a walk." She stuck the oar into the sand. Two feet or so. She could get them a little closer. Leo didn't budge, didn't even acknowledge having heard. He opened and closed his fist.

"Hey, stand up," she said. "Stand up. I need to get the oar."

She nudged his shoulder. He knelt. Then stood, looking out at the marsh, fighting the urge to hang in half. She hated that most—the dangling.

Low man wins. One of Leo's old peewee football sayings. He was never good at following formations or moving in the clunky gear.

Gia stood behind him on the bench so she'd be taller, then hopped down. Closed her eyes as heat welled behind them. She had seconds before he turned around and the whole thing was over. *Think,* she begged her brain. *Your room. Ray. Your money.* That thermos on the seat between her and her father. Her mother washing the puke bucket. Lorraine's shoes disappearing under the flooded street . . .

Her hands shot forward, pushed at the small of his back, shoved him hard enough to make him lose whatever balance he had, then shoved again until he was over the side of the boat. Then she scrambled back to the motor, forcing distance between them as he flailed, standing, pulling his wet shirt away from his skin.

"I'm sorry, Leo." She stretched her voice over the wind, over the swallowing water. "There's a tent with food and water and clothes and blankets. I don't . . ."

Her voice trailed off, and she stared up at the clouds: white, story-book puffy, out of place.

"Just go to the tent."

But Leo just stood there, knee deep in water, the tie still hanging from his neck, his face twisted, trying to work it all out. His mouth was moving, but Gia couldn't hear him or didn't want to. She looked away, past the water, past the marsh, where Manhattan was hazy in the distance, full of people in dress pants and collared shirts like her brother was now, only they weren't standing in water, hadn't just been pushed off a boat by a thirteen-year-old girl who thought she could save Leo with an island and Moon Pies. It was too much. He trudged toward her in the water. She started the motor and took off, the boat crashing less through the water now, the wind pushing at the front of the boat, forcing it back when the canal and the dock and her house were forward, away from the island, the tent, and her brother.

At dinner, she shrugged when her father asked where Leo was, if she'd seen him, if he'd gone to school. She didn't say anything when her father took his keys from the hall table and went for a ride.

But at night, she stared at the ceiling and thought about him in the water, wondering if he'd changed into clean clothes or if raccoons had gotten to the food first and if there were enough blankets, as she pulled her own under her chin, then over her head, dark as an island without lights, hoping to drown out the echo of wind. She couldn't sleep and doubted Leo could either.

She was the only one who knew where he was, holding the other end of a tin can on a string, only the line buzzed with wind and waves and laughing gulls. She would go back first thing tomorrow and keep the secret from her parents a little longer, because if he came back in a week, cold and tired but fixed, it would be worth it.

The "why" of it nagged at her because she couldn't think of one honest reason for doing this, only that it seemed fitting and fair, but certainly not to the boy in the water—or who he used to be—or the girl in her bed with a secret too heavy to settle. It bounced inside her all night, landing in strange places—a sudden memory of a boy throwing a Ping-Pong ball to win a goldfish, wrapping a girl in toilet paper at a birthday party, letting her hold the reins on a sled down a hill, kicking the broken shell of a robin's egg into the gutter—until she couldn't remember what was real and what was imagined.

~

The first morning, Leo threw rocks at the boat and shouted things the wind carried away. When the first rock hit her squarely in the thigh, Gia motored off. Clearly, he was fine. She slept a lot better that night.

But on the second morning, her father had worked an overnight tour and slept for a few hours in uniform on the couch, shoes and all, before going out to ride around. Her mother took the big yellow phone book from the hall closet and dialed every hospital listed, describing Leo over and over again until Gia wondered if it wouldn't be better to just tell them he was trapped on an island—if that wouldn't be a relief. But Gia said nothing, and on the last call, Agnes rubbed her temples in small circles, straightened, and forced a smile.

"Your birthday is coming up," she said. "What would you like for your birthday dinner?"

Had she ever been asked, or had the usual trays of lasagna and eggplant parm and meatballs just shown up every year along with Aunt Ida and Uncle Frank, Ray and Tommy, and Lorraine? It was her first birthday without them, and it made the whole thing sadder, more permanent.

"Eggplant," Gia said. "And an ice cream cake with cookie crumbs in the middle."

"Not one from the bakery?" Agnes suggested, rubbing the space between her index finger and her thumb like she always did when a headache was coming on, and Gia noticed the time, three p.m. Her mother should've been at work but wasn't. How many days had there been like this because of Leo now? All those hours were money and bills.

"Oh," Gia said. "I can ask Lou."

"Forget it." Agnes pressed her hands to the table and sprang up. "I'll get you an ice cream cake if that's what you really want. Vanilla and chocolate?"

Gia nodded, surprised by the raw emotion in her mother's voice, the change of heart. Agnes paused by the doorframe, where the telephone cord was still swinging.

"You deserve it," she said, looking at Gia. She must've grown a little, because she was nearly eye level with Agnes now. When had that happened?

Agnes slipped the phone book back into the hall closet, and it made Gia pray all the more that whatever she was doing on this island would work.

~

Leo never knew her birthday until someone reminded him, at which point he'd show up for dinner without a card or present, sing for candles, mumble a happy birthday, and disappear when it was time to clear the table. She was a first-frost baby, starting as nature closed down for winter, but now as she ferried another boatload of food, water, and toilet paper to the island, she felt older, alone on her boat, doing something brave and important without adults.

She cut the motor as the island came into view. Sister Island. She coasted down a shallow slope to land, waves carrying the boat the rest of the way before it dragged to a stop. She hopped out, salt water splashing against her knees, and pulled the boat farther in. Leaving supplies in a new spot meant he'd have to crawl out of the tent and find them to survive. Everything was gone each day. Even the playing cards, thermos of hot chocolate, T-shirts. It was working. She unloaded the boat, sidestepping the three-pronged sandpiper print and bits of frayed rope littering the beach. The flashlight glowed in the tent in the distance, wasting batteries. She would call out to his zipped tent when she left. At least he was here.

Tonight, she would tell her parents about Sister Island. She imagined they would stare at her in silence, processing that she, Gia, had figured out something that worked. Her father would raise one proud eyebrow. Her mother would bring out the pots and pans and make spaghetti, and Gia wouldn't mind if Agnes asked her to bring some to Leo. She would point to Sister Island on the nautical map near the kitchen phone where the tide charts were taped to the wall, and the small green dot on the island would stand out above the others.

The sun rounded to the horizon, where the ocean would swallow each day, however many days it took. Maybe one night after dinner, he'd thank her, and there'd be a little gift on her birthday. A scallop seashell with a hole to thread a cord through. She carried the last water jug to the sand and heaved the boat back into the water.

On the last shove, the water rippled behind her. A single splash like a fish jumping from a wave, airborne, then disappearing beneath, only this time it pressed a cold finger down her spine that numbed her toes.

Leo was behind her, knee deep in the water, leaning on a long stick, the kind that would pop a hole in a hull, damage an outboard. His face was greasy, his hair at every angle.

"Hey, Gia." He forced a smile, but he was looking past her at the boat.

She tightened her grip.

"Thank you for taking me here. It worked, you know. I'm clean now. All better. And I'm thinking I'd like to go home. See Mom and Dad because they're probably worried. Go back to school again. And maybe, because you did this to me, we could go to New Park, because you love New Park. The salt on the crust is your favorite, right? Or how they burn the bottom a little bit? We could get a whole pie and split it."

But there was a desperation in his careful words that cut right through her. And his grip on the stick unnerved her. The boat rocked into her shoulder. She pushed it away. The water was getting deeper. It was the same desperation of forcing a part that didn't fit, jamming it again and again until it snapped.

"So I'm thinking I can ride back with you. We can get the tent another time."

He took a step toward the boat.

"One more day, Leo." Gia swallowed. "Just one. They know you're here," she lied. "And they're really happy it's working, so just one more . . ."

Something flashed across his face before he wiped the slate, started over, but it was enough to dry the words on Gia's tongue. The boat rocked harder. She was losing her footing in the sand, and the water was deeper now. She wouldn't be able to hop in as fast. Not with him inching her deeper.

Leo opened his arms. Maybe for a hug. But it was Leo. She tugged at the boat, jumped, but Leo cracked her with that stick. Right against her spine. He lifted her by under her arms and tossed her aside. She splashed face-first, gasping a mouthful of salt water, eyes stinging, ears fogging, fumbling in the moving water. Her hand darted for the boat. But the water was suddenly cloudy. Too cloudy to see. She couldn't lose the boat. There was no air. Waves washed at her, forcing her out, forcing her in.

The first breath broke through her lungs, making her dizzy, as Leo caught the boat. She was soaked through, cold to the bone. Leo lifted himself into the boat. It tipped as he tumbled inside, the bottom filling with water before it righted. He dropped the outboard and started the engine.

"Wait—" But there wasn't enough air in her lungs.

She crawled to shore, shells scratching her palms, and tried to stand but fell over with the weight of her wet clothes, the pain down her spine.

He couldn't come to shore with the outboard down. Seagulls laughed overhead, and the sound cut through her. Already she was shivering.

"Wait," she tried again. The sound disappeared in the wind, lost under the motor's hum. Her motor. Her hum. He was filthy, his wet clothes hanging all wrong as the boat left the island behind. "Backstabber. Bastard. Rat bastard." The words exploded from her mouth. She shouted and shouted, but Leo didn't turn back. The boat crashed through whitecaps, cutting toward land. A broken oar floated at the water's edge. Her eyes teared. She was his sister. And he'd left her for dead.

The rules she'd trusted broke inside her. Gia crawled toward the patchy marsh grass, wet clothes gathering sand, her father's words about always knowing where she was echoing. She lay flat, taking the weight off her spine, lessening the tingling in her fingers and toes, then sat up and hugged her knees to her chest, wishing she were a buoy rocking in the water and crying in the wind as boats returned on the right, passed on the left. It would get dark and cold. As a buoy, she'd be anchored. As Gia, she was not. The water jugs and soda crackers wouldn't last long. *Think,* she begged her brain.

Dry clothes.

The inside of the tent stank of sweat and metal. She unzipped the flaps so the wind could blow through and tossed his clothes in a filthy pile outside. He wouldn't come back. Wouldn't bring supplies. Wouldn't know where to find her if he wanted to. She licked salt from a saltine to offset the bay water in her mouth. The sun dropped and the marsh grass shivered in the wind as she changed into the clothes she'd brought for her brother; unwrapped a Moon Pie, one of the last; and ate it in small bites, feeling terribly stupid at her core, because for everything she'd thought of, she'd missed the biggest threat of all.

Chapter Thirteen

Gia gathered the remaining supplies into a plastic bag and stashed them at her feet. At least he'd barely eaten. She ate a bag of Fritos, knowing this food was her last until she got out of here, which only made her hungrier, made her think of Nonna pouring manicotti batter into a crepe pan, stacking the steaming shells on a plate, filling them with cheese, rolling them up in a baking dish. Or the ravioli she'd let Gia press with a fork. She'd never taste anything exactly like that again because Nonna was gone forever.

At night, the marsh was a different place. The water was moonless, lapping quietly, kicking up with the wind. Wind in the marsh grass sounded like whispers, spooking her into believing she wasn't alone. Things shuffled in the grass, on the shore. *Please, not sand snakes,* Gia prayed. Raccoons scratched outside the tent for crumbs. The tent made her feel exposed, the nylon exterior so unlike the sand, grass, and water around her. One of the poles collapsed, sagging around itself, so Gia crawled into the grass with blankets, laying one on the sand and one over herself, a barrier between her and mosquitoes lured by her body heat. She didn't want to admit it, because it was her marsh, but she was terrified. She imagined her mother slamming cabinet doors in the kitchen, pissed that after working all day and another longer-than-expected commute home, clutching her purse the entire way, Gia couldn't be bothered to help with dinner. Counting Gia's punishments as she sliced onions. If she'd noticed at all.

Her father was working, which meant he didn't know she was gone. She wished, prayed, his car could ride over water and circle the marsh, the headlights lighting up the grass where Gia hid. In her brother's baggy clothes and blanket heap, she probably looked like washed-up beach trash. *And that,* Aunt Ida would say, waggling her finger over the rim of a gimlet, her hair-sprayed curls frozen in place, *is what you get for running around on the water, thinking you're more than thirteen, which you're not, and if you spent half as much time helping your mother as you do tomboying, you wouldn't be in this situation.*

No one was coming. She was stranded. Just like Lorraine had been that night. Her throat throbbed, and she swallowed back the lump lodged there. Lorraine, like Gia, must've thought she'd never go home. Every minute more important than it had ever been. Each one excruciating.

The night crept on. There was too much noise. The temperature dipped, and Gia shivered, curled into a ball to trap heat, pulled the blanket over her head to ward off mosquitoes, and breathed into the blankets, warming herself. By six, the sun would be up. Her mother would twirl the kitchen phone cord around her wrist, calling her father at the station, then Lorraine. *Is she with you?*

Time passed. An hour. Ten minutes. She wasn't sure. Her father patrolled the little marsh in his star-pointed hat and badge, flashing the picture of Leo and Gia in the water, her mother on the boardwalk with the frayed rope of his tattoo tied around her waist so he could find his way back to her. *Sleep,* he whispered. *I'm watching.*

Leo braided cordgrass into a rope, cut the tent into strips of fabric. *We'll make a boat and sail home.*

It won't work, Gia argued.

You wait, he said, while Lorraine ran her fingers through Gia's hair under the blanket, the smell of her perfume a reminder of home. Gia breathed deep.

The smell of perfume changed to rain, a light pattering on the blanket. The wind kicked up, knocked the tent flat. She could drag it back to her spot in the grass, use it for cover, but she was too scared to peel back the blankets and see how dark it'd gotten, how dark it would stay for the next few hours.

See if this is useful. Uncle Frank lumbered over, offering her an old umbrella with the spokes missing. Ridiculous. She would look like a mushroom cap with that. The rain picked up, soaked through the blanket, and then stopped as the storm rolled to another part of the bay. In the distance, Pop Pop played his accordion, singing off-key in Italian, the old songs that Gia remembered only the feeling of, while Aunt Diane picked flowers off her housedress and left them in a circle at Gia's head, pressed her finger to her lips. *Shhh.*

A boat chugged on the water, slowly, so slowly Gia almost didn't hear it. Her breathing stopped. Cold rushed in as Gia jumped up. Darkness in every direction was disorienting, but she'd flag down the boat, and it would take her home. She'd be back before anyone suspected she'd been anywhere other than Lorraine's all day. She held her hand out in front of her face, wiggled her fingers while her eyes adjusted to the dark. Where was the light on the water? But there wasn't any. Was she dreaming? No, there was a boat, a big one, cutting a slow line between the marsh and the dark. Shadows moved on board, silent. A cigarette glowed bright orange, dulled, flared.

Morse code. Her father crouched beside her, one hand on his holster as the other pulled Gia down slowly. *H-I-D-E.*

The engine cut out. The boat bobbed. There was a flurry on deck. Three men, arms flashing, working on something like when her father and Uncle Frank pulled in a big catch, thrashing and slippery, desperate for water. Only nothing moved here, just grunts and soft swearing as the men hoisted it to the railing, heaved it overboard. It plunked into the water and sank slowly.

"Good riddance." The cigarette flared again. Their breathing was loud. One spit over the side of the boat.

The saltines she'd eaten rushed up her throat. It had been a person. A dead one. Sinking to the bottom in tarps. The boat drifted. The three men looked out at the marsh.

She reached for her father's hand, praying he'd pick them off like bottles on a fence, then yank her up by the arm when it was time to go, holding her hand the whole way, but there was only sand. *Please,* she prayed, imagining herself wrapped in plastic, dropped from the boat.

One nudged the other, whispering. They'd seen the tent. It was too close to the water. The boat gassed, changed direction, coasted closer. A flashlight swept the grass. Gia squeezed her eyes shut, hollowed her breath. There wasn't room for her heart or bones or blood anymore, just fear. The flashlight lingered on the collapsed tent, the pile of clothes, like someone had left in a hurry, not like a girl was hiding in the marsh.

Her breath through the blanket made her think of breathing through a tarp, of the face inside. She wanted it off her head. Not yet. Not till the boat went away.

"Junkies," someone said. "Kids."

But there were fresh tracks. Girl-size feet in the sand, unless the wind and rain had blurred them, unless her marsh had kept her safe. The flashlight beam swept again, and Gia willed herself still, hoping none of her showed through the grass. Mosquitoes circled overhead, excited by fear, humming loudly, too loudly, as they lowered and stabbed through the blanket, drank blood through straws.

Now she knew what her father had meant about other threats on the water.

He was right. He'd always been right. The lump in her throat hammered. *Leave,* she prayed.

175

The boat was closer to shore now, as close as it could get without bottoming out. Something splashed. Legs trudged through water. Someone kicked around in the sand, shook the tent. A zipper. Pissing into the weeds.

Gia did not breathe, didn't trust herself not to scream. Didn't trust herself, her brother, her cousins, anyone. Not these men. There was nothing that wouldn't betray her. Desperately wishing she could crawl down a hermit crab hole, wash out unseen like a seashell or a piece of trash. Instead, they circled her now—Uncle Frank, Aunt Ida, her mother, her father, Leo, Ray, Tommy, Lorraine—rolled the soaked blankets around her tightly, twisted the ends into knots, and stuffed the insides with stones that pressed the air from Gia's lungs, turning the world a directionless black. The men would hoist her into the water, where the stones would sink her until there was no more Gia. How could she be over when she hadn't really started yet? There would be no more tomorrow or yesterday. It would not matter that she'd once hunted chemicals or loved swimming. She would never be anything when she grew up. Uncle Frank tied scraps of rope around the blanket. They cut into her neck, her stomach. Nonna urged them to make it tighter. Leo lit a cigarette. Laughed. *We should all go this way,* Aunt Diane mused. *Same as Lou. Why is she any better?*

She'd always thought if she was good, did the right thing—maybe not always, but most of the time—was good to her parents, didn't steal, did her homework, worked honestly, and took care of her animals, life would promise good things back. But it wasn't true. It didn't matter. It just didn't. Because life picked. The world picked. Nature picked which sparrows fell from trees and which did not. It had nothing to do with how good one was over another. And she deserved this. Everything. For failing Lorraine; her brother, even if he was beyond saving; her parents. For believing Ray. She should have paid attention in church, gone to confession, and counted Hail Marys as penance. She thought of her father's tattoo again: the frayed rope. An anchor held nothing it wasn't tied to. It sank. Even if she was completely still, a raccoon could rattle grass, draw the flashlight. She wondered if her father would give her a funeral or if he'd hold that back like he'd threatened Leo, if her mother would pack up the macramé owl in Gia's room and tear down the World's Fair poster, toss Gia's seashells and pebbles into the trash, failing to see the curve in one that made it look like a galaxy or the cut of another that looked like a dolphin. Just junk, all of it, all of Gia's wasted hours.

There were stars on the other side of this blanket. Ursa Major and Orion's Belt, but she couldn't remember any others. *How quickly we forget the world we knew.*

The weeds rustled, but she wasn't afraid anymore. Fear had run out of her in rivers that sank, Gia imagined, trickling through the sand in imperfect lines, some absorbing into the roots, others washing toward the bay, until she was a castaway shell, its inhabitant long gone. Just carbon.

"Nothing doing," he called back to the boat.

Water sloshed. The motor started. They were leaving. Gia's eyes were wide under the blanket. Her breath came out in quick spurts as she kicked the blankets away.

You see? her father whispered, his starched uniform close to her nose. *This is why. Not because you're a girl.* He pointed to where they'd been, where the boat had bobbed and, somewhere, the body still was. She prayed it wouldn't float up. She imagined jeans, a sweater, sneakers, and socks soaking up the water as her father rubbed mud over her face until she was only eyes peering through the grass. *I see,* she said, tears prickling, rolling the mud away in rivers. *I see.*

The sky gradually lightened, exposing her further. In the early light, another boat darted across the water in the distance, slowed to a stop, worked a trap. A bayman, pulling a trap from the water, forcing Gia to look away because she did not want to see what was on the other end of that line.

Gia crawled out of the grass, afraid to call out in case he heard her. In case he didn't. What could she be after the life had leached out of her? After she'd said goodbye to her own self? She could scream, piercing the sky and startling the fisherman, who'd drop his trap and watch her from the boat in his yellows, still as anyone could be in a boat.

But she crawled back into the marsh grass instead, back to the wet blankets, then thought better of it and pulled a handful of spartina to brush away her footprints in the sand. She would leave everything exactly as it had been in case they came back. Not that it mattered. There wouldn't be another boat except garbage barges and people like last night. But she couldn't trust anyone. Not even the bayman. She watched as he motored off, oblivious to the girl on the island, a shadow in the marsh grass.

~

That night, she decided she would swim. She ate the last of the Moon Pies and Fritos. She would leave when the sun came up and walk into the water until the sandy bottom sloped away, knowing most of the bay was not deep and she could rest her toes in the mud if she needed a break. She was a good swimmer. And if she swam, it wouldn't matter what kind of people were in the boats, good or bad, because she would get herself home. Just Gia.

It was a clear night. Manhattan made a haze over the stars, over the black, over the flaws in her plan. What if she got tired? What if it was farther than she thought? Had she ever actually swum a mile? What if the boat came back? Or a side stitch. A storm. What if, like last time, she missed the most dangerous piece? But the thoughts drifted past. There were no boats tonight, only stars, and there was nothing left to lose. It seemed fitting because maybe she'd already died. And tonight, there were no shadows of her family to guide her, just the shell of Gia.

In the morning, she lit the tent on fire and watched it burn for a while. Then she pulled the sleeve off one of Leo's spare shirts and tied it to a water jug. Maybe it would float. Maybe not. She slipped her hand through the loop and waded out. The water was colder than she'd thought, but it would warm as she swam, as the sun came up. She would follow the buoys. The water jug banged along with the first few strokes, jarring her arms until she released it and it floated off soundlessly. The farther from shore she got, the more the waves picked up, filling her mouth with salt water every few strokes. Without the water, she was thirsty. By the time she got to the first buoy, she wasn't any warmer. Her fingers pruned. There was too much water, and the waves picked up, bouncing the buoy, making the rope hard to catch. She'd forgotten about rip currents and undertow. The rope was covered in barnacles. They cut into her hands and feet, salt water stinging in hundreds of sharp cuts.

Put your foot down. Just put your foot down. But the ground was not where it should be. The spots she could reach suctioned at her feet, pulling her lower. She flapped wildly to free her foot, and suddenly it wasn't mud but hands free from tarps. Bloated underwater bodies. How many were there? How many bodies? How many boats? Pulling at her legs.

There was too much water in every direction. She could swim back, but she'd burned the tent. A plume of smoke curled into the sky, laughing at her in the distance. She'd never make it to the next buoy. Not if she couldn't breathe. And how many were there after that? Too many. She was cold and tired, floating in Leo's clothes, the most alone in the world she'd ever been. It was hard to believe she'd ever had a family or a name, had ever had dreams that woke her up at night. There was only a gray sky and gray water, one reflecting the other, and she just wanted it to be over.

She floated on her back, staring at the sky as waves carried her in any direction, praying only that those hands couldn't reach her if she floated on the surface. That she wouldn't get sucked into the undertow of a garbage barge, or that if she did, it would be fast. *Stupid girl,* she thought. *Stupid, stupid girl.*

The sun was hidden behind the clouds. It would be nice to feel the sun on her skin one more time, to close her eyes and blink back the colors it made inside her eyelids, her own private show to drift away to. It was just starting to roll out when she heard a motor cut out and an oar drop into the water. She should right herself. Swim off. But it was over. She was on to another unknown fate, and the best she could do was stay numb about it.

The boat was watching her, maybe to make sure she was real, that she wasn't a trap. It was a bayman.

"I don't want no trouble," he said, as kind as he was threatening.

Gia nodded. She couldn't speak. She'd used up all her words and just wanted to be home in her bed, inhaling the clean smell of her sheets, to hear her mother making breakfast downstairs, if those memories were even real. She would help with dinner and never complain about it again. She would clean out the bunny hutch without being told. She would wear dresses and stop asking about the boat. He lifted her in and put his rubber coat around her. It was warm from his skin, like her mother's hug would be when Gia finally came home. The worry in her voice enough to make Gia sorry for every terrible thing she'd ever said or thought about Agnes.

"Where to?"

She pointed. A sack at her feet slithered with whatever was inside. The boat smelled like fish scales and metal. Gia breathed through her mouth to keep it away, pointing when it was time to turn beneath his yellow jacket, feeling as exposed as an egg fallen from a nest, yolk spilling on the sidewalk.

The boat slowed at an empty dock. He helped her step up, holding the dock to steady the boat. She gave him back the yellow jacket. His face was a blur. She hadn't asked his name. He hadn't asked hers. Two nobodies.

The boat bobbed in the water. He pushed off the dock and headed back for the bay. She stared after it, then at the parakeets on the line, wishing they'd drop like the sparrows had just so they would shut up, as quiet and dead as she felt inside, breathing through a plastic sheet.

The muscles in her body found the right streets. She paused outside her house, staring at the weather-beaten shingles. They'd been white once, but now they were stained with rainwater, a discolored set of greens, grays, and browns. The gutters rusted. The tree branch her brother had lopped off had a haphazard look to it, like everything else about their house, where things were fixed with duct tape and stains were lazily dabbed at with soda water on a washcloth. Nothing was ever replaced. Nothing was ever made new. The rabbit hutch leaned a little to one side, the wooden legs unevenly cut, slapped together. The lawn grew in patches, flooded too many times to grow in properly despite her father flinging grass seed. It was ugly.

No wonder Aunt Ida and Uncle Frank, even Ray and Tommy, looked down on them. Even Uncle Frank's cast-off trash things were nicer than anything in their house. The only reason they'd come here was to save them from having Gia's family in their house, where they'd junk up the nice furniture, the rugs. She had done that once, hadn't she? With one of Aunt Ida's crystal wineglasses, a wedding gift. She'd filled it with grape juice, pretending it was wine, and put an olive on a plastic cocktail sword, too, then dropped the whole thing when she'd screamed "Happy New Year!"

Leo had killed her in the marsh, left her for dead. It didn't matter if he'd planned it or not. The point was, she'd been disposable, like the rest of her family, sent to America to work, sent to the South Pacific to fight, sent to burning Brooklyn, left on a marsh. She stared at her house with the sagging porch and the leaking roof and thought of the girl named Gia who used to live here once, with a brother and two parents, two grandparents. Then she thought of the man in the tarp, dropped over the side of the boat, sunk to the bottom of the shallow bay. They were the same, him and her, rolled up and thrown away, a tarp thrown over her sun, her sky, the world an empty black, a watery quiet.

The front door flew open, and her mother rushed down the walkway, calling her name.

Gia's face pressed into her mother's stomach, where she'd come from, carried for months until she was ready. Her mother was crying. Tears landed on Gia's shoulders in warm splashes. She touched one to make sure it was real, too numb to know for sure.

Her mother led her by the hand into the house.

There was noise. Lorraine came from the living room. Aunt Diane too. Her father in the kitchen doorway, pulling at her arms and legs, bending her head forward and back, digging through her hair to inspect her scalp. There was a new lock on the front door, gold and brassy, the kind bought from a dusty shelf at the hardware store, the same color as a king's crown. Her father carried her up the stairs, set her down on the bathroom floor, then fell to the background as the women rushed in. Her mother closed the door, started the shower water, peeled away her clothes, and dropped them on the floor, pausing at the mark on her back before helping Gia step into the shower. Lorraine and Agnes circled her with soap, washing her hair. Neither caring that water splashed them, too, leaving wet marks on their clothes. There was a towel, a hairbrush, a braid, a clean nightgown over her head, the bed she'd imagined on the island, her feet leaving wet puddles on the floor.

Her mother didn't leave. She kissed her forehead and whispered prayers. Gia closed her eyes. It wasn't that she saw the body falling over the side of the boat; it was that the water fogged her ears and her vision went dark, flashes of light catching through the tarp weave as she was cocooned in plastic, water weighing above and below her small body. She was only thirteen. She saw that now, how little the number thirteen really was. She could count it in her father's pacing steps outside the door, one to thirteen again and again. At some point, she dropped off and sank like the body had, into an endless black.

~

For days, Gia did not speak. Food arrived on a tray: buttered toast, plain noodles, chicken soup, mugs of tea getting colder by the hour. Agnes pressed her hand to Gia's forehead, but it was always cool. There was nothing wrong that chicken soup could fix, just like there wasn't a cure for closing her eyes, sinking through water, and settling on a soft, sandy bottom. The idea was stuck there, rippling through her thoughts whenever a shadow passed over the sun, in the early morning before it was light out, as the light went away. It was there when Agnes ran a bath and the water sat in the tub, in the hum of a mosquito that had slipped through the screen.

She snatched at mosquitoes, real and imaginary, squashing them in her hand, squeezing, squeezing, squeezing to stop that terrible hum, brushing the dead dust away on her comforter, surprised to feel soft cotton instead of sand. But as everyone orbited her, all she wanted was to be alone, as alone as she'd been on the marsh. She didn't deserve Agnes's rosaries or her father opening the windows or his shadow in the doorway at night, standing guard, or Lorraine slipping in after school, whispering stories about a boy who opened his mouth and swallowed the universe, washed it clean, while a dried plant in a bowl burned near the window. She hid a pink crystal in the sheets by Gia's feet and promised it was for healing, listened to her heart with her nursing stethoscope, but Gia said nothing. Her silence became something they tiptoed past.

On the third or fourth day, her father carried a chair into her room, plunked it down hard enough to wake her. She hadn't known she'd been asleep. She'd been dreaming about the chickens they used to keep in the yard, how she'd sprinkle bread crumbs through the mesh and they'd peck at it, digging through the dirt to scrape up more, how they'd still run after their heads had been cut off, how Leo, Ray, and Tommy had poked at the back of the headless chicken, waking some bone-deep instinct to move until it flopped over. That had happened in real life,

Gia realized as she blinked her room into focus, and she forced away nausea at the cruelty of it, at their fingers raking through red-orange feathers, prodding it forward.

It was bright outside. A perfect sun. It caught the stray gray hairs on her father's head, the same color as fishing line. Gia couldn't look at him or near him. There was too much she didn't want him to see.

"You're probably wondering where your brother is." He sighed. Gia pressed her eyes shut because she was *not* wondering where Leo was and didn't care what kind of stinking, wasted place he'd slithered off to.

"I brought him to a halfway house in Brooklyn because he can't live here anymore. I don't know what he did. I don't care why . . ." But his voice cut out, his face twisted so that all the features scrunched toward each other. He put his head in his hands, animal sounds escaping from the hollow space. His back heaved, and his heels ground into the floor, broken for her. It should've moved her, but she only felt impatient, annoyed he was intruding on her silence, talking about Leo.

"He's not coming back. Not until he's fixed. And I hope that brings you a little peace."

The hope in his voice disgusted her. He was not the fixer of everything. How could he be with only eight years of school, most of which involved nothing but counting and tracing letters? She wasn't being fair, but that water was in her lungs, that empty sky, all that darkness. There was no room for anything else, not words. Not sympathy.

And what was a halfway house? Leo wasn't halfway to anything. Definitely not halfway to better. No one who left his sister for dead and stole her boat just to get a fix was halfway to anything good. Couldn't he see that? Why couldn't he see it the same way she did? Maybe because Leo hadn't tried to kill him yet.

He stood up as if there were some urgency, clearing out before he'd given Gia a chance to speak because it would hurt less when she didn't, but he paused by the door with the chair in his hand.

"You're a good soldier," he said.

Alone again, she thought of one of the orange-peel boats she'd launched from her porch to Lorraine's on tidewater with one of Leo's little green army men inside. It had floated for a bit, drifting down the street past a fallen stop sign with two points of its octagon sticking out above the water. It never made it to Lorraine's house, but there was only so much you could expect from newspaper sails on orange-peel boats.

Chapter Fourteen

Gia didn't go to school. No one asked her to. She slept whenever she felt like it, took stray bites of food here and there, and left the plates unwashed. She peeled back a curl of wallpaper from beneath her light switch in one long ribbon, exposing the yellowed glue underneath.

When her parents went to work, she walked to the canal and sat on the empty dock. The rope was still coiled, waiting for the boat to come back. She remembered having a dog once when she was very young that must've run away; for months the leash had hung by the door. She was not mad at the bay. She felt sorry for it, forced to swallow that person, forced to keep a secret; she felt sorry that something so terrible could happen to a place that was meant to be good: a resting place for migrating birds, a breeding ground for horseshoe crabs and oysters and mussels, a place that absorbed storms and teemed with life. Yes, it knew death, but not like this. She pulled her knees to her chest as water rippled past with a sadness Gia hadn't noticed before. How many others were there? How many other terrible secrets was the bay keeping?

The halfway house lasted for four days. "What do you mean, he's not there?" Agnes shouted into the phone before dropping her voice. The thermos she'd been rinsing in the sink overflowed, and then there was a flurry of phone calls—to her father at the station, to local hospitals, to her father again—until Gia got bored with it. That was the nice thing about being a ghost: it made everything that would have hurt duller.

That night, her father took the doorknob off her door and popped a new one into place that locked from the inside, gave her a key on a loop of twine. So much for Leo not coming home. He ignored the wallpaper on the floor.

Otherwise, no one talked about it, at least not to Gia. But there was more food in the refrigerator than usual. New locks on the doors. Fresh sheets on Leo's bed. A fourth towel hanging in the bathroom. A new toothbrush. A heavy safe with feet drilled into the closet floor in her parents' bedroom, as if her parents didn't agree about where their son belonged. Agnes, Gia suspected, was still leaving milk out on the porch for her son, the stray, while her father built a fort. And he was doing something else too.

Gia sat on the porch next to the rabbit hutch and watched people come and go. Her father was doing something inside one of the new houses; she was sure of it. They had windows and doors now, siding and shingles, gutters. The lawns were full of dirt, bundles of drywall under tarps, buckets of Spackle. Soon they would have walls. She saw him in his uniform through an open door, talking to someone inside, looking over his shoulder to sweep the neighborhood. And why was he in uniform? The questions were surprising, seeping in through cracks in the numbness.

That was yesterday, and it had sat wrong all night.

Today, Mr. Angliotti moved boxes to the curb for trash pickup, cleaning out the basement in the same navy trousers and moth-eaten plaid shirt he always wore. "Can't take it with you," he'd said, shrugging, that morning as Gia had walked to the canal, the hose battering the rosebushes. He was a ghost, too, living a shadow of his former life like she was.

Trip after trip, craning over each box before taking the next step, bending slowly to line boxes on the curb. It was painful to watch.

Irritating, almost. He stopped to wipe sweat from his brow, and Gia's mouth smarted with the memory of salt water up her nose and on her lips, of sand scraping her scalp and sand fleas bouncing near her face, of Leo's disgusting clothes on her skin.

Gia's arms and legs were awake now, pulling her down the street. She was too restless to sit still. Helping an old man move junk to the curb was something the other Gia would've done, something she could help with without making worse.

She met Mr. Angliotti on the curb. Sweat beaded on his forehead, above his lip. His face was bright pink, his shirt damp under the arms. She reached for the box.

Mr. Angliotti eyed her through a milky cataract. Gia's heartbeat quickened defensively. Yes, the rumors about Leo were true, but she was still good, wasn't she? Or was she guilty by association? She was willing to just accept it and go home. What was the point of trying to prove otherwise? Mr. Angliotti hesitated. She'd been in his house dozens of times to babysit his grandkids, had brought her old toys over for them. Gia's disgust for her brother intensified.

"Well, OK." Mr. Angliotti ran his hand over a wisp of hair on his bald, sunspotted head and handed her the box. "Everything's in the hallway. Just get 'em to the curb. Take whatever you want. I don't need it anymore." Mr. Angliotti sighed. "Everything changes . . ."

She couldn't listen to him grumble about how good the world used to be. Not today.

Framed pictures of Mr. Angliotti's grandkids smiled down at her. There was a mirror next to the hallway coat tree, a new color TV in Mr. Angliotti's living room. War medals. Trinket boxes. A carved wooden clock. What had the man in the water left behind?

She made trip after trip, sweating through her shirt, her muscles burning, especially the sore spot on her back where he'd hit her with that stick, but Gia didn't care. She imagined the things in her room being packed into boxes: her macramé owl, her poster of the World's

Fair, her seashells, the chain of egg cases from a thorny skate, the new tubes of makeup. The key to her room hung around her neck, warming to her skin, as she passed the tree stump where the sparrows had fallen again and again. Only she didn't hold her breath. It seemed silly now.

Mr. Angliotti offered her cookies from a tin when she was done, admiring the empty hallway as Gia swept the dust. It was amazing how unnecessary speaking was, how people didn't even notice.

"Come back tomorrow. I'll pay you."

But Gia shook her head. She didn't want money. Not ever again. And she wouldn't come back. Mr. Angliotti's door closed behind him. The lock clicked into place. Did he always lock it, or was it because of her? She imagined him watching through the peephole just to make sure she was gone, like the trash heaps along the Cross Island Parkway, capped with fresh soil and clean grass but filthy and contaminated underneath the hills that disguised the garbage.

～

On Saturday, every light was on at Our Lady of Grace. Five o'clock Mass had finished, and everyone filed down to the church basement, where canned goods were stacked on folding tables, waiting to be sorted and loaded into vans for soup kitchens for Thanksgiving. A bag full of canned peas cut into Gia's wrist, leaving a throbbing welt. Vegetables were in the far right corner, fruit on the left, everything else at the front, but Gia was not looking for the right table. She was looking for her brother.

Because someone had rummaged through the boxes on Mr. Angliotti's curb earlier that morning and thrown a bunch of stuff into the street before garbage collection had come. And someone had picked at the new lock on the front door with a sharp object while Gia was at the doctor until they'd given up and broken the window, reached through to open the front door, taken the money from the grocery jar in the kitchen, and kicked down the door to Gia's room for the money she used to keep under her mattress.

"Should we call the police?" Agnes had asked as she'd swept the broken glass into the dustpan, and Gia had almost broken her silent streak to ask if she was an idiot.

That morning, before Leo had broken into the house, Eddie had turned down Gia's quilt to kiss her cheek and tell her he loved her, as Gia had pretended to sleep. Later, Agnes had taken Gia to the doctor, a pediatrician, who'd looked in her ears and mouth, up her nose, asked if she'd had her first menstruation yet, an idea that made Gia queasy as he pressed on her stomach for organs. Her mother explained that Gia had not spoken since the "incident" while Gia stared at a small smudge on the ceiling that could've been a squashed bug or a curl of cigarette smoke or a splash of blood, working out how long it would be before she could sleep again while the doctor whispered about shell shock, silence, nightmares, coming out of it eventually. Wrong, wrong, wrong, Gia thought as Agnes nodded along. Silence was not a choice. It was all that was left.

Until she'd seen the front door swinging, her mattress thrown aside, the trail of him fresh. Now, her whole house felt contaminated the same way the bay did with a body floating under the surface. She could not curl up in her bed and listen to the house hum anymore because his presence cut through the silence and made it hum with hate. She was not *looking* for him as she pushed through the church doors; she was hunting. She wanted to stand in front of him so he'd know that she—Gia—was alive despite him, that she'd saved herself in the marsh after he'd left her for dead, and wasn't that something? She'd made it. Then she'd never speak to or think about him again. She was old stock too.

Everyone was here. Her mother, Aunt Ida, Mr. Angliotti, the nuns. All but Lorraine, who was probably at the house with the pillows. Her mother had even dressed up in her favorite black dress, her face circled by short curls, sorting cans mostly alone. The women from her card club popped over to say hello before moseying off to Aunt Ida's table on the other side of the room, her mother a citronella flame to their spindly wings, as little kids spun cans on the floor.

Gia skirted the room, sidestepping conversations, searching for her brother and thinking about how ridiculous this was. Only humans were stupid enough to feed animals that could not feed themselves.

Upstairs, people set up poinsettias and pine garlands at the altar. The air was cold, heavy with high tide. Gia walked the first few blocks home, jogged the last. The houses were dark except for Ray and Tommy's, where the lights were on and Ray's car was in the driveway with Antonio's behind it, blocking part of the sidewalk, acting like it belonged there when it really didn't. Cars pulled up to the curb, and kids hopped out in their best jeans and fringe jackets, walking all over the front lawn, Tommy ushering them inside. He'd thinned out, grown a little, his face less Gerber Babyish but still not manly. So they were having a party. How nice.

She sat on the porch. Across the swimming canal, construction materials had been cleared from the patchy lawns, the windows and doors installed and locked. They had new aluminum siding and clean gutters with drainpipes to let water race down dirt lawns to the canal. They would be lived in by Christmas. The more finished they got, the more final it seemed that her swimming canal would go away, but Gia didn't care anymore now that she'd never swim with Lorraine again, or even Ray and Tommy, or Leo. It was just her, and part of her was gone, just as the others were.

Crazy Louann rode by on her bike, humming "It's a Small World" and sprinkling cat food from the basket, honking the horn. Was she happy, Gia wondered, alone with her cats, as Gia was alone on the steps? More kids tumbled up the mum-lined walkway, laughing, throwing their arms around one another. Two kids were making out in a car in front of the house as cats slunk out from under parked cars and snatched a few bites before disappearing again. Nine lives each. That was the world, Gia thought; take your bite and leave.

Mr. Angliotti's front window glowed. A sunrise orange. Or a candle in a jack-o'-lantern. But Mr. Angliotti was at church, and there were no cars out front; it couldn't be his children visiting. The light in the window pulsed. How could it be that bright?

Gia crept closer. The ground oozed under her sneakers, mud clinging to the backs of her legs as her brain squawked: a thousand birds crying, flitting between trees, calling out danger on the ground. This was stupid. The rhododendron bush scraped her arm, her bones begging her not to take another step while music pulsed from Ray and Tommy's party.

The back door swung with the breeze, one glass pane gaping, exhaling black smoke. The ground was covered in mud and broken glass. The air was heavy with smoke. Not the pleasant smell of campfire smoke or barbecue coals but burning. Plastic, fabric, plaster, wood, paint, clothes, rugs, wires—fire turning everything to embers. Gia froze. Smoke burned her eyes, her nose and lungs, as heat curled the hair on her arms. The memory of that oar cracked across her back. Leo was in there. She was sure of it. He hadn't found whatever he needed at her house, so he'd come here.

She couldn't go in there. Couldn't drag him from whatever room he was in. She imagined a backpack of Mr. Angliotti's stolen things at his feet, war medals, a needle. A bottle cap.

But her father would. Her mother. They would duck the smoke, crawling from room to room, because they'd made him, because they wouldn't be able to live with knowing they hadn't been brave. This smell would haunt her when she was old in her bed, same as the marsh and that body sinking below the surface would, knowing she'd stood here with the heat on her face and done nothing. That was the difference between them, wasn't it? He'd left her for dead on that island, but it wasn't in her. She was her father's daughter.

"Leo!" Gia's voice was unfamiliar, startling. She did it again, screaming into the smoke. It carried weirdly over the crackling. Something popped, and sparks flew. His name filled the air around her over and over again. She should call the police. Or the fire department. Panic flashed through her. They wouldn't be able to cover this up. Her father's entire career destroyed by his son. Everyone would know. It would ruin them.

She was inside, crawling under the smoke, thinking of her father kicking down doors in dark hallways and rushing from room to room with a gun and a flashlight, his partner at his back. The bathroom door was open. Something slid. There were pills under Gia's palms, sticking to her skin, bottles on the floor, the medicine cabinet door ripped off and tossed aside so that the broken mirror reflected a girl on all fours and a boy curled into himself mumbling, rocking, knowing he'd screwed up bad.

It was pathetic. This was not the boy who'd held his breath to swim under boats.

"Get up!" she yelled, pulling him by the collar.

His eyes met hers, wild and unfocused, and Gia saw herself finally, as her brother had as he'd darted away on the boat or stuffed stolen candy into her backpack, or when she'd jumped off her sled and stared at the sky, that beautiful blue, Gia quietly changing, quietly growing, with a stillness he envied. She had never been less than he was. She'd always been more.

The smoke sank. She grabbed his collar, made him crawl toward the open door, surprised by his deadweight, until they were in the yard. Mud seeped through his clothes. They had to get out of here before anyone came back from church or took a smoke break outside the party.

"Crawl," she hissed. He did, slowly, the same way he might've when they were kids playing horse and cowboy and she'd ridden on his back. He would've died in there. She pulled him by the back of his shirt, pushing away the thought that she should've left him like he'd left her.

The house was lit up now, flaming orange in the windows and eerily dark everywhere else. She prayed no one would come home yet. They were almost there; then she'd call the fire department, and fire trucks would scream up the block. She spit the taste out of her mouth. It was black on the sidewalk.

She dumped Leo on the hallway floor and ran for the phone, spinning the numbers as fast as she could. Her words came out in a jumble. A fire. The address. Her face smudged with smoke in the hallway mirror, hair stuck to her in damp strands. The operator asked her name. Nausea doubled her over. She slammed the phone down so hard it bounced out of the receiver.

There were sirens in the distance. Gia sat on the floor as the house consumed itself.

There were things in the flames: outlines of doorframes, a falling beam. She should wash her face, change her clothes, but all she could do was watch it burn. Tears stung the smoke out of her eyes. It ran down her face in black rivers, her chest tight. What would her father say? Her mother. In her pretty dress.

"You did this," she hissed. Her voice cracked. Leo mumbled to himself. The worst part was it would keep happening. He would steal again, break more houses, burn things down. Gia hated him for it, this lying, bottomless thing he'd become, while everyone cleaned up around him.

The block filled with swirling lights. Firemen hopped off the truck, ran hoses, opened a hydrant as people ran back from church. Word was out. Gia couldn't watch when Mr. Angliotti got here, when he stood outside the house he had lived in his whole life with his parents and then his wife and children. Water sprayed. Firemen shouted. More trucks. People covered their mouths, rumors starting in their heads. Such a terrible thing. In her heart, she was the terrible thing.

More lights and sirens screamed up the block in blue-and-white cruisers this time, cornering Aunt Ida's house, driving onto the lawn and surrounding the doors. They shouted through bullhorns for everyone to come out with their hands up, lined kids against the aluminum siding, and patted them down as the police filed inside to search Aunt Ida and Uncle Frank's home. They led Ray and Antonio out in handcuffs, shoved them roughly into a cruiser, and slammed the doors hard as the other kids were let go one by one and police filed out of the house with cardboard boxes.

Tommy was on the porch with his hands under the mailbox, eyeing the cop pacing behind him.

Don't dart, you moron, Gia prayed. If the cops cared about anything he had to say, he'd be in the back of that cruiser too. But if he ran, they'd crush him. Nightsticks and all. All he had to do was stay still.

But he ran. He barely made it to the curb before they were on him, his face smashed into the dirt, kicking, kicking, kicking until the cops got his arms behind his back, cuffed his wrists, and his sneakers went still. Ray pounded at the window of the cruiser. The other kids streamed past in flashes of fringe. The cops stood up, dusted themselves off. The parked cars shuffled away, like the street game where a ball was under a cup and you had to guess which one, where no one won except the dealer. Ray's car was lonely in the driveway. On the ground, Tommy was still. They left him in the dirt as the cruisers drove off, one by one, carting away whatever they'd come for, until the police threw Tommy in the back of one too. It took two cops to lift him.

Her mother burst through the door and turned on the light, where Leo and Gia were on the floor, covered in mud and smoke. The light snapped off.

"Oh my God," Agnes said in the darkness, stepping over them both, heading for the kitchen, where she put her head in her hands and sobbed into the hollow space.

Chapter Fifteen

All night, it smelled of ashes.

"You did not see anything, do you understand?" The panic in her voice cut through Gia's numbness as Agnes closed the curtains and forced Gia into the shower, where the smell washed out of her hair, her skin. Soot ran down the drain in dark puddles. But it was inside her, too, burning her nose, throat, lungs, the places she used to be happy. She nodded. The warm water wouldn't stop the shivery feeling. It wouldn't go away.

"And neither of you was at that party?"

No. At least that was true. Agnes probably wished she were yelling at them for throwing beer cans in Aunt Ida's bushes instead of setting Mr. Angliotti's house on fire as she threw Leo in the shower and told him to take whatever he needed to stay quiet and not leave his damn room. Then she mopped the hallway while water boiled on the stove for tea to soothe Gia's coughing. Leo passed out in his room. Agnes put a blanket over him, rolled him onto his side. She didn't ask what had happened.

Gia was layers of an ocean. Numb at the outer layer, where the sun should've warmed her, where she should've been teeming with life. Underneath, she was a cold nothing. She sipped her tea, but it didn't help. Agnes stood on the porch, a silhouette in the smoke, watching Aunt Ida scream at the cops about what they'd done to her house and where were her sons? The car with Ray and Antonio was gone. It was odd that they'd put them together. Never once had her father questioned her and Leo together for anything half as bad. No one got the truth that way unless they didn't want it.

When Agnes carried tea to Leo's room, Gia decided she would move out and live with Lorraine. If Leo lived here, fine, but not Gia. She wanted to read and go to school and wave at neighbors when she rode her bike instead of keeping her head down as people whispered about him. *The one whose father is a cop. Imagine—how embarrassing. Your own son.* She couldn't be part of it.

She stuffed a handful of clothes in a backpack. The effort made her light headed, forcing her head between her knees. Then tears burned as soot washed out, her body fighting to heal. Why, she thought, couldn't Leo's just do the same?

She crept down the stairs as Agnes argued into the kitchen phone. "What do you mean, he's not there? He left this morning, and he never gets his days mixed up. Yes, I'll hold."

Gia crossed the street in the blankets her mother had put around her. Mr. Angliotti sat on his lawn in a plastic chair, the house a black frame in the darkness, matching her shock. The smell of it was everywhere, stronger than low tide.

An officer held a glass of water for Mr. Angliotti. Her father. He drank it in one long gulp and let it fall. It landed in the grass, but neither picked it up. Gia inched closer, slowly because it hurt to breathe and the smoke made her light headed. The trail of flattened grass where Leo had crawled was nauseating. She wanted to slide under her father's free arm, breathe into his coat as he squeezed her shoulders, smelling like coffee from the station. She wanted to memorize her father just as he was before he knew. Eddie put his coat around Mr. Angliotti. He was not the great fixer of everything, but he tried.

If she were Leo, this would be a moment to put something in her veins, because it was unbearable. She stared at a streetlight until it made stars, like that exploding transformer months ago. Her mouth filled with acid. Was that when it had gone wrong, the day they'd sold the bike? She forced the thought down, because there was no magic medicine.

She was shivering again, so hard her teeth chattered. Eddie gave Mr. Angliotti's shoulder a squeeze. Something fell inside the steaming house, but Mr. Angliotti was still, staring. Her father split away, and as the distance between her father and the old man grew, the kindness in him hardened off, like a dead thing stiffening into a horrible shape. He plowed past her without noticing.

"Dad?" she whispered. He stopped cold. She had not spoken to him since the island, and the surprise on his face was painful. Why did he have to look at her like that, like he already knew? Gia was shaking. The blanket fell off her shoulders into a puddle at her feet. The knapsack slid down with it. He knew.

"Oh, Jesus, Gia." He put his hands on his head and paced. "Jesus, Gia," he begged. She'd never heard his voice like this before. It terrified her. "Tell me you had nothing to do with this."

Gia could not breathe. Air would not pass her nose. It would not reach her lungs. She tried again until there wasn't enough air to keep standing. She sat in the street, her father pacing and pulling at chunks of his hair until he doubled over, clutching his stomach.

"Gia, please . . . ," he begged. "What will they find in there?"

Gia sobbed. She hadn't thought of that. What would they find? God, they would know. The pills on the floor. The stolen things. Girl-size footprints preserved under fallen debris. She would go to jail. No, she couldn't go to jail. She was only thirteen. She couldn't go to jail, could she?

"What did he do?"

Gia could not stop shaking. The words would not come.

"Gia, answer!" He shook her shoulders to snap her out of it. Her neck bounced forward and back. Her mother ran down the walk, her bathrobe flying, that pretty dress underneath.

"Eddie, come inside," she urged, pulling at his elbow.

"Agnes," he said, that same cry in his voice.

Her mother's face gave it away. They were still, staring at each other, Gia forgotten on the ground, before the air around her father changed, prickling Gia's skin.

"Eddie, stop." Agnes reached for his arm, but he shook her off, charging up the walkway.

"Gia, get up," she urged, already running after Eddie.

Gia couldn't move. Her father flung the door open, took the steps in leaps. In the glow of her brother's room, her father was a spiderlike shape that landed on Leo in his bed, his fist cracking down. The sound of it traveling through the open window broke through her. She'd never seen her father hit anyone, let alone her brother. Agnes screamed for him to stop.

But he couldn't. Gia covered her ears, humming to drown out the sound. Behind her, Mr. Angliotti was still in that lawn chair. She could not go inside. She sat in the street on her blanket, covering her ears, her face in her knees, praying a car would squash her. She almost did not see the front door open at Aunt Ida's or Aunt Ida carrying blankets and a tray to Mr. Angliotti, kneeling beside him to set it down. It was not real, the glass with the straw, the plate of food, nor was it real when Mr. Angliotti followed Aunt Ida to her house down the mum-lined walkway, the plastic lawn chair abandoned. *Why don't you fix my father and Leo too?* Gia thought bitterly. She wished the fire had been at Aunt Ida's house instead, crumbling the marble heads and the new shag rugs, burning up Ray's room while they watched on the lawn in their only clothes, so they could feel how unfair it was to have your life snatched away.

Inside, the noise stopped, and the silence was worse, final. Aunt Ida's door opened again, and Aunt Ida, Gia realized, was coming right for her, still in her church outfit, though her blouse had come untucked, her skirt wrinkled.

"Gia," she said softly, her voice breaking. "You shouldn't be in the street. God forbid . . ."

She looked off toward the swimming canal, bit her lower lip. Gia dug her fingers into the blanket Nonna had crocheted, gathered it around her.

"It's so late, and . . ." Aunt Ida's voice broke off. "It's time for bed."

She was all tears, a blurry face. "Where is my boy, Gia? Where did they take him?"

Gia stared. Silence stuck in her throat again, same as after the marsh. Aunt Ida wrapped her arms around herself, asking where her son was, and Gia couldn't take it, couldn't take the delicacy of someone who didn't deserve to be delicate.

"Leave," Gia said finally, then louder, and again, pushing it from her throat until Eddie crossed the lawn. Aunt Ida whirled on him.

"You did this," she hissed, jabbing a finger at the air. "I don't know how, but it was you. You did this, and I know it."

But Eddie just stared, his silence making the size difference between them more obvious as Aunt Ida jabbed her useless finger until she gave up and took off back to her house of bleach and polish, which used to be the prettiest on the block before the new houses made it look squat, before kids walked all over the new rugs and police tossed everything around despite Aunt Ida's careful dusting and vacuuming, making the sum of her work a great big fat zero.

"Go inside, Gia," her father said. "Please. Just go inside."

Then he took off down the smoky street, and Gia knew the night was not over.

Chapter Sixteen

Gia got up. The world turned to salt and pepper briefly. She left the blankets and her knapsack in the street because she couldn't remember what was inside, why she'd packed it in the first place. Where would they be? Where would they go? There were endless places. The marsh, Leo's weeds. All in plain sight. She walked toward the canal, drawn there in the same way she always was, and squatted by the water's edge, dipped her fingertips.

The new houses watched over the scene on the other side of the swimming canal, smug with their air conditioner cutouts and shiny new windows, probably enjoying how quickly Mr. Angliotti's house had leveled because it had been made by the kind of people who'd never live in the new houses.

Only one was missing windows and doors. Only one had a car parked out front. The others were still, but not this one. Shadows moved inside. She knew that car.

Gia was a moth, flapping stupidly, paper wings warping as the light intensified and drew her closer; she knew there was no other choice. The real Gia split away until she was more like a tree trunk watching a leaf from its own branch drift to the ground. From above, she could watch the girl in a flannel nightgown and Keds tiptoe across gravel, pause behind a car, crawl under a dark porch full of pebbles and debris, where a wire cut her hand and blood pooled on the cuff. The nightgown tangled, but she kept crawling toward the voices above the beams and plywood. The girl on the ground used to be afraid of snakes and centipedes, of dark basements. Now, nothing could hurt her, not when the real her was high above and safe.

Plywood bowed under someone's weight. More than someone. Many someones. *Count the voices.* Yelling. No, arguing. She could tell from the tone of it but couldn't tell how serious it was: if they were arguing over money piled on a card table with cigarettes burning in ashtrays that broke when the last hand was drawn and everyone threw down their cards, or if it was the kind of tension that struck out from the inside suddenly: A fist. An elbow. Skin on skin. Bones smashing.

Five. Five men in the room and one invisible girl.

"This one? No. He's a punk kid with a smart mouth. Thinks he's a big shot, but he won't roll."

"What are you, his lawyer?" Laughing. But not from everyone. Only from two.

"Look at him. He's shitting his pants. Playing tough but eating his mother's sauce every Sunday, sleeping in his big-boy bed, you know what I'm saying? Never been inside. Don't know nothing from nobody. This one, though? That's a different story. He knows better."

"He should. But he don't."

"So what I'm saying is, cut this one loose. I'll vouch for him. If he makes trouble, and he won't, I'll set him right. Because the way I see it, if you hurt this kid, it brings more heat, you know? He's not gonna disappear quietly. Not in this neighborhood. Do whatever you want with the other one."

Her father. He was right above her, shifting his weight in a way that made the floor bend as the man bent words. *You know this voice.* Bedtime stories, whistling "Edelweiss" over coffee, only now it was filled with broken glass. Nails.

And he needed help. People didn't shift when they were on solid ground.

Another voice: "You don't shit where you eat."

Good riddance. She knew this voice, too, waited for the splash of water that didn't come, the gurgling of the bay as it swallowed that heavy tarp. Her father had to get out of there.

"Listen, this is a good kid. A stupid kid, but he'll clean up. He'll give back whatever he took from you. Make it right. Work it off till he's square. Let him speak for himself. He'll tell you he's sorry. Won't you, Ray?"

Ray. Her father was trying to save Ray. Gia squeezed her eyes shut, closed her hands around a pebble, as a chair scraped forward.

Whimpering. Same as when Uncle Frank grabbed a misbehaving son and brought his free hand down on his backside, shutting the boy right up.

More whimpering, louder, without words, like screaming into a pillow. Something was happening. A chair scraped forward. Had they done that as kids? Tied their arms and legs to chairs and raced from one side of a line to the other? Yes, and now the chairs above were inching across the plywood, racing for somewhere else.

Suddenly she imagined her father asleep in his bed and being rolled into the blankets, carried to a boat, a single cigarette tip glowing the whole way through. *No,* she thought. *No, no, no. Get him out of there. Think,* she begged her brain. She needed something else, something to distract them. Something to break the tension and catch them by surprise so her father could make a move. Something reckless. She needed Leo.

Dirt and insulation scraped at her skin as she crawled out, tangling in her nightgown. She stumbled to her feet when there was no longer house above her, prayed they would not hear as she slipped into the freezing canal, swam across, and ran for home in the lingering haze of fire smoke. She burst into Leo's room and saw him but didn't really see his bruised face, swollen lip, and torn T-shirt in the dark room.

"Explode a gas tank." The words burst out. "Can you explode a car?"

"What's going on?" Agnes was in the doorway, but Leo's head jerked up as he balled the sheet on his bed under his arm. Of course he could explode a gas tank. They pushed past Agnes, told her to stay put. Leo trailed behind her, not because he couldn't outrun her, even like this, but because he was following her in her soaked nightgown. She thought, vaguely, how embarrassed she'd been that day at the canal with her dress suctioned to her new body and that man watching, but here she was again, drenched, stealing a bottle of lighter fluid from under the barbecue and a packet of matches, running back toward the canal and swimming across, Leo with that bedsheet above his head to keep it dry, as she prayed it wasn't already too late. She'd been gone five minutes at most. Was that too long?

It was quiet. The people inside could not see the new pair of sneakers walking slowly across the dirt lawn, could not see the shoes stop near one of the window cutouts and rise up on tiptoes, could not see those same sneakers run back toward Antonio's parked car and open the gas tank. Leo bit down on his swollen lip, uncoiled the bedsheet, stuck it into the gas tank, and doused it with lighter fluid.

The match set off a line of fire, racing for Antonio's car as someone yelled, "Shut up!" and a chair was kicked over, hit the ground hard. Leo was too close to the car, his face full of shadows and angles, watching the fire race, eyes darting to the house and whatever was happening inside. Shuffling, stamping, more yelling. Gunshots. A smoking hole where the bullet disappeared into dirt. Leo barreled toward her. Gia gripped at pebbles, digging her fingertips into the earth, calling out her need like the trees in the story. And then the pebbles were gone. Leo threw her into the water, balled her nightgown into a fist, and didn't let go as Gia kicked for the surface.

The car exploded.

Under the water, the sound was muffled, but orange burned above, curling the leaves on a tree, spreading through the unfinished houses to all the things inside.

Eddie limped into the canal, dragging Ray behind him, wincing at the water. Both of them waded across to where a cop car was now waiting, and Eddie shoved Ray inside. It took off without lights and sirens. Eddie kept going but stopped to pick up Gia's backpack in the street, Nonna's blanket, turned them over in his hands like a new tool on a Swiss Army knife. He waded back across the canal with them above his head, wadding the blanket into a ball, squirting the rest of the lighter fluid on it.

Leo crouched on the pebble beach. Suddenly Gia was beside him, watching, as Eddie struck a lighter and the blanket flamed through an empty window. Her father was a shadow in the flames, and the car burned hot on Gia's face as Eddie waded back across, his arms above the water.

Leo nudged her to go, but she couldn't look away from the burning house, wondering if they'd still fill in the canal now. Numb set in with the cold until Gia couldn't tell if any of this was real life or some kind of dream, if she'd stuck out her tongue at some point and Leo had put a melting smiley face there that had brought out all the monsters in her head, her deepest fears, because only then would it make sense that her father had risked his life just for Ray. Only then would it make sense that the men in the boat were here, just steps from her house, that they were probably still in that burning house, and if they were dead, her father had done it. Of course he had. Because he'd done it at war. She couldn't believe he'd aimed that navy machine gun at the ocean and come back alive. But now it was true in a new, terrifying way. They were the same, him and her, because she hoped those men were dead. That they'd never again roll a person in a tarp and drop it into the bay as casually as flicking away a cigarette butt. That they'd never catch her. Or Lorraine. Or even Leo and Ray. Marsh grass or not.

Leo was gone from the pebble beach, her father from the street. It was just her. She pressed her eyes closed, welcoming the endless black. For the second time that night, fire trucks raced to their block. The houses were a haze of smoke, making it hard for anyone who'd heard the bang or the gunshots to really know what they'd seen, and so shades closed as Gia wandered home in her soaking nightgown, teeth chattering, knowing she'd never swim in the canal again. Aunt Diane rushed down the front steps faster than Gia had ever seen her move and pulled her inside, tugged the nightgown over Gia's head, and forced clean clothes on her. Aunt Diane washed Gia's bleeding hand in the sink, because Aunt Diane had seen everything.

Lorraine flashed out the door, running to Gia's house, where Eddie was dragging one leg up the sidewalk, pressing Gia's knapsack to his lazy leg.

"Take this," Aunt Diane said, filling a bag with towels and gauze from an old army box under the sink.

She shoved the bag into Gia's stomach, knocking her backward. Told her to go.

But Gia just stood there and Aunt Diane just stared as Gia took in the painted blue cabinets, the crumbs on the counter, the wet shoes on her feet, the sirens and yelling outside her head, the quiet within.

"Am I dead?" Gia asked finally.

"Not yet, baby," Aunt Diane said. "You got a lot more life ahead of you."

For a moment, Gia was disappointed, because how many horrible things could chip at a person before they were only a shell, dust instead of the stars in the universe we were supposed to be?

Aunt Diane hugged Gia, and she knew Diane understood because she'd seen just as many horrible things. The real Gia floated back down to the one in Aunt Diane's arms, and so when she said, "Your father needs you," the real Gia snapped to, dodging fire trucks and racing across the street on two thin legs with borrowed air in her lungs because her father, *her father*, had just saved stupid Ray, and now he was limping up the walk with one arm over Lorraine's shoulder, but she couldn't carry him alone. Gia wedged herself under her father's other arm as her father called out like an animal in a trap.

Agnes rushed toward the steps. They dragged him into the hallway, got him on the floor. Gia dumped the bag of things near Lorraine as she cut fast at the pant legs.

"Two," her father croaked out.

Lorraine rolled him, searching his leg for something she couldn't find.

She looked at Agnes for a very long time, the two of them deciding, until Agnes nodded and pulled at the belt on Eddie's waist until it snapped free. She folded it into a thick wad and told Eddie to bite down. Then she thought twice and grabbed a bottle from the hutch, told Eddie to drink. The liquid disappeared. He bit down on the belt as Lorraine forced apart the two bleeding halves of his leg with tweezers. Gia thought of Eddie lining cans on the fence, letting them shoot into the marsh, digging around for the cases after to see how they'd split. Now Lorraine was doing that in his leg, and she was only a nursing student who smelled like incense and had probably been sitting on a cushion listening to tambourines when this had happened. The sounds her father made cut right through her. She fell back to the living room, where she could hear but not see. It was too much to do both at once.

"Gia. Gia, listen, OK?" Leo crouched beside her, and Gia realized she was sitting on the floor, holding the carpet between her fingers, picking at it like blades of grass. "I'm sorry, OK? I'm sorry. I've done some real bad shit, and everybody knows it. I don't want to do it, OK? I don't want to make it all wrong anymore. I made a mistake, and now I can't take it back, Gia. But I can't make it right here."

Agnes looked up, glaring at Leo over Eddie, then forced her attention back down to the tweezers and whispered something to Lorraine, told Eddie to take another drink. Leo was still talking, but Gia's head was radio static as Lorraine dropped a bullet piece onto the floor. It was embarrassing to see her father in his underwear, biting down on his own belt. She was too numb to do anything but see facts. They were straight arrows, as clear and sharp as jellyfish stings in the ocean.

"Shut up, Leo," she spit. "You'll do whatever you want to do anyway."

But he'd saved them. *No, you saved them,* Gia's brain corrected. It didn't make sense. Nothing did.

"Gia, just listen, please . . ."

But all Gia could see were bullet fragments on the floor, Agnes filling a pot with water at the sink, digging in the drawer for a clean dish towel as Lorraine threaded a needle, stabbed it through the raw flesh, and stitched, closing holes. Agnes wiped blood from Eddie's leg, dabbed the stitches with ointment, hid the whole ugly thing away with gauze.

Leo covered his head, still squatting, crying into the cove of his chest. If she was not so numb, she would've held his head up and made him watch.

The women carried Eddie upstairs while Gia wiped the floor, ran the bullet fragments under cold water in the kitchen sink, and put them in her pocket.

"I love you," Lorraine told Agnes by the front door. "You've always . . ." Her voice broke as the two women hugged, both exhausted, their knees buckling under the weight of each other. Gia looked up from the spot she was mopping, struck by the emotion of it, and she knew. Lorraine was leaving. Not tonight. Or even within the next few weeks, but she was going away.

The fire trucks were done, pulling away from the other side of the canal. Agnes stood in the doorway as Lorraine crossed the street. Dawn was breaking, the sun cutting an orange circle above the horizon through a haze of smoke and ash. The parakeets were gone from the line, and Gia wondered if they'd come back or if they'd gotten sick of the danger and taken off for good.

"Leo." Agnes kept her eyes on the sun. "It's time to go."

Leo looked up from the floor, straight at Gia, wild eyed and younger looking, like a bird dropped from a nest whose wings suddenly wouldn't work. Gia looked away.

"Get your things," Agnes said, her voice as calm as the orange light rising behind the trees. "You have ten minutes."

There were footsteps on the stairs. Drawers opened and closed. A zipper. Agnes dialed the station and told them Eddie had the flu and would likely be out for the week, then dumped the bucket of bloody water down the kitchen sink and refilled it, all before Leo came back down.

"Gia, listen for your father, all right? If anything happens, go get Lorraine."

She did not look as Leo walked down the front walk and climbed into the passenger seat, as the engine started, as Agnes pulled away from the curb. Later, she would learn that Agnes drove him all the way to the Port Authority in Manhattan, the farthest Agnes had ever driven alone, and bought him a bus ticket to Florida because it was happy there and she couldn't send her son anywhere she'd never been herself. Leo boarded without protest, took a seat by the window. Agnes came back to a parking ticket on the windshield. She laughed as she ripped it into a million little pieces and scattered them over the filthy sidewalk, and Agnes told Gia she remembered those pieces scattering, blowing in every direction, more than she remembered anything Leo had said on the ride from home to away.

～

The news reported a burned-down house with two unidentified bodies inside. The police and fire departments were investigating. Two days later, the bodies were identified as Sal DiGiovanni and Antonio LaRocca, both known affiliates of the Mafia. The investigation was ongoing, but it appeared to be an internal dispute following a police sting on a local drug ring. Gia swallowed a lump, tucked the newspaper under her arm, and carried up her father's breakfast tray, glad he was asleep when she brought it in because she couldn't quite match the man throwing a flaming blanket into an empty house with the man who used to make Mickey Mouse pancakes. Agnes must've been struggling, too, because she made eggs and toast, poured coffee, and helped Eddie change the dressing on his thigh now that he was feeling better enough to be embarrassed by anyone else helping, but otherwise, she sat in the kitchen, lighting cigarettes, letting them burn out after the first few frenzied pulls, waiting for the phone to ring.

Gia wondered if Agnes was more afraid they'd get caught or more afraid that they wouldn't, or if she was worried about Leo in Florida, who'd called to say that he'd made it there, yes, but he'd gotten rolled at the bus terminal and could they send him some money—just a little— to hold him over until he found a job. And Agnes had listened with the phone away from her ear, squeezing her eyes shut, before placing it gently down in the holder.

"You know," she'd said, when she'd finally opened her eyes again and didn't look quite as pinched. "I owe you an ice cream cake, don't I?"

She hurried to the drawer and pulled out money from inside the oven mitt. "And I think we could all use a little ice cream cake, don't you?"

Her hands were shaking. The mitt fell, and the money fell with it. A five fluttered under the table, singles around the fridge. Agnes scooped up the money and pressed it into Gia's hands.

"Go, would you? Get the best one. Let them write your name in icing and tell them to make it pretty. Whatever you want, OK?"

Agnes wrapped her arms around her waist, forced a smile.

It was still shocking to go outside, where black pits sat in either direction. Aunt Diane was on the porch in a floral housedress, barefoot in December, smoking a cigarette. She nodded at Gia, and Gia nodded back. She wasn't so bad, Aunt Diane. Maybe that was why Lorraine had always taken care of her. She searched Aunt Diane's face for a clue about what else was in store for them, but it was as chipped up and unrevealing as a river rock.

She passed the bakery just as Big Lou was feeding the meter, trying to ignore her but fumbling with change so stupidly he dropped coins into the gutter. So she wouldn't get her job back, and that was fine. Who could stuff cannoli after everything anyway?

Inside, Lorraine was behind the counter, too busy to notice Gia outside, hurrying from one tray to the next as the line grew. Her hair was pulled back into a bun, but she'd tucked a spray of tiny pink flowers into her elastic. She'd seen them growing in a pot at Lorraine's new church, the buds green and only hinting at the pink inside, but seeing them in Lorraine's hair felt like a tiny miracle, a glimmer of hope. Gia unzipped her coat, surprised by the sudden warmth those flowers had filled her with. Even if Lorraine was leaving, moving on to somewhere else to bloom, maybe that was OK. It would have to be.

At Carvel, the girl behind the counter handed Gia a pen and paper, told her to write out in block letters what the message on the cake should be. Gia stared off for a while. What did you write when you didn't even deserve ice cream cake or the bed you slept in? When there wasn't anything to celebrate anymore?

Edelweiss, she wrote finally, thinking of them in the living room with the couches pushed back, dancing in socks. It was the only word she could think of.

~

The next day, the phone rang again early, and Agnes jumped up so fast she threw the chair back with the motion. It landed on its back like a dead bug.

"Yes? Yes, he's here. Gia, get your father. It's the station."

But Eddie was already halfway down, swinging his bad leg over the steps with his full weight on the banister, sweaty and disheveled from several days without a shower. He really did look like he had the flu. Gia stepped back.

"Martino." His voice came from an unused place. Then he coughed, and Gia realized his lungs were hurting from the smoke just like hers. He looked in Gia's direction as he listened, without really seeing her.

"Thanks," he said finally. He put the phone down in the receiver and rested his head against it for a moment before looking toward Agnes, who was biting her cuticles down to the quick against the refrigerator.

"They booked him," Eddie said heavily. "Ray. Possession with intent to sell. No bail. He'll go to trial or take a plea, but he's looking at time."

A line of red welled near Agnes's nail.

"And if you think that's too harsh—"

"I don't," Agnes snapped, staring past the dusty seashell collection on the window to where Aunt Ida's house would be. "I hope I get to pick his jurors."

And with that, Agnes was up the stairs in a flash, moving at the speed of a typewriter ribbon again, and upstairs the shower hummed, and Agnes got ready for work because it was early enough that she could still make it on time if she was quick about it.

~

Two days later, a family moved into the first finished house. The moving van pulled up on Saturday morning around the time Gia was walking to Big Lou's to ask for her job back because she didn't know what else to do with herself anymore. At least at Big Lou's she could put the money she earned in the grocery jar, help her parents. The truck unloaded new furniture wrapped in plastic while a woman in heels with a flippy Jackie Kennedy haircut pointed toward this room or that from the porch or opened the windows to air the place out.

"It smells too new in there," she said, laughing, ignoring the burned-out shell two houses over. Gia guessed there'd be cookies baking in the oven before the last box was unpacked. That night, there were two cars in the driveway, both new and shiny, that came and went at odd times. By Monday the woman was out there again with landscapers, pointing at the sandy stretch that should've been a lawn, and by Tuesday there was fresh sod in December, the lawn a brilliant summer green. It didn't matter if it didn't last. They'd replace it until the real lawn took root, as many times as it took.

The following week, a big tree appeared in the window, covered in white twinkle lights. On Christmas morning, a kid in pajamas with a coat thrown over them rode a new bike with a bow into the street, speeding up real quick, burning rubber to stop, until his mother called him back. Gia was glad she'd forgotten about Christmas Eve, and it was too late to stab a lemon at midnight Mass for Ray. He had enough punishment coming his way.

When that kid rode his bike down the driveway, Gia understood what Ray's biggest mistake had been. He hadn't seen the changes, hadn't seen even what Antonio had, that the neighborhood was changing and it wasn't theirs anymore. It would be Wonder Bread and new cars and automatic laundry machines and crime, yes, but not in their own back-yards. The drugs Ray had brought in were like the citronella candles her side lit to keep mosquitos away on nights when the moon was perfect and the breeze was warm and everyone had just come back from a swim, only there wouldn't be any more swimming, and the old houses would eventually be knocked down, replaced with the new. The new people were like the men in white suits who'd swept away the sparrows, only this time, her people were the sparrows: day laborers and city workers who'd done OK in America but never *made* it, hadn't quite moved far enough away from the bricklayers the new side couldn't stand. It wasn't their neighborhood anymore, and Ray had helped them take it away.

She felt bad for Ray in prison, only there had always been a cap on how far they could go. She just hadn't seen it.

Chapter Seventeen

Gia came home from school and slid her bag of books to the floor. It'd been easy to go back after the new year when everything was starting fresh. Everyone knew. No one asked questions. She was oil in a water bowl and preferred it that way. Only Sister Gregory had put a hand on Gia's shoulder during a spelling test her first week, left a copy of Cormac McCarthy's *The Orchard Keeper* on the corner of her desk.

After Leo had left, Agnes had cleaned. Buckets of soapy water turned black as she washed everything: the tops of cabinets, moldings, fan blades, the inside of the Tiffany light above the kitchen table. They steamed the rugs, nested the pots and pans in the cabinets, mopped, organized food in the pantry. Gia dumped her dresser drawers, made a giveaway pile for church, refolded her clothes. Agnes opened every window, cool air seeping through until everything had absorbed it, even hours later when the windows were closed. The door to Leo's room stayed shut.

And when they were done and it was still quiet, they carried the buckets and cleaning supplies over to Aunt Diane's and did the same. Lorraine had thrown the windows open and closed her eyes when the air had rushed in, breathing deep, memorizing the cold smell of salt water. Gia wondered if washing away dust was a quiet way of saying goodbye.

They weren't trying to scrub Leo away, more like bring the house back to life, but it still felt empty. Even today, like watching the first stars come out at night or a sunrise in the morning. Empty and everything.

Gia warmed milk in a saucepan and spread peanut butter on toast. The smell of cleaning soap was still strong. Breakfast dishes were upside down in the drying rack. Her father ate regular food now instead of broth, and his stomach was doing fine. There was no need to look for Leo in the middle of the night, but Gia still woke up at odd times, the house quiet around her, settling with an unfamiliar purposelessness. Eddie walked with a limp now, and the effort to hide it on the job sent him straight to bed at night, even though he was still on desk, just wasn't complaining about it anymore. They were still waiting on the fire report as bulldozers loaded what was left of the two houses—one on their side of the canal, one on the new side—into overflowing dumpsters, but Eddie thought they were in the clear now.

Peanut butter stuck to the roof of her mouth. She drank her warm milk and opened her notebook on the table. She was so far behind. Reading felt too slow now, the words swirling as she tried, sentence by sentence, to focus. She could see, almost, Leo's point about things being heightened when he was high, more vivid, covering a stronger palette of emotion that made everything else dull in comparison. She did not want to admit it, but he was right. Everything was dull.

Something fell in the living room, a soft thud, like a paperback from the arm of a couch. Her skin prickled, alive again.

"Mom?" Gia called out.

Silence. Gia pushed the chair back quietly, took a knife from the butcher's block.

"I'm here," a small voice from the couch said. Her mother.

"Why didn't you say anything?"

But her expression stopped Gia cold. Her legs were curled beneath her, in her favorite brown skirt and ruffled sky-blue blouse, as she stared at a spot on the ceiling, biting down on her index finger hard enough to leave teeth marks as blood rose beneath them. The light was fading outside, but the lamps were off, turning the room the color of a rinse cup for paintbrushes. The thud was a shoe that had hit the carpet after slipping slowly from her mother's foot. It was impossible to tell how long her mother had been sitting like this, if she'd even gone to work.

She should shut the curtains and hide this. Call her father.

"Should I get Lorraine?" Gia hovered in the doorway, afraid to touch her mother's side of the room. Silence.

"Or Dad?"

Gia twisted her hands, wringing the skin, fighting the bone and muscle beneath, her chest a spiderweb of tension, weaving, weaving, weaving.

"Are you sick?"

Agnes turned, her gaze slowly settling on Gia, her face muddy in the fading light. "The police called."

Gia's stomach lurched. There were gaps, her father said, in his bulletproof vest, places his tactical gear didn't cover, but a bullet was better than a knife, cleaner. The police radio terms he'd taught her sped through her head: DOA, 10-31, 10-35. What if they'd taken him off desk? He was limping, couldn't run if he had to. Or if they knew about that house—picked him up at the station and cuffed him in front of everyone. They'd found blood under the floorboards or too many footprints on Mr. Angliotti's lawn. Or the wound Lorraine had dressed with gauze and peroxide had gotten infected and spread to his blood.

"Is Dad . . . where's Dad?"

"The Florida police." Agnes flattened against the couch, staring out the window at where the parakeets were on the telephone wire again, green against a purple sky. And Gia could not help it, but she was glad it was not her father, that he was at work behind a stack of papers with a coffee cup leaving a ring on a file folder, stuck on desk, his badge over his heart.

"January always gets a nice sky," her mother said, lost in the window world.

Whatever Leo had done was worse than before, worse than the fire or the marsh. Whatever it was, her blood was cold, and she felt empty, dread spilling over her insides. She wished she could go back to her toast and homework, back to normal again, instead of feeling the ache in her spine where he'd slammed her with that stick.

"I'm calling Dad." Gia moved for the hallway phone.

"No." Her mother shook her head, still staring out the window, where birds flew in small circles without gravity or the same weight that anchored Gia to the living room. "No."

"Mom?" She didn't want to know, but she would have to. Whatever it was had already happened.

"The police found him this morning. He overdosed. On the beach."

Each sentence was a separate, impossible fact. Gia's head buzzed, ears ringing. It was good that they'd found him, the police with their badges and star-pointed hats, carrying pictures of their children in the lining, their mothers or fathers or wives. Their children. Like her father. Someone like her father had found her brother.

"So he's in the hospital?" Gia rushed on. "Or he's coming home?"

But her mother only stared.

But he couldn't. Not Leo. Not her brother, who'd taken down fences on his motorcycle and only gotten scraped, who'd once fallen off the roof but caught a gutter on the way down, who could hold his breath underwater for longer than anyone, long enough to untangle ropes under boats. He was always fine, scaring everyone else with his dangerous things. And yet her father had threatened this, and now it was true.

"How do they even know it's him? He doesn't know anyone there. No one knows him." There was no air in Gia's chest. "How could they know if they don't know him?"

"It's him, Gia." Her mother's voice was flat.

"But how do they—" Leo's smiling Confirmation picture sat on the mantel. He was in a suit, the only time he'd ever worn one. He couldn't be gone when he was smiling in that frame. When he was in Florida with palm trees and the ocean. Cuban sandwiches. Orange groves. Days of endless summer. Baskets of hush puppies and fat slices of key lime pie and flowers bigger than human heads. They'd checked, pressing their faces alongside blooming hibiscus, pressing sand into buckets with ocean water for sandcastles. He was there to heal.

Her mother was staring off through the window.

"January blue," she said. Gia could not take it. She grabbed her coat and rushed out. Cold air slapped her face hard enough to make tears sting. Then she was on her bike, riding down the street. A car rounded the corner, but Gia cut it off. The driver honked, yelled something Gia didn't hear. Handlebar streamers fluttered like telltales on a sail, and Gia pedaled faster, thighs burning, until she was at the dock, only there were no boats in the water now. They'd been dragged to land and stuffed under tarps for winter.

She threw her bike down and dangled her legs off the dock, ignoring the bird shit on the broken boards. The tide was out, and moss grew at the high water mark. Gia shivered. He was supposed to be a better person one day and put this behind him, but he couldn't do it. He was weaker than she'd thought, weaker than he had let on. Gia peeled back bits of wood and dropped them into the canal, where they dipped and floated.

Would it be different if she'd said something sooner? Or led Leo out of Ray's basement? *Come on,* she might've said, *let's catch a movie. Let's bowl. Let's go to New Park and see who can eat the most slices.* But he wouldn't have listened. She couldn't pretend he was that kind of person now just because he was gone.

Gone. Gia held the word on her tongue. Gone like one season to the next or the years Gia was little. Gone like first or second grade. The pets they used to have. Gone like Aunt Ida and Uncle Frank, even though they were still down the block. Gone like Pop Pop, his home across the ocean. Nonna and her signs. Her boat. Even Lorraine. She could add her brother to that list now, only it didn't fit. It didn't make sense. Because he'd always been there, her brother, all the way back to when she'd been in her mother's stomach—he'd been running up and down the steps, sleeping in the same bedroom down the hall.

A plane took off from the airport and headed to sea. Gone like departing planes, like today would be. She needed her father. Gia closed her eyes, imagining this dock wasn't New York in January, that the water was not mud green, that the maple trees were palms swaying in the warm sun, the water crystal blue. She could swim if she wanted to. Orange trees grew on sidewalks. The world was full of tropical flowers in pinks and whites, and little lizards warmed on the dock, the sun warming her too. That was supposed to happen for her brother but hadn't. Why would it if her island hadn't worked? It was disappointing to realize she'd been so stupid both times to let hope fester quietly under the surface.

Had he known he couldn't stop? Dogs and cats ran away to die. They made themselves disappear. Was that what Leo had done? Had it been easier away from home, like it was easier to be herself away from her family—all the best and worst?

Gia hugged her knees to her chest, imagining her brother on this canal, his pants rolled up, barefoot, coiling rope on his arm, kicking off from the dock with a cooler, the sun reddening his nose, with a bucket of teeming bait. Or revving an engine he'd finished after all those stray parts had finally fit together, how confidently he'd pulled them apart because he could fix it better.

Or fighting, flushed from the effort, limbs tangled, her pride at knowing he was the best, cheering on something she'd never do, though they'd been cut from the same cloth.

They would have laughed about it one day, sitting on the front lawn while his wife carried coffee and cake to the folding tables, a little kid hanging upside down off his lap to look at the moon. *Remember that time I left you on the island?*

The sky was indigo with feather clouds. Her mother was right. It was beautiful.

And what hurt the most and felt most unfixable now was wondering how much she'd ever really known her brother, if at all. Now, she never would.

There would be no more new memories, Gia realized sadly, only the same repeating ones, the most recent of which were not very good. She wished it were possible to pick and choose your memories instead of jumbling them together. To keep the better ones and let the rest go, wash them out to sea like her marsh did.

Chapter Eighteen

"Mom?" Her mother was at the sink, pinning her hair into rollers, like any other night. Gia had not brushed her teeth, changed her clothes. No one noticed. Besides funeral things, her mother didn't speak. No, they did not need a priest. No, they did not need a service. Sadness evaporated off her like a puddle after a rainstorm, the air heavy with it, with more waiting underneath.

And as for her father, well, she didn't know where he was, but it wasn't here. The station. Overtime. Anywhere but here.

"Did you know this would happen?"

If I give him money, he won't steal. Maybe it wasn't as dumb as it seemed, like feeding change into a pay phone before the call ended or into a sidewalk horse while a kid rocked on top.

Her mother rolled another curler. Mint-green tubes were lined up on the sink next to scattered bobby pins. The contrast was unnerving.

"Doesn't matter," she mumbled, not looking at Gia.

"Why didn't you say something sooner?" Gia begged. "Because a man is always right? If you knew better, why didn't you say?"

Her mother ran her fingers under a trickle of water. It was sickening. Even now, Agnes kept her thoughts in her head. Even now, her hair had to be perfect.

"Answer me!"

Gia swiped the pins and sent them scattering, bouncing on the bathroom floor. But her mother only pressed her eyes closed, balling her fists, breathing heavily through her nose.

Agnes shoved the bathroom door shut so hard it crushed Gia's pinkie. She was white light, blinding, as she pulled her finger from the door, balled her hand around it to quiet the throbbing under her nail and in her head. Kicked the door so hard it shot nerve pain up her leg, into her back. Gia screamed without words, just high and shrill with hurt. Not that her mother cared. Not about Gia. She wouldn't have been the same loss to Agnes.

Gia slammed her door, hating the pink wallpaper with tiny, delicate flowers, the white bedroom furniture with spindly legs, the window seat meant for a daydreaming girl with two neat braids down the back of her head, a different kind of daughter.

Her poster of the World's Fair Unisphere in all its metallic glory was a big middle finger to those petite wallpaper flowers. To the dresser's mirrored tray, sitting neatly on the lace runner, with only a tube of lip gloss instead of pretty perfume bottles.

Gia peeled the wallpaper back, pulling it away in one long line until it snapped free. She scraped another piece with a scissor, then another, until her room was streaked with yellow glue, the discarded paper all over the floor. It could sit there forever without anyone noticing, even when her mother left clean clothes on the bed.

Wasn't someone supposed to talk to her? To see how she was doing now that her brother was gone? That was how it happened in movies, Maria from *The Sound of Music* strumming her guitar and singing things Gia felt inside, but Maria was not coming. Not even Lorraine anymore.

Her fingertips were numb. The whole room looked like a sick lung, but it was satisfying. Leo would've found it hilarious, Gia surrounded by strips, funnier than the time she'd dropped that crumb cake that had been cooling on her mother's dresser, a handful of butter crumbs in her fist. But that wasn't going to happen now, and it wouldn't have happened before either. He probably wouldn't have noticed. What fun was wallpaper compared to motorcycles?

Gia clicked her lock into place, threw the window seat cushions on the floor. They weren't comfortable, never had been. She lay down on the smooth bench, cold wood seeping through the back of her shirt. She smelled. Maybe her mother didn't want to say goodbye without looking like herself. It would be the last time they were in the same room together. Maybe she just wanted to be his mom one more time.

The dress Gia was supposed to wear hung from the closet door. It was black with blue buttons down the front. The tag dangled under the armpit. The blue buttons were wrong, too happy considering in two years she'd be the same age as Leo. In three, she'd be older than he'd ever been, and then she'd do things he'd never done. The list would get longer and longer.

Her mother was still in the bathroom. The door was closed, and the light was on. Gia imagined her mother against the tub, pins and rollers scattered on the floor, a box of tissues at her feet. She should knock and say she was sorry, pick up the pins, arrange the rollers on the sink, but she was tired of doing things adults were supposed to do. It made her inconsolably sad, like she'd woken up in the wrong part of her life, so she tucked clean clothes under her arm and went to Lorraine's.

She wouldn't have to explain. She would just fill the tub with water and wash her hair with Lorraine's shampoo, scrubbing herself clean. Right now, someone was dressing her brother in a suit he'd never worn, combing his hair, straightening him into the best version of himself, tucking his feet into fancy shoes despite the marks on his arms. It was all wrong, but Gia would play her part.

She didn't ring the bell. She went straight upstairs, where the door was open and Lorraine was sitting by the window.

"Saw you coming," she said without turning around. Gia preferred being invisible.

Lorraine's outfit for tomorrow was on the bed: slacks and a white blouse. Gia swallowed the lump in her throat. How stupid had she been to smooth that dress?

"I have to take a bath." It was ridiculous when her own house was across the street, but Lorraine didn't question it. She slid from the seat like a cat down a fence, landing soundlessly. It was only when she turned around that Gia noticed she'd been crying.

Lorraine filled the tub and tossed in a handful of dried flowers for healing that soaked up water, blooming back to life, as Gia slipped out of the clothes she'd been wearing for the past few days and stepped inside. She didn't care that Lorraine was still there as she pulled the curtain closed and dunked her head.

"I keep thinking," Lorraine said after a while. "We had a barbecue once at your house, like usual. I don't know if you were born yet or if you were just really little, but Ray and everyone thought it was hilarious to throw things on the barbecue when your dad wasn't looking. Like sticks and leaves, just stuff no one would notice. Then Ray undid his shoelace and dropped that into the flames. We thought it was so funny when your dad and Uncle Frank checked the grill. We're rolling, and everyone kept asking what was so funny, which just made it funnier. And then Leo . . ."

Lorraine stopped. The faucet dripped ripples into the tub. It was rare to hear a story she hadn't heard. It had more meaning now because he was gone. The bathwater steamed on her face.

"He threw his whole shoe in, right on top of the hamburgers and hot dogs, but it wasn't funny. We knew he'd just gotten us in a ton of trouble, but he had this huge grin like we should be rolling. Sure enough, your dad walloped him, made him work it off. The thing is, he just couldn't understand why he was in trouble. He didn't think. He was just . . ."

Lorraine struggled for the right words.

"Onto the next thing?" Gia suggested. Like a pinball working the maze. All lights and motion.

"Exactly. There were no consequences. He never really learned from anything. He just bounced."

There would be no more stories over what Leo had survived. Gia let that sink it.

"Your mom told mine it was a car accident."

"It wasn't." There was an edge in Gia's voice. She was on the verge of tears now.

"I know," Lorraine said quietly.

Gia collected a palmful of flower petals.

"Do they work?" Gia asked quietly. "Do they really heal anything?"

Lorraine was quiet for a moment. "If you want them to."

"Lorraine?" Gia worked up the nerve to ask the question she'd been dreading most since the night of the fire. "Where are you going?"

It was silent, but the air changed.

"India," Lorraine whispered.

"India," Gia repeated, rounding her tongue over the letters, as far away from here as anyone could get. How many planes did it take to get there? They must have to fill up their gas tanks like her father had on their Florida trip, guzzling gallons of fuel to keep them moving. Only this time, Lorraine was going alone. And she really was going. Gia hadn't imagined it. She wished she were wrong, but the air felt right with it. It was true, all because of that place with the cushions and the accordion and those pretty words that made Lorraine almost happy again. Gia was jealous, maybe, that that place hadn't been magic for her too.

"When?"

"Soon."

Suddenly, she was too alone in the tub, the walls closing in, the overhead light too muddled through the steam to see clearly. Gia's hand fished around the shower curtain, where it dripped a puddle on the floor. Lorraine's hand found hers, and together they sat in the bathroom until the warmth in the air was all but gone and the water in the tub made Gia shiver.

~

The funeral was the uneventful thing her father had promised it would be. Gia stood between her mother and Lorraine under a cove of evergreen trees, their branches fanning with the breeze under a perfect blue sky. The pine box holding her brother was lowered into the ground by men in gray jumpsuits using canvas straps. There was no priest, no words, just creaking straps and handfuls of dirt, her mother crying softly, rows of identical pearl stones in every direction. Her brother's stone would come later. For now, he had an index card on a metal spike stuck into pebbly soil.

Gia had taken her brother's brontosaurus, a souvenir from the World's Fair. That was the first time Gia'd ever had a belgian waffle piled with strawberries and whipped cream, powdered sugar fluttering off the top and trailing behind them as they'd carried it to the Unisphere and gobbled it down beneath those fountains. She'd meant to leave it for him, the plastic warming in her pocket on the ride, its legs poking into her skin when she shifted. He'd slipped it into his pocket from a souvenir bin, and he'd held it up outside the Unisphere and made it roar.

"Brontosauruses don't roar," she'd told him. "Nothing that eats leaves does."

But he'd just shrugged and buried its face in the waffle. Roaring. Roaring. Roaring. Full of strawberries. Full of whipped cream and powdered sugar. Roaring. Roaring. Roaring. Already, she couldn't remember his face in that moment, only that she'd laughed and he'd laughed, too, the sun peeking out behind gray clouds as he'd licked whipped cream from his fingers, neither one caring who'd eaten more than the other, the whole plate piled high enough for both of them.

Gia didn't have the heart to toss the dinosaur into the dirt. Not even after her mother tossed the cellophane rose she'd bought from a gypsy at a red light. Gia closed her hand around it instead and kept it in her pocket. She looked at her father, her mother, Lorraine, the two men in gray jumpsuits, the evergreen branches bobbing in the wind. In the distance, another open hole gaped in the ground, and Gia wondered who her father had been punishing when he'd said there wouldn't be a proper funeral if Leo died this way.

It was a cemetery for war veterans all the way out on Long Island. Her mother sat in the passenger seat, staring out the window, perhaps knowing she'd never be able to come here alone, not without driving on highways. There were times on the ride back that she shot forward in her seat with urgency, memorizing this tree or that one, a curve in the road, some clue that would lead her back if she had the chance, while her father stared straight ahead, never once glancing through the rearview mirror.

Only once did her father pull off the highway, following a road full of hills that dipped suddenly, dropping Gia's stomach with it. Homes peeked out from clusters of trees, the air fresh with earth. Brown leaves skittered across the road. Someone had made a fire, tossed in armloads of dead leaves, while chickens pecked on overgrown lawns and frost lingered on the grass. He pulled over next to a squat bungalow with a wagon wheel marking the house number against a wooden fence, got out, and lit a cigarette. The curtain peeled back, and a dark face watched their car idling in the street, leaves and pine cones crunching as he paced, puffing, maybe wishing he could stay here in this cedar-shingled house near her brother instead of driving them all the way back to the empty house, a reminder of how they had failed.

Lorraine watched it all with her hands folded in her lap, never moving. Gia hadn't seen her eat or sip water or do anything human all day, just tuck stray pieces of her hair back into the elastic at the base of her neck when the open window shook them free.

After the World's Fair as the Grand Central rolled out before them, Gia had blurted out that she wanted to be a scientist. She wanted to go to the moon. She wanted to dust off dinosaur bones in the middle of a desert. She wanted to invent a picture telephone and rocket shoes and a TV you could smell.

"Girls can't be scientists," Leo had said, laughing. "They won't even send 'em to war, and you think they'd send 'em to the moon?"

"Tell you what, big shot." Her father eyed Leo in the rearview mirror, where Leo had one leg propped on the back seat. "Take your foot down; then let's hear what you want to be."

Leo stared out the window for so long Gia didn't think he'd answer. The streetlights had halos, and Gia was so tired each light blurred into the next. Heat crashed through the open windows, and finally Leo answered.

"Nothing."

Her father laughed, but it was a dry, unhappy sound.

"Not an option."

But Leo had stared out the window at shadow shapes, as if he'd known something they didn't.

Death, Gia realized, wasn't a tide that washed in and out on moon time. In all her life, she couldn't think of anything that washed out without washing in again. Except this, and the thought of it coming for her felt like taking the red ribbon Nonna had left under their mattresses to ward off the evil eye, tying it around her neck, and pulling at the loose strings until it had choked off any promise of what had come before as the car rolled over the open road.

Chapter Nineteen

Night hadn't given in yet. It was still inky black, the streetlights hazy orbs, so quiet Gia could hear herself breathe, enough to make her nauseous because she hated quiet now. She curled into a ball on the couch, waiting.

It might be too late already. Lorraine's house was dark, with only the faintest glow of the hallway night-light drifting into Lorraine's room. Aunt Diane must've bought that light when Lorraine was little, afraid of her sleepy eyed near the steps. Or maybe it hadn't been Aunt Diane but Agnes, picking up an extra when she'd bought one for Gia and Leo, replacing the bulb whenever she'd changed it for her own children.

Already, it felt less like Lorraine's house and more like Aunt Diane's shell.

The stairs creaked behind her under her father's weight. She must be right if he was awake, too, setting up the percolator, sensing another change rolling in with the tide while Agnes slept, holding away another loss with shapeless dreams.

Aunt Ida's door opened first. She and Uncle Frank hobbled down the walkway, her arm laced through his, with Tommy trailing behind, to make the long ride upstate for visiting hours where Ray was waiting for trial.

"If he makes it," her father had said.

"Why wouldn't he?"

"They don't want him to talk, Gia. Can't put a rat on the stand."

That body plunking over the side of the boat had a face now. That was the last time they'd talked about it. Gia didn't want to hear any more.

Tommy had regained the weight he'd lost and was back in sweats again. It didn't make her happy, just heavy, like climbing a tree in all her winter clothes, as the taillights flashed and the car pulled away from the curb.

When the front door opened across the street, Lorraine was barely a shadow. Only the streetlights confirmed that she was really there at all in her jeans and old flannel top, looping her arms through the straps of an army backpack. It was too small for her to be leaving for good, but when Lorraine locked the front door and slipped the keys in the mailbox, Gia's stomach lurched. She hadn't thought there were any feelings left in her to well up, but they rushed in now: Lorraine's hand trailing through the water when they swam in the canal, makeup brushes over Gia's closed eyes, falling asleep back to back on Friday sleepovers, waiting outside the bakery for Lorraine to finish work, untying string from cookie boxes, how Lorraine always burned her mouth on the first triangle bite of pizza. She was leaving and Gia was staying, only there wasn't any anger in it. Just a mild shock, like waking up to realize the power had gone out or the water had come up from a storm she'd slept through. She couldn't stop it, just like leaving a calendar page on the wrong month wouldn't stop time, so she pulled her shoes on and lingered by the door.

"Don't you want to say goodbye?"

Her father stirred the spoon in his mug behind her and took a sip, his eyes suddenly wet. Maybe it was just steam, but he shook his head, and Gia understood: there had already been too many goodbyes.

He cleared his throat and pressed change into her hand. "Call me when you're ready, wherever you are. I'll pick you up."

Lorraine was halfway down the block, lost under the army bag on her back. She'd sewn a patch of embroidered flowers to it: *War is not healthy for children and other living things,* the flowers and script bright against the gray camouflage. Everything she needed was in that bag, zippered shut. Did Aunt Diane know her daughter was leaving for good, going on an airplane, crossing oceans? Gia had traced a line on the map from New York to India with her finger, crossing the Atlantic Ocean; the Mediterranean Sea; the Arabian Sea; maybe even the Bay of Bengal, which fed the Indian Ocean; and a puzzle of imperfectly drawn countries, the jagged lines a squabble of yours and mine.

It was worse, maybe, when someone was leaving because they wanted to, but they were still physically here, the best parts of them closed off because they no longer wanted to share. Lorraine would never come back. When she stepped off the plane and smelled new unraveling flowers for the first time and woke up to new birdsongs, knowing that coming home meant collecting empty bottles beside her mother's chair and heating TV dinners, Lorraine would sink her feet into the new earth. She was a tree, like the one in her story, her roots calling out to the others, only no one had heard her. Including Gia. So when Lorraine looked over her shoulder as Gia fell into step beside her, she hoped Lorraine understood the apology in it for not taking her to the marsh that night and hiding in the spartina, letting it weave around them under a maze of hidden stars and mosquitoes that would pull the blood from their arms and legs without apology.

They walked in silence. Lorraine looked at her feet as if they were moving without her permission, or to the brightening sky, the houses they'd known since they were kids, trick-or-treating, babysitting, chasing stray dogs and cats.

The walk to the airport was full of tall weeds. Lorraine's hair was pulled back into a ponytail, brushed and clean but not styled anymore. Not since. She wasn't wearing makeup, but she was more beautiful without it. Inside the weeds, people slept. The grass rustled as others walked, their heads just above the tallest places, like ghosts in an abandoned world. Neither flinched at their stained clothes, the smell of their unwashed bodies, because they knew now how close any of us were to becoming people in the weeds. Choices.

They were getting closer. There was so much Gia wanted to say, and also nothing.

Cars pulled over to wait on the highway. Morning was just breaking, but the airport was already awake with people stepping from taxis, trailing luggage larger than Lorraine's backpack, their skin illuminated in the glow of fluorescent lights, holding them all in a tank without time.

They paused at the door.

"Check on my mother sometimes. Maybe tell her a story or something."

Gia stared at the sparkles in the concrete. Quartz. Almost as tough as a diamond. She wished she were half as strong, because Lorraine leaving was unbearable. Gia crossed her arms over her stomach and held tightly.

"And you can take anything you want from my room."

People pushed past with luggage. Fancy suitcases with leather tags, swinging through the revolving doors in a blur.

"You could visit me. The world is bigger than just here. And I want to see it, Gia. Some people believe we get more than one chance at life, that we keep coming back, but what if we don't? I'm glad it happened, Gia. All of it. Maybe it did all happen for a reason, and I just can't see it yet."

Gia nodded, but even at fourteen, she felt rooted here. The pull of everywhere else wasn't strong enough.

Lorraine was out of words. She shifted the straps on her shoulders, the flannel scrunching beneath, and startled at a plane overhead, maybe because they'd never been this close to the airport before, had never buckled a seat belt onboard and gone anywhere else except Florida and back, bouncing in the back seat with mesh bags of fresh oranges at their feet, making *Help us, we're kidnapped* signs for the window, breaking pecan logs in thirds and sucking sugar from their teeth as Eddie drank cups of gas station coffee and drove. Falling asleep on each other, a tangle of arms and legs, unaware they'd ever grow up and untangle. Gia threw her arms around Lorraine one last time, wishing they could go back to those car rides or float away on the canal, somewhere Lorraine could forget without going away. She smelled like soap and water. Clean and warm. A fresh start. Then she pulled away and spun through the revolving doors, a flash of green flannel in a ticket line.

Gia wished a supersonic jet could take Lorraine off so that everyone would know. It was too big an event, too blinding. Let the supersonic jet scream it over the water, rattle the picture frames, wake babies in their bassinets, and set off car alarms so everyone would know something had happened even if they didn't know what.

She sat for a while watching planes before dropping change into the pay phone. Her father answered on the first ring, didn't say hello, and didn't ask any questions as Gia sobbed into the receiver. Only when the operator asked for more change did he say to stay put. He'd be there soon. Gia sat down outside the phone booth, not caring that she was sitting on the dirty ground as people rushed past.

Gia did not remember getting in the car, only that it was him and her driving slowly through the neighborhood, looking for people in the shadows, except there was no one left to find. Gia pulled her knees to her chest and buried her face. She couldn't stand passing Aunt Ida's house without Ray and Tommy, or her own, where Leo wasn't, and now Lorraine's.

When they were kids, they used to ride the cleaned-up bikes Uncle Frank had brought home from the dump. They'd fit the spokes with plastic covers and put streamers on the handlebars and ride down the street after the mosquito trucks, laughing in the white cloud and rubbing it over their skin so they'd be bug proof. In her memory, they were shadows in that cloud. Arms and legs, silhouettes of bikes, a splash of color from someone's shirt, Gia trailing behind on her smallest bike and pedaling as fast as she could, the cloud settling bitter on her lips as she called out for the others to wait up, though they never did. Eventually the truck would outrun them, and they'd be left panting in the street. Bikes stopped. Laughing as the cloud dissipated and the light resettled again.

But now as the car turned onto their street, she was somehow in the lead, no longer trailing behind, only it still felt like she'd been left behind, all of their journeys taking them elsewhere. She was glad that Lorraine was free to cross oceans. Only she wished it had been something more beautiful that had made Lorraine fly away.

EPILOGUE

In 1971, President Nixon declared a war on drugs. *You're a little late,* she thought. But the academy was buzzing about it. There were rumors of a federal task force, but to Gia, it was only newspaper promises. As long as there was demand, people would take risks, like Ray, five years into his sentence, probably making deals and building an empire on the inside. Maybe not. She didn't know. Ray felt far removed from her now, but she sometimes wondered if he was glad her father had saved him when the first shots had gone off or if he wished one had gone straight through him, if his opinion shifted depending on the day, each one ticking past in a blur.

The following Sunday, Gia was sitting next to her mother in church when Father Gentile asked for a moment of silence for the young men in Vietnam, soon to be joined by one of their own, Thomas Edward, a good son to his parents, Frank and Ida. If Tommy had gone to college like Aunt Ida wanted, he could've deferred, but he'd gotten a job fixing electronics instead. Funny, Gia thought, that while they could've grown up and sought each other out, they just hadn't. But it was enough knowing Tommy was in the shop tinkering with parts and soldering irons while Gia trained. Aunt Ida's usual spot in the third pew was empty, and Gia wondered if Tommy was going or if he'd already gone. It bothered her that Father Gentile, who'd put Communion wafers on all their tongues and absolved their early sins, hadn't mentioned her. Agnes slipped her hand over Gia's, the pulse in her wrist beating strongly. *I approve,* it said. That was enough.

The **FOR SALE** sign in the front yard, hammered in two days after Eddie had filed his retirement papers and put a down payment on a five-acre farm on Long Island, was less startling now, as were the "new" houses, the filled-in swimming canal. Sometimes when the street flooded, she could almost pretend nothing had ever changed. Lorraine's old house was a sunny yellow now, the front lawn strewed with bikes and a blue plastic swimming pool full of floating grass. After Lorraine had left, Agnes had packed up Aunt Diane and moved her into Nonna's old apartment. "You can't live on your own anymore," Agnes had told her as she'd shoved things into boxes, but Gia suspected Agnes had needed someone new to take care of. Agnes had wavered a little on the day they'd signed the papers for Aunt Diane's house, when the couple had pulled up with a little boy and a little girl trading Cracker Jack pieces in the back seat. Now she set aside candy for them on Halloween, looked forward to seeing them in their Easter clothes or Christmas outfits, their first-day-of-school pictures, even as she packed the house, emptied the garage, fretted over how to dig the peony bush out of the ground without breaking the roots because she couldn't leave it behind. Nonna had planted it. And their new house was almost finished.

On weekends Eddie and Gia lugged tools and lumber, hammered a frame of two-by-fours, hired an excavator to dig the foundation and a water well. It was the kind of project he might have wanted to do with Leo one day, but aside from pausing on the beams every so often to stare out at the surrounding forest of pitch pines or to listen as a blackbird called, he never showed it. It was a small house, but there would always be room for her, he'd promised, and extra room in case there were grandkids one day. He'd shrugged at the idea as Gia had lined up a saw over a pencil mark. She'd laughed, but the idea of a little one running on this lawn of leaves and pine cones scattered with yellow buttercups, as they built a house under a tree with a lightning-strike scar, was touching. Another generation. Another chance.

There had been a little while after high school graduation when Gia had been unsure of the future, the whole thing stretching endlessly, too many days to fill. She hadn't seen Lorraine since that day at the airport, but Lorraine had met someone, a scientist, and together they taught families to use water purifiers, treated illnesses. It was right, Lorraine carrying a small bag of medical supplies from village to village, asking little kids to stick out their tongues outside their homes instead of in a sterile hospital somewhere. It reminded Gia that she couldn't work in an office forever. It was time to start over. If Lorraine could do it, so could she, so she'd dropped her new boat into the water and started rowing, building strength until she could row for hours.

She'd thought about becoming a researcher. They were out there every morning as she rowed past in her unnamed boat: studying oysters and mussels and periwinkles, tagging osprey, each studying a piece that connected back to the whole of the bay. But she could never study the marsh like they could. Not when, at heart, she was a protector, and the bay needed her.

Because the bay would soon be a wildlife refuge protecting the water, its shorelines, islands, dunes, brackish ponds, and woodlands, and all its creatures. It would never be a port, and the airport couldn't expand. Trash dumping would be illegal. Though she doubted anyone would ever be able to stop the baymen in their rubbers from pulling up eel traps, not when the bay was in their blood like hers. For them, the water went beyond rules and regulations. It was life. Not a place for the things she'd seen that night on Sister Island. That, she realized one morning on the water before the sun had fully risen over the horizon, was her moment. Even outside of her bay, there were 150 miles of waterways surrounding the city, needing someone who understood water and the secrets it kept.

"Dad," she said one fall night after they'd packed away the tools, debating whether to tell him now or wait until they'd driven home, but here was their future. Home was the past. It felt fitting. "I made it into the academy."

Her graduation was set for early July, just after his last day. She imagined slipping behind his desk with its piled papers, mugs rimmed with coffee, Sweet'n Lo wrappers, a phone with a tangled cord that rang and rang, and turning the calendar page from his last one, circled in red, to her first.

Her father was quiet for a long time, staring into the darkening pines, where a squirrel skittered past, rattling the leaves, until it was quiet again and the squirrel was gone.

"I wish you would've been a teacher." He sighed, rubbing his fore-head with his palm. "Because it won't be easy."

But she wasn't a teacher, and they both knew it.

"Do you know where you want to be?"

"Harbor Patrol," she said.

"I could make some calls," he said.

"No." Gia shook her head. She couldn't be a cop's kid dropped into a good position. They'd never respect her. "I want to earn it."

In one of the distant houses, someone had made a fire. Woodsmoke filled the crisp air, reminding them that they'd have to pause building once the cold weather came, but there were enough other things to work toward now. The academy, for one, and dismantling their old lives.

"It won't be easy," he said again.

And Gia understood. There would be jokes about bench-pressing and what her man thought about his woman being a cop, if there was one, and could she still perform her duties on the rag? But the truth was she could outrun all of them and jump fences faster, the nimblest of the bunch, even if female officers were required to wear skirts and low-heeled pumps, even if they made her carry her gun in a handbag. Every morning she took her boat out on the bay despite the weather, preferring rowing to running. It built a quiet strength in her. She couldn't deadlift, but so what? Over the next few months, Eddie made sure she could load and unload her piece faster than anyone. And it was in her blood. Her training had started the first time Leo had put her in a headlock. And she knew, deep down, what the others wouldn't until their moments came: that she was brave, truly brave, in the way most people only hoped to be.

On graduation day, it didn't matter that Father Gentile hadn't mentioned her graduation at Mass. The world was changing, maybe not as fast as she would like, but slowly and surely. All around her was a sea of metal stars, affixed over hearts that would try to be brave and honest and answer when called, to do their best in the worst of the world. Sometimes they'd get it right; other times, they'd fail spectacularly because people were not like dunes or tides, readjusting with the seasons. They were fixed points, Gia believed now, and could only sway so much during their short time on Earth.

She stared at the flags on the dais, past the tip of her star-pointed hat, the crowd behind her pulsing. Her parents were in there somewhere. There was applause now. People standing. Cameras flashing as the captain congratulated the rookies. Hats flying. Confetti falling, raining down on her, just like when she would throw a handful of velvet flowers over Lorraine in two weeks at her wedding, all the way in India. It would be beautiful, Lorraine in a pale-gold dress, henna spiraling her hands, a sea of flower petals, all to wish her into a new and beautiful life, far from the coffee-and-cake Sundays their parents had imagined for them. But today, she stared through everyone in the audience as she had through marsh grass that night on her island, staring out at a world she hadn't understood then, still didn't, but she was trying.

And then she thought of her parents anchoring their small boat beside Uncle Frank's, the kids swimming between, splashing for sandbars, and filling buckets with clams and Leo cannonballing and swimming beneath the boat. And the bridge he'd walked on years later, their two shadows in the blinding sun, only now it was she who was tightrope walking the ledge, bridging the world they'd come from with the way it was heading, carrying memories of Ray and Tommy, Lorraine and Leo, and the hopes of her grandparents when they'd sailed across the Atlantic and stepped foot on new soil, and it filled her with pride so strong she could feel her heart beating furiously beneath her own metal star, against the two broken bullets in her breast pocket to remind her of the person she wanted to be on the job and off.

I will make you proud, she promised them all, pressing her toe against the bottom of her shoe, imagining she could press all the way into the earth to call out her need and that the world would answer.

ACKNOWLEDGMENTS

A Frenzy of Sparks is about a family, and it wouldn't have been possible without the inspiration and support of my own . . .

Dad, first and foremost, I will always be incredibly grateful for the time we spent together while I was writing this book. It's a special thing to imagine the adult you've known your entire life as a little kid.

Mom, Michael, Jenna, and Emma, I will always appreciate how honest you are with me. You've been my earliest editors, teasing and supporting and sussing out the essence of what I was going for both on the page and off. Dad, this goes for you too.

Robyn, I've lost count of the reads but will never forget the sanity and wisdom you poured into this book. I will always be grateful we met by chance as kids at Hofstra—and we were kids—and of the writing journey we've been on ever since. Thank you for G-chatting at all hours to toss ideas back and forth.

Abby, remember when this was a proposal and I sent you the same outline . . . a hundred times? Well, it worked. Thank you, my friend.

To Alicia Clancy and the Lake Union Team: You're magic. Thank you, endlessly, for believing in me as a writer and trusting me to bring another story into this world, even when it was only an idea.

Rachel. The enthusiasm in your voice when you talk about my writing gets me every time. Thank you . . .

To the fantastic readers and fabulous Bookstagram community who welcomed *A Lily in the Light* with so much love it made me want to write a hundred more—thank you!

Rob, I saved you for last because in real life, you're always first: first to tell me I can do something I'm doubting, first to congratulate me on the wins, first to joke about the setbacks until I have enough kick to keep going again, first to order a pizza when all else fails. Thank you for always believing.

Finally, *A Frenzy of Sparks* was inspired by my uncle, who overdosed long before I was born. I know very little about him, but there was always a pervasive, unexplained sadness in his absence, and I will always wonder about the life he could have had. For those of you who have lived similar stories to Gia and her family, may you also find moments of peace.

BOOK CLUB QUESTIONS

1. The 1960s were a turning point for women's rights. How is Gia impacted by these changes, both in how she views the world and in how she can participate in it? How does Gia deviate from the roles expected of her?

2. How has understanding of drugs and addiction changed since the 1960s? How would Gia's family have coped differently with Leo's addiction if it had happened now instead of in 1965?

3. The theme of opportunity repeats throughout the story. What are some ways the characters had opportunities they didn't recognize at the time?

4. Gia's relationship to the boat and the bay changes throughout the story. What do the boat and the bay symbolize for Gia? How do they reflect other themes within the story?

5. There are several potential turning points for Gia, Leo, Lorraine, and Ray. Which are most impactful for each character? Do you agree or disagree with their choices?

6. Parenting in the 1960s was very different than today. As children of working parents, Gia and Leo had a lot of freedom. How do you feel their parents contributed to the development of both characters and the choices they made?

7. How does the setting of the marsh alongside one of the biggest cities in the world shape the story? How does Gia's changing neighborhood shape the story and these characters?

8. How do Gia's observations of nature and her reading of *Silent Spring* influence her understanding of the world?

9. Ray's decisions led to many serious consequences for each of the characters, whether they were active participants in the choices he made or not. Who, in your opinion, has suffered the most for those decisions? How much do you blame Ray for his actions?

10. In what ways does the title, *A Frenzy of Sparks*, reflect the story as a whole?

ABOUT THE AUTHOR

Kristin Fields grew up in Queens, which she likes to think of as a small town next to a big city. Fields studied writing at Hofstra University, where she received the Eugene Schneider Fiction Award. After college, Fields found herself working on a historic farm, teaching high school English, and designing museum education programs. She is currently leading an initiative to bring gardens to public schools in New York City, where she lives with her husband.